MW01426636

SECRETS OF MILAN

BOOK TWO OF THE NIGHT FLYER TRILOGY

❧

EDALE LANE

PAST AND PROLOGUE PRESS

CONTENTS

Acknowledgments	vii
Prologue	1
Chapter 1	3
Chapter 2	10
Chapter 3	17
Chapter 4	24
Chapter 5	30
Chapter 6	38
Chapter 7	46
Chapter 8	55
Chapter 9	61
Chapter 10	68
Chapter 11	74
Chapter 12	81
Chapter 13	87
Chapter 14	94
Chapter 15	101
Chapter 16	106
Chapter 17	114
Chapter 18	120
Chapter 19	128
Chapter 20	135
Chapter 21	142
Chapter 22	151
Chapter 23	158
Chapter 24	166
Chapter 25	174
Chapter 26	181
Chapter 27	188
Chapter 28	195
Chapter 29	204

Sneak Peek - Book Three	211
About the Author	213
Other Books by Edale Lane	215

Secrets of Milan

By Edale Lane

Published by Past and Prologue Press

All rights reserved. No part of this book may be used or reproduced in any manner without written permission of the publisher, except for the purpose of reviews.

Edited by Melodie Romeo

Cover art by Enggar Adirasa

This book is a work of fiction and all names, characters, places, and incidents are fictional or used fictitiously. Any resemblance to actual people, places, or events is coincidental.

First Edition June 2020

Copyright © 2020 by Edale Lane

Printed in the United States of America

❀ Created with Vellum

ACKNOWLEDGMENTS

Launching a writing career is a vast undertaking; add in creating and working to establish one's own label as well, it can be overwhelming. Fortunately, I am blessed with several talented and supportive individuals to guide, assist, and advise me on this journey, and I wish to take this opportunity to thank them. I acknowledge J. Scott Coatsworth, Mark Marco Guzman, and Other Worlds Inc., along with Stephan Zimmer of Seventh Star Press and Tomorrow Comes Media for generously lending me their expertise. I also wish to thank my team of beta readers, particularly Lisa Forest Walker whose insights and comments proved very valuable. Next, I recognize my partner Johanna White who has been with me every step of the way, despite us typically being hundreds of miles apart. Finally, I want to thank all of you readers, without whom these pages containing the creation of my heart would merely languish unloved and unappreciated like the castaways on the Island of Misfit Toys.

PROLOGUE

November 1502, Bern, the Swiss Confederation

"Milan, we have heard of this Night Flyer ravaging your city. Does he pose a threat? Need he be eliminated?" The deep voice boomed through the high vaulted windowless stone chamber cast in dim candlelight. Twelve figures, nine men and three women, garbed in smoke-gray hooded robes, circled a round oak table in the center of the room. A blue and white tapestry hung on the wall bearing the image of a rearing horse with no rider. The den had the musty smell of a seldom used root cellar with stale air and an imposing sense of antiquity.

A man spoke confidently in reply. "We have nothing to fear from the Night Flyer. He is merely seeking retribution upon House Viscardi and poses no threat to the public or to our plans."

"House Viscardi, you say?" inquired a female voice. "This may actually work to our advantage."

"Sì, Rome," replied Milan. "Prague, rest assured, the Night Flyer is unwittingly acting in our favor."

"I agree he could be an asset," inserted Paris, with typical French superiority in his timbre.

"How so?" asked a male voice dipped in a Spanish accent.

Milan explained. "Viscardi is a prominent arms dealer. Getting him out of the way is desirable no matter how you look at it."

"Agreed," pronounced Prague, the first man who had spoken.

"Vienna votes non-action on the Night Flyer. Let his course play out," concurred another.

"As does Cologne."

"Can he truly fly?" The awe and excitement in the woman's voice was apparent, and her curiosity was clearly mirrored in the rest of the enclave as all eyes turned in anticipation toward Milan.

With a nod and a humorous grin, he replied. "Indeed he can, dear Florence; indeed he can."

The figures in smoky robes and hoods marveled, nodding at one another, making flying gestures with their hands, and commenting upon how unbelievable was the idea until Prague called for order. "Gentlemen, ladies, we have much to discuss at this meeting. Let us move on to the matters at hand."

CHAPTER 1

Mid-December 1502, Milan

Everything was wonderful… until it wasn't. As Florentina stood before the looking glass getting ready for the day, she tried to figure it out once more. After splashing water on her face, she blotted it with a cotton hand towel. She frowned at her dusky olive complexion, her too large nose, and her thin lips. Even her lively, amber-infused brown eyes, keen to catch every detail and nuance, were ordinary in her estimation. She sighed and ran a brush over her long, brunette hair hanging past her shoulders. Her build was slender and sinewy, not at all how a woman's body was supposed to look. But her physique had been no different when Maddie declared her love.

"I'm so excited!" bubbled Angela, Florentina's roommate who was five years her junior. Now she had an attractive female shape and the desirable blonde hair and ivory skin to accompany it. "Don Alessandro is giving me three days off for Christmas to go home and visit my family!" She danced about, dressing in her servant's uniform as she chattered. "It will be the first time I have seen them since coming to work here months ago. And I have money to shop for gifts. Mama will make her holiday pie and there is always singing and a special Mass in the village."

She spun up to Florentina, glowing with the thrill. Florentina had no family. Her father had been murdered six months ago, and even though she had exacted her revenge upon Don Benetto Viscardi, destroying his business, his fortune, and his mansion and sent him crawling off, tail between his legs, to a salted and useless vineyard, it didn't change the fact she was without family. But that wasn't exactly true either. Don Alessandro, his sister Madelena, and her two precious children were her family now… at least she previously thought so.

"I am so happy for you," Florentina said, forcing a smile, choking back tears she would not allow to fall.

Angela continued to gush, oblivious to Florentina's misery. "He told the entire staff we could choose between having Christmas or Epiphany off, because someone has to still be here—although Bianca said she wasn't going anywhere; this was her home, or something of a similar nature."

Florentina watched from the mirror as Angela crossed the small, sparsely furnished chamber to peer out the window into predawn gloom. "I wonder why it is always so dark in winter? I wake at the same time and it is light out in summer." Although her current profession was as a tutor, Florentina was in no mood to explain the rotation of the earth and how it affected daylight hours through the changing seasons. "I guess that's why we have the winter solstice. Anyway, I know Epiphany is when we usually exchange gifts and all, but I truly wanted to go to the carol singing and Christmas Mass at the church in my village with all my old friends. It won't matter if we exchange presents early."

"I'm sure they will all be glad to see you and hear about life in the big city."

Angela's eyes lit with her smile. "Do you think? Oh, Florentina, you are such a wonderful friend! Look at the time; I have to run. Talk to you later." Florentina sighed in relief at the young maid's departure.

She went about her morning routine in a haze, selecting a simple wool two-tone dress with a scoop neck, a band above the waist, and long full skirts appropriate for giving the children's lessons, all the while attempting to determine what had gone wrong. Two weeks ago, her alter-ego, the Night Flyer, had saved Madelena from an assassin and revealed her identity to the woman she loved. After shock, hurt feelings, and lots of tears, Maddie understood she had only kept this secret to protect her. Maddie kissed her as she had many times before and declared, "Tonight I will show you a new way to fly," and she delivered. It was the most fabulous night of Florentina's life! The energy and fire, singular sensations, ecstasy and bliss were beyond imagining, but what was more, their joining had not merely been a physical zeal ending in release, but a metaphysical melding of two souls. She could not have imagined how intense the sensation had been and was certain the experience had been mutual. In the throes of passion Madelena had tried to give it voice, vowing her love, practically singing her own pleasure, surrender, and victory. That night Maddie had whispered in an almost reverent tone her awe at her feeling of completeness, of their total unity.

Then there was... nothing. Like a puff of wind extinguishing a candle, Maddie was just gone. Florentina was certain she was avoiding her, always busy, prepared with excuses, assailed by headaches, and quite emotionally distant as well. She was polite enough, pleasant, but seemed sad and worried. Florentina wanted to ask, to demand an explanation, but she didn't wish to pressure Madelena; she would tell her when she was ready... wouldn't she?

Florentina looked once more in the mirror. *Maybe she was merely emotional after the attack on her life, simply grateful I had been there to intervene. If she regrets the course the night took, she may be embarrassed to talk about it.* She sighed and turned away from her ordinary reflection. *It doesn't matter. I nevertheless have a task to perform—two, in fact. And I'm still a member of the household. She hasn't thrown me out. I'll pretend my way through breakfast as I have been doing, give all my attention to sweet Betta and Matteo, then search for clues to the secret society, the evil organization who would dare send an assassin after a woman.*

* * *

MADELENA STROLLED INTO A VACANT BUILDING, her footsteps echoing as she scrutinized the cracked plaster on the walls, the dirt-streaked windows, and the dust laden floor as the first winter morning light filtered its way around and through the dim hall. The structure lay in the middle of the Vittore District along a street recently renamed Via de Leon by the French magistrate and would require significant renovation to be transformed into Margarita's Hope House. The only current furnishing was a work table and two benches near an east-facing window, and Madelena gravitated toward it. There she began to leaf through diagrams and plans. She had skipped breakfast with the family for an early meet with the architect, but arrived before him.

If it weren't for the Night Flyer, for Florentina, I wouldn't have even thought of establishing this charity house, she pondered, a knot tightening in her belly. *What am I going to do? I can't avoid her forever.*

Two weeks ago, an assassin had come to her balcony to kill her—God knows why—and the Night Flyer happened to be there to fight him to the death to save her life. It was then she discovered the city's mysterious criminal—or benefactor, depending upon one's point of view—was none other than her children's tutor, with whom she had begun a romantic liaison. She had been baffled, confused, offended, and relieved all at once, and somewhere in the flood of emotions she had taken Florentina to her bed and made unrestrained love to her.

The encounter had blasted Maddie with a far greater impact than she had expected, being experienced with both another woman and her late husband. It was electrifying and soothing, riveting her with arousal and satisfaction, intoxication and climax, savage need and tender serenity. She bonded with Florentina on more than a physical plane, and she felt closer to the singular woman than she ever had to another person on this earth. She had loved her before, but now something stronger than love bound their souls together.

When she had awakened the next morning, Fiore, her affectionate name meaning "little flower," lay with her head on Maddie's shoulder and an arm draped around her waist. It was the most joy she had ever known… and then the assault of dark thoughts and emotions began. Fear drew its sword first, thrusting it into her gut. *She is embarking on a dangerous mission to seek and destroy powerful, violent men, a group of them with money to hire assassins, with secret plans and strategies, and all she has to go on is a diary written by a madman. She will surely be killed, and then what? You lost a husband to these malefactors and now you shall lose her too, only this time the pain will be greater because you love her more. You will be shattered and immeasurably alone.*

Next shot guilt. *She means more to you, more than did your lawful husband and just think: if he hadn't died, you would not have her, would not have this deep transcendent relationship. Does that mean you are glad he died? And if so, it makes you a horrible person.*

The jabs of fear and guilt were relentless, and Madelena had done the only thing she knew to do–she ran away. She needed to find a method of handling this before she could face Florentina again, so she avoided her whenever possible. None of it was Fiore's fault, but she didn't know what to say or do. *Maybe if I start distancing myself from her now, it won't hurt as much if... when they kill her,* she had thought. *I can't go through such loss again, not with Florentina—she is my everything!* But the guilt still hung around her neck like an anchor. If she could just stay busy enough, perhaps she wouldn't have to deal with it.

"Good morning, Donna Madelena," sounded a cheerful greeting, "And a joyful Novena to you."

Maddie looked up into the jolly smile of a rotund man sporting the square, wiry brown beard as adorned many an artisan's face. "Francesco, thank you for agreeing to meet me so early," she greeted.

Madelena had not chosen the costly designer dress embellished with countless hours of handwork silk threads weaving intricate patterns through the cloth to flaunt her family's wealth, but to proclaim her position of authority. Similarly, a ruby pendant hung below her throat, occupying the opening of the V cut to the dress's neckline with matching earrings adorning her lobes. She had replaced the wedding band which had spent much time in its box of late. It was difficult for any man to take his direction from a woman, but for a woman of means he would make an exception; therefore, as she often did when conducting business, Maddie dressed for power. Her flame hair was pulled back, braided, and housed within a netted snood matching the evergreen and gold of her gown, a hue darker than the leaf green of her eyes.

"It is my pleasure." He bowed slightly at the waist and she almost smirked as he raked his gaze down her sculpted curves, but refrained by drawing in a deep breath and lifting her alabaster chin. "The building was a shop with apartments above prior to your purchase."

"Precisely why I believe what I have in mind will function well." She pulled one of the sketches from the stack, laid it on top, and he stepped nearer to peer at the paper. "I want the carriage house out back converted to a kitchen with a covered walkway leading to the rear door here," she pointed. "And this patio needs flower boxes, outdoor furniture, and shrubberies—hydrangeas for color. There's already a compact room near the front door which shall be an office with a seating space adjacent. Then the remainder of the main floor should be divided into a dining section," she said pointing to the sector closest to where her new kitchen would be, "a common area with seats around this hearth, and about where we are standing now a work room where the residents can be taught marketable skills and crafts."

He nodded thoughtfully and rubbed his bearded chin. "Upstairs will be the sleeping quarters, which shouldn't require much alteration," she continued. "Be certain there is a water closet and bathing room on both upstairs floors, and at one end of the hall a sickroom for residents who may be afflicted with a contagion. And I want all these walls re-plastered and painted with bright, cheery colors, the flooring refinished, and draperies along the windows. I am creating a home here, a place for these unfortunates to feel worth and pride."

Francesco smiled and shook his head. "You will make it so fine they shall not wish to leave. What you envision is indeed superior to many rented rooms in the city; where is their incentive to acquire jobs and move on?"

"In their renewed sense of self-worth and to have something belonging to them alone rather than shared with many. You let me worry about getting them out; your task is to create the space I have envisioned."

"Yes, Donna Madelena, I believe I can produce everything you have asked for, but at a price."

Maddie glanced about the sizeable room in the growing light, seeing the end result in her mind's eye. "A trifle," she replied in an unconcerned tone. "It is a tribute to my mother and God's work to help the less fortunate, well worth the cost. How soon can your workers start?"

"It is Novena, then the Twelve Days of Christmas begin and Epiphany… perhaps January seventh."

Maddie frowned. "Doesn't anyone wish to earn money with which to enjoy their celebration? Surely you can find laborers who will make some progress this week, before festivities begin in earnest." Madelena needed this project to get her out of the house. She wanted to shop for furniture, linens, draperies, carpets, light fixtures, but there must be somewhere to bring the purchased items.

"Well," he laughed heartily. "If you are insistent, I'm sure I can at least start on the first floor, but the kitchen is a bigger job and I can't possibly secure the skilled workers to construct the oven and such until the holiday is over."

"Grazie. It is bad enough people will spend Christmas cold, hungry, and homeless. I do not wish to keep them waiting all winter."

"You are an odd woman, Donna," he said shaking his head, "and I mean that in a good way. Most women of your station do not indeed consider those beneath it, and the widows I have known are often bitter over their own misfortune, but you… You work beside your brother in your family business and devote your time to projects benefiting those you do not even know. Many would regard you an angel or a saint."

"I'm no angel nor saint." The rebuke was swift and cut the air like a knife with a much harsher tone than she had intended. Guilt continued to claw at her belly and fear to rip at her soul. After a calming breath she added, "I suppose I am a bit odd though."

CHAPTER 2

A week before Christmas Milan was bustling with shoppers and merrymakers, decorations of evergreen boughs and citrus fruit in the piazzas, and venues attracting customers with a woman dressed as La Befana with a broom in one hand while doling out candy from a sack to children with the other. Gaming halls and taverns overflowed more than usual during this season as well. The Sforza rulers had planned and implemented elaborate celebrations throughout the city during their reign; the representatives of the French King Louis XII now administered Milan, and they allowed most of the traditions to continue, albeit not as lavish. But at three hours past midnight, even the most enthusiastic partier was at home in bed.

The Night Flyer perched on the peak of the fabulous Duomo's roof, the magnificent cathedral that dominated the heart of the third most populous city in Europe, if one considered Venice and Milan a tie. In black leather leggings, black silk blouse, gloves, and boots, with a matching coif and face mask an observer would never guess the enigmatic outlaw/vigilante was a woman, much less a child's tutor employed by one of the most prosperous merchant Houses in the metropolis. But Florentina de Bossi was no conventional female. She had learned volumes from Master Leonardo da Vinci during his years in Milan, since her father had been his assistant. Leonardo's work was in such great demand he couldn't possibly have time to complete every order himself, so Luigi de Bossi, along with his daughter, spent each day in the master's workshop inventing, crafting, carving, and doing whatever was needed.

Leonardo had inspired the weapon she carried, a small crossbow with a revolving cylinder for rapid-fire shots, and he had exhilarated her with the dream of flight. Using copies of his sketches and her own experience as a test pilot for his prototypes, Florentina had designed and built a one-person glider kite which resembled a pair of wings. It utilized the strength and lightweight of silk, a folding skeletal system akin to a parasol's, and a backpack that strapped over her shoulders and snapped to her belt. Pulling a lever deployed the wings, which she could control with hand grips, while tugging another cord would fold them back into place.

She had created the Night Flyer to fulfill the family vendetta and punish Benetto Viscardi for poisoning her father over a perceived slight; she kept the persona to aid in her search for the covert syndicate Viscardi feared, the order scribbled about in the diary of a dead man, the terrible collective who was trying to kill her Madelena.

From her vantage point, she scanned the misty square as fog rolled off the placid canals. Streetlamps formed eerie glowing orbs, which failed to brighten the sleepy avenues. The night would be comfortably cool if not for the humidity closing the cold in. The piedmont south of the Alps and the Po Valley did not experience the severe winters endured in the north of Europe, but did face more unpleasant weather than the southern end of the Italian peninsula. *Where to search?* She wondered. *What is the sign of the horse Galeazzo Monetario wrote of in the journal?*

Uncertain where to try after a fortnight of vain explorations, Florentina decided to simply fly and allow the wind take her where it may. She pulled the lever deploying her obsidian wings, took a running start, and let them lift her feet off the roof tiles. The enterprise of flight never ceased to exhilarate and thrill, to fill her with awe and wonder. The Night Flyer leaned to her left to glide over one of the shopping districts, sharp eyes watchful for clues. At once, she noticed movement below and the scuffle of shoes on cobblestone. Steering for the nearest rooftop, she drew in her wings and lighted on the terracotta shingles. After securing them into their pack, she scrambled down a drainpipe and dropped to the ground.

Florentina double-checked her gear. The grappling hook with its length of rope and sheathed dagger were on her belt and the specialized crossbow hung securely from its cord. She had no explosives, smoke bombs, drugs, or potions with her tonight, but presumed she was well armed enough. Rounding the corner, the Night Flyer spied two drunk men staggering along, arms around each other's shoulders, struggling to remain upright. One began to sing. "God bless ye mas'er o' this house, like–hick–mistress too," he bellowed, slurring the words of the Missa, or Italian carol. "All ye li'le chil'en that 'round ye table go," his friend joined in on a totally dissonant pitch.

Florentina cringed at the clashing tunes, a shiver running down her back. Leonardo was a musician as well as a painter, inventor, and every conceivable aptitude, and had taught her the finer points of music. Then a third man materialized in an adjacent doorway. He wore a dark waist cloak, and a cap pulled down on his head. She watched as he bumped into the two drunkards, grumbled for them to watch where they were going, and then skip away down the lane.

Smooth, she thought, *but not smooth enough.* Just as the thief was checking the contents of the coin pouch, the Night Flyer stepped into his path with arms crossed over chest, feet planted shoulder width apart. The pickpocket glanced up, then wilted, turning sheet white with terror. He dropped the pilfered purse, coins clinking on the stones, and started to run. After only a few paces, a lasso caught about his neck, and he jerked to a halt. "I, I, I'll cut you in," he stammered, grabbing at the rope and tugging to loosen it. Florentina spun him around by his elbow and thrust his slight frame against the nearest wall. "Ha-happy Novena, Night Flyer. You're looking well."

"Silence!" she hissed in a low tone ambiguous to gender. However, Florentina used a Venetian accent in this role to further disguise her voice.

He gulped wide-eyed as he stared at the city's new legend. "You keep the coins."

She glared at him with a steely gaze and called out, "Hey fellows singing such a fine carol!" The revelers who had reached the far end of the block stumbled to a stop and glanced behind them. "Sì, you two. Come back for your money. You must have dropped your coin purse." She held it up in one hand while keeping the other tight on the rope. Then she gave it a mighty toss in their direction.

"Thank ye," one managed while the other fell down when he bent to retrieve the pouch.

The Night Flyer's attention returned to the thief. "Now you are going to tell me everything you know about underworld organizations, crime circles, and secret societies. Who uses the symbol of a horse?" He stared back at her with a blank expression and a gaping mouth. "Tell me what I want to know!"

He blinked and kept his hands at the rope encircling his neck. "I have no idea what you are talking about."

"A powerful criminal element, a gang who stay to the shadows, who hire assassins to do their bidding. You are a criminal; don't you keep apprised of your business?"

"See here, I am but a pickpocket. I have nothing to do with assassins. Besides, you are a much more capable outlaw than I; how could I have more information than you possess?"

This approach was getting her nowhere; he was the third thief she had shaken down this week and none of them had a clue. "Why are you out here stealing from drunks? Why not do honest work?" She scrunched her brows and frowned at him, but lifted the loop from around his neck.

He laughed nervously, in obvious relief. "Why should I work twelve hours a day for the money I can collect in two minutes?"

The Night Flyer drew back her right fist and punched him in the jaw, popping his head against the solid wall. "Because that man worked for twelve hours a day to get those coins and they are rightfully his, the fruit of his labor, you selfish loathsome toad!" She sighed when he crumpled into a whimpering heap on the ground. It was more out of frustration she had struck him than anger. Seeking the alleyways at night was getting her nowhere, and she was further annoyed by Maddie's avoidance of her. She had not felt this lost and powerless since she held her dying father in her arms. At least then she knew who to blame, where to turn for her vengeance. She had no idea who this enemy was.

"Don't kill me!" the pitiful figure pleaded.

"I'm not going to kill you, you oaf," she groaned. "Think how you would feel if someone stole from you. Take up an honest profession."

"Man," he moaned through frightened tears, "people been taking from me since I was born."

* * *

DON ALESSANDRO TORELLI, leader of House Torelli and estimably the wealthiest merchant in Milan, pulled out a brocade cushioned chair for his lovely, petite wife and took her arm as she eased into the seat. He stood a head taller than most men, with a robust build, wood-brown hair grown to his collar as was the fashion, a smooth carved face, and intense umber eyes. Alessandro bent down and greeted Portia with a light kiss on her full, rosy lips. He noted the exquisite woven netting that bound her silky blonde hair and the gold circlet holding it in place. She wore an everyday dress suitable for breakfast while he donned business attire consisting of a long-sleeved azure silk shirt worn under a fitted fern green velvet doublet which extended past his belt to thigh length over rust hose.

The dining hall door burst open to a pack of noisy children streaming through it. "There's a carol singing tonight in the Piazza Duomo and everyone is going!" Bernardo excitedly proclaimed. Alessandro's youngest son Bernardo was an eager lad in a gangly stage with a voice which altered from squeak to deep in the blink of an eye. He tossed back light brown hair he had yet to comb that morning as he bounded toward his chair to the left of his mother's. The spacious, high ceilinged dining room sported an ample stone fireplace on its interior side and a row of windows facing the boulevard on the opposite wall. The mahogany table was large enough to seat eight with ease, more if necessary.

"There will be instruments playing Papa!" Pollonia, the burnished haired beauty who would soon blossom into a genuine woman chimed in, her fair face glowing in anticipation. Though other fathers had married off their daughters by her age, Alessandro was in no hurry to rid himself of such a loving, attentive child.

"Is that so?" he responded in bemusement as he took his seat, knowing it would only fuel their enthusiasm.

Behind his children bounded two little ones, Matteo age seven and his sister Betta age five. They were tugging on their mother's hands, dragging along a disheveled looking Madelena. "Can we go, can we go?" They chanted.

She looks tired, he thought with concern as he considered his younger sister. *Something is bothering her which she hasn't told me about.*

"Yes, you may go," she sighed in surrender as she uncharacteristically plopped into her chair at the other end of the great mahogany table. "Florentina will take you."

Alessandro watched as she glanced over her shoulder at the intriguing and ingenious woman coming through the doorway. He was privy to the secret of their relationship and had no objections as long as they remained discrete. He noted Florentina was carrying an object of some kind and rose from his seat.

"Aren't you coming?" pleaded the most adorable blonde-haired piccolo with the biggest, roundest blue eyes he had ever seen.

"I can't, Sweetie," Maddie replied in gentle tones. "But Florentina…" She paused as Florentina walked past carrying something about the size of a chess board loaded with figures. Alessandro met her before she reached her spot at the table.

"I wasn't sure where to display this," she said as she handed it to him. "I was going to put it in my room, but then I thought—"

"What an exquisite *Il Presepe!*" Alessandro declared as he took it from her and set it down for examination. Everyone's attention was riveted on the work of art.

"My father carved the pieces," Florentina explained. "I just painted them and constructed the barn. I guess I was about Bernardo's age at the time."

"Wow!" exclaimed Betta, fascination filling her cherubic face.

Maddie echoed her daughter's sentiment. "I've never seen one so detailed, so artfully crafted."

Alessandro laid a hand on Florentina's shoulder. "Thank you for sharing this beautiful tribute to the Nativity, Florentina. We shall display it on the mantle in here so we may all enjoy it at every meal."

"Hey, there's real straw in the manger," Matteo noted as he pushed chestnut curls out of his astonished brown eyes.

Bernardo had bounced out of his seat and scurried around the table to get a better view. "The tall wise man looks like you, Papa."

Alessandro smiled as he lifted the piece and placed it on the broad, polished mantle above the dining room hearth. "I don't think Luigi de Bossi knew me when he and Florentina made it." Everyone recognized the honor of having their likeness painted or carved into a manger scene.

"Florentina, it is so beautiful!" Portia gushed. "Thank you so much for letting us all enjoy it."

"You're welcome," she said humbly as she slid into her seat at the table. "Thank you for allowing me to participate in your family's Christmas season."

"But of course," Portia replied with a genuine smile. Alessandro had invited Florentina to fill a place at their table vacated by his eldest son

Antonio. He knew Portia would be melancholy to be reminded every day of his absence, and since Matteo had wanted to sit in his cousin's spot to Alessandro's left, Florentina had taken the boy's chair on the other side of Madelena from little Betta's seat.

"You *are* family," Alessandro said in an assuring tone. Then he glanced at his sister, noting the odd fog of despair in her verdant gaze.

Bianca, the Torelli's full-bosomed, middle-aged cook, entered from the other end of the spacious hall bearing a broad tray laden with their morning meal. "You don't mind taking the children tonight, do you?" Maddie asked with a glance toward Florentina as Bianca set the tray in the center of the table.

"Grazie," Alessandro said to her. "It smells divine." With a quick curtsey and bow, she exited.

"No, I would love to take the children to the caroling tonight," Florentina answered and Ally watched her search Maddie's expression. "We would love it even more if you were to join us."

Madelena turned her attention toward pastries and orange slices. "It is the end of the year audit. I will be too busy making sure the books are balanced, but you all go on and have a wonderful time."

No one mentioned Antonio, but Alessandro was certain he was on everyone's mind. His son had stubbornly defied his wishes and joined the army. Now he was spending his Christmas in Napoli, in a siege with the French military, the Spanish threatening attack at any moment. There seemed to him to be two major avoided issues: the danger facing Antonio and what was off between Maddie and Florentina.

CHAPTER 3

*D*on Benetto Viscardi sat alone in a gloomy upstairs room, heavy drapes pulled almost closed allowing in only a sliver of light. Uncharacteristic ashen stubble dotted his chiseled chin and fiery anger burned in his slate gray eyes. He clenched his fingers into a fist, which he pounded on his thigh. *He thinks I'll just fade away and become nothing, but I'll get what's mine back. I will make the Night Flyer pay! There must be a way, something I can do to regain my power.* But having passed the fifty-year mark, he comprehended it was too late to start over.

With a sigh, Benetto rose, trod to the window and pushed aside the drapes enough to peer out. Small patches of snow remained in shady areas, spotting yellow-brown grass. He gazed out of the medieval manor house over hills striped with dormant grapevines clinging to their trestles. *Salted. Ruined. Bastard couldn't even leave me this one thing.* He paced the wooden floor, prodding his devious brain for a plan. *Can't afford to keep the servants—only have two now,* he grumbled to himself. For two weeks he had brooded, cutting himself off from his family, indulging in self-pity, recycling anger, bitterness, and hatred until they played on a continuous loop. When he slept, he had nightmares of nameless, faceless villains in dark robes laughing as the Night Flyer knelt over him with a knife to his throat. *They say confession is good for the soul,* he had said and demanded, *Speak the names of the men you have killed.* No matter how he tried to make it stop, the voice returned, repeating everything he had spoken as Benetto's world went up in flames.

"They only got what they deserved," he declared aloud in his own defense. "I only killed those who crossed me, or betrayed me, or did not fulfill their end of a bargain. You must show people who is in charge, you have to…"

He stopped, wiped a hand through his untended salt and pepper hair, and exhaled a breath. "The Night Flyer is a dead man." But the once commanding arms merchant had no clue to his identity and no means with which to discover it.

A rumbling in his gut reminded him he had not eaten yet, so with irritation painted across his face he trudged downstairs. There he witnessed the unreal: his wife and daughter were… decorating! How could they even think of celebrating? How dare they act as if all was normal? This rickety old manor had a thatched roof–thatch! And they are ready for Christmas?

Benetto whirled through the great hall like a dark tornado, sweeping the fir branches, oranges, and lemons arranged in neat groupings to the floor with a vengeance. "What do you think you two are doing?" he bellowed. Spying an old family *il Presepe*, he grabbed for it, but young Agnese was too quick for him and scooped up the manger scene, stealing his opportunity to smash it.

Daniella startled at his shout and dropped an orange that plopped and rolled without direction across the wood slat floor. The chubby woman with her expensive blonde wig and stylish dress spun, cringed, and raised her arms protectively. Her nervous blue eyes went wide, and she scuttled away from him. The Night Flyer's voice reverberated in his mind again. *Even your own wife and daughter are terrified of you.*

"Foolish woman," he scolded, but halted his wrathful advance. "I am not going to strike you." But he had; in the past, on occasions, he had slapped or hit her, but it had been because he was angry, and she merely convenient. It had seldom been her fault, and he usually apologized afterward or bought her a gift or something to satisfy. But had those tokens satisfied, or were they just to sooth his own conscience?

"Papa!" Agnese wailed from a safe distance, clutching the wooden representation of the Nativity. "You are ruining Christmas!"

"*I'm* ruining Christmas?" he retorted in defensive denial. "You think it is my fault a vandal and thief burned our home to the ground and we are stuck in this hovel? I don't feel like celebrating and I'll have none of these gay trappings about."

"The manor isn't so bad," Daniella ventured timidly. "It could be worse."

"Worse? How could it be worse?" he roared. "My business is gone, the fortune lost, the mansion destroyed. We have nothing—nothing but a centuries old cottage and a vineyard which can't produce edible grapes."

"But we are alive, Papa. He could have killed you, all of us, but he didn't."

Benetto's fingers moved to the half-healed cut on his chin. *That is to remind you,* the Night Flyer had said. *Every time you look in the mirror and see that scar, remember you were given a second chance.*

His expression softened toward his daughter. She was indeed lovely and kind, just coming of age to marry. As he studied her haunted face, he wondered what had gone wrong, how this gulf had formed between them since the time she was a little girl and would run to hug her papa. And it seemed to him her long golden strands were fading back to the earthy brown they had been when she was younger. "I simply don't feel like celebrating," he replied at length.

Tensions were starting to ease off when the front door opened and a fit youthful man in traveling clothes and cloak stepped through and dropped a trunk on the floor. Agnese's face lit with her smile as she cried, "Niccolo, you are home!" She set down the Nativity decoration and raced into her brother's arms.

Daniella was right behind her. "Niccolo, son, we are so happy you made it home for Christmas," she cooed as she embraced the handsome young man and greeted him with a kiss.

"Tell us all about Bologna and your studies at the university," Agnese urged.

But Niccolo's features remained stony, and his ebony eyes glared across the room at his father. After granting his mother and sister each a kiss on the cheek, he released them and crossed to Benetto.

He knew the look in his son's face and assumed a defensive posture, raising his chin as Niccolo was now taller than he. "As is customary the university students were all sent home for Christmas break," Niccolo recounted with ire seething beneath the surface of his words. "Only when I got there, all I found was a pile of ashes. Strangers had to tell me where to find you."

"Son, there was no time for a letter to reach you," Benetto began in a calm, reasonable tone. "You would have already departed for Milan before the message would have arrived."

He nodded curtly. Then the assault commenced. "What am I supposed to do now? Is there money to complete my education? And why should I bother? I was going to learn all the newest trends in the business world, law, and accounting, and then return to be your partner. One day Viscardi Arms and Weapons would pass to me. What is there for me now?"

"Son, there should be enough funds to finish your studies and with the skills you are learning you can start out for yourself, be a journeyman with another merchant or a banker and work your way up as most men do."

"Do you know how long it will take? You never think of me or Agnese," he accused.

"Just a minute," Benetto retorted, heat building in his gut. "This isn't my fault. It was the damned bastard, Night Flyer. Didn't they tell you who burned the warehouses and mansion?"

"Oh, yes, everyone told me," he fumed.

"Then you know it is that criminal who is to blame and are aware the magistrate and the guild wouldn't intervene to help us. It was the Night Flyer who stole your future!"

Niccolo pushed back a sweep of black hair from his face, a cold stare bearing into Benetto as he stepped closer. Then in a chilling voice he probed, "And who created the Night Flyer, Father? Someone you cheated, someone you lied to, someone whose relative you killed. You angered the wrong person, and he took his revenge."

Benetto stared at his tall, dark, handsome son whose dangerous temper mirrored his own and found he had no reply. He was aware Daniella and Agnese were standing behind Niccolo, holding close to each other, no doubt afraid to interfere. Did they think the same as his son only were too frightened to say so? Certainly they did, and why not? Evidently it was true. He could blame the thief, the secret society, even the weather, but in the end it all came back to him and a scripture verse he learned in catechism a lifetime ago: *whatsoever a man sows, that shall he also reap.*

"Look what you've done to poor Agnese," Niccolo continued. "She is as innocent as a lamb, but how will she ever find a decent husband? Who will want to wed her now, with nothing for a dowry and a failure for a father? She'll be lucky if she needn't resort to marrying a dirt farmer!"

Guilt poured through Benetto like streams through a canal. He tried to stave it off with anger as he clenched a fist but could not find the words to rebuff his son. Then he heard a strange sound come from his daughter's lips; it rang with confidence and defiance, a strength he had not witnessed in the timid mouse before.

"Antonio will want me," she professed with straight posture and a firm jaw. "Antonio loves me and he won't care about any dowry or the financial troubles of my House."

Niccolo turned to the side shifting his gaze from father to sister. "Antonio?"

"Torelli," Benetto said with a weary sigh. "Fool boy has joined the army, and she has this fantasy he will come riding back on a white horse and carry her off to his castle."

"It is no fantasy, Papa; you'll see," she insisted.

Niccolo shook his head. "The Torelli mansion is a bit like a castle at that. Enlisted in the army, you say?"

"They sent him to Napoli, to the war with Spain." Benetto, at once overcome with exhaustion, sat in the nearest parlor armchair.

"When Papa found out we wanted to court each other, he forbade me to even speak to Antonio. So instead of going to university, he took a commission as a junior officer in the French artillery to prove himself." *When did this girl acquire such boldness?*

Niccolo's irate features melded into bewilderment, and he crossed back to Agnese and took her hand. Then he turned a cocked head toward Benetto. "The Torellis are a wealthy family, well respected in the community, an ideal match for Agnese. Why would you oppose it?"

"Because I can't stand that arrogant Alessandro; never could," he said. "And Antonio is too young and immature, as evidenced by fool-hearty choices which put his life at risk."

"I recall Antonio. We were peers, Father," Niccolo stated. "He is only a year or two younger than I am."

"We love each other," Agnese declared.

"Love, love," Benetto mumbled as he wiped a hand down his lined face. "What good is it? What good is love if the boy gets himself killed? Besides, love fades. It withers and dies, and then what have you left? Best to be wise when choosing a husband; better yet, follow tradition and allow your father to decide for you. Agnese, I know you have been cross with me, but I do have your interests in mind. I want a respectable older husband for you who is settled in his career and can take excellent care of you." One may well have heard a heartbeat in the silence as all waited for Agnese to reply. Benetto feared the worst, given her sudden surge of resolution.

"It is very sad you discount love Papa, just as it is very sad you do not wish to celebrate Christmas or do anything besides sit in your room and talk to yourself." Her voice was tenderness, that of the child he once held in his lap, such it almost compelled him to weep. "Without love, what is the point? Without happiness, why bother to live at all?"

* * *

SAME DAY, *Barletta, Napoli*

Antonio Torelli sat on a barrel sipping steamy liquid from a cup. He was wrapped in a green tunic over a black and white long-sleeved shirt and matching two-toned leggings with a red beret perched over his straight wood-brown hair. Rich umber eyes gazed out at the busy camp filled with French soldiers, Swiss mercenary pikemen, and Italian attachments such as his. The base smelled of horses and campfires, latrines, and soup in large kettles. Behind him was erected a canvass tent he shared with three other standard-bearers, the rank he held as a most junior officer. They had arrived about a week ago and typically sat around doing nothing while those in charge discussed plans and options, deciding who should go where.

He doubted there would be sweets and feasts for Christmas, no gifts for Epiphany, but there were plenty of priests assigned to the army so there would be Mass celebrations. He had already witnessed a group of enlisted men singing carols and Papi, a very animated, straw haired junior officer, recounted all the traditional tales from La Befana, the Christmas witch, to St. Francis and the first *il Presepe*.

"Good day Antonio," greeted a skinny, ruddy lad his age dressed in the same attire.

"Good day, Roberto," he replied. "What news is there?"

The wiry fellow with ginger curls pulled over a crate to sit by the fire with Antonio. "They are saying we may be sent somewhere else. The generals are divided between keeping a massive force together in one place or divvying us up to attack or reinforce other strategic spots around Napoli."

Antonio hummed out a nonverbal reply as he took another sip. "What do you think we should do?"

Roberto laughed. "I'm just a standard-bearer, same as you. They don't pay us to think; they pay us to follow orders. Hey, you're a merchant's son, right?"

"Sì," he replied amiably.

"My father's a banker. I guess neither of us needs the money, only I have two brothers ahead of me to inherit. I thought I may make a go of becoming a condottiere. What about you?"

What indeed? he pondered as his thoughts turned toward home, his family, and Agnese.

CHAPTER 4

Madelena and Portia, dressed in their finest, rode down the stone-paved street in an open carriage toward the Sacchi mansion. The weekly gathering of their ladies' circle each Saturday was not hindered by Christmas being only four days away. In fact, Julia was more than eager to show off the decorations she had displayed in her home for the occasion. The mild, dry morning exhibited all the signs of there being a warm Christmas. Maddie could remember a foot of snow one year and a balmy day where she needed to break out summer clothing the next. One never knew what to expect where weather was concerned.

As Portia chattered and waved to shoppers on the sidewalk, Maddie dreaded the social meeting. She had once thought these youngish upper-class women who shared her station were her friends, but she was now seeing them as opportunistic busybodies whose only concern was to flaunt their wealth and beauty. They never discussed topics of genuine interest to her and she felt less and less comfortable in their company, but she was trapped. If she were to suddenly leave their association, stop attending at all, she was certain rumors would begin to fly. They had excused her absence for the first months following her husband Vergilio Carcano's death as it was a proper mourning period for a widow to remain in her home, but afterward she was obligated to return. No, that wasn't right… it was only after she had met the fascinating and adventurous

Florentina, she had realized how tedious her weekly women's brunch had become.

"Look at this, Maddie," Portia exclaimed as they approached the front entry. "A holly wreath," she commented. "And see the evergreen and red candles in every window!"

Madelena studied the exterior of the extravagant house and its seasonal décor. The cream-colored stucco was bright and accented with rose painted wood window and door frames to match the roof tiles. The three-story edifice was similar to their own estate, and from earlier visits she knew it included an inner courtyard with gardens like theirs.

"I have no doubt Julia will have every decoration imaginable," Maddie replied just as the door opened and they were ushered inside by a maid.

The front hall boasted a large *Il Presepe* bookended by arrangements of nuts, citrus fruit, and fir boughs, but in Maddie's estimation it was not as artistically crafted as Florentina's. This one was larger, but only comprised the Holy Family and the Magi and lacked detail. On the mantle rested an assortment of Christmas themed statuary, most carved of wood and painted. They included La Befana with her broom and an enormous bag stuffed with treats and toys over her shoulder and a representation of a snowy bearded man dressed in red and white robes holding a staff in one hand with the other raised as if giving a blessing. Being unfamiliar with this likeness, Madelena moved forward to examine it.

"Donna Julia had that St. Nicolas sent all the way from Cologne to add to her collection," the maid offered. "This other one here is from Paris," she added, pointing to a porcelain figure of the beloved saint. "Donna Julia and her other guests are in the ladies' parlor. I'll show you in."

Maddie and Portia had been to this house dozens of times, but it was proper to be escorted, so they dutifully followed the maid. Upon their entrance the radiant powdered face of a younger woman about Madelena's height shone beneath an embellished updo of golden honey strands. Leading with her impressive breasts, which threatened to leap forth from the gown with a cut to accentuate them, Julia opened her arms to greet first Portia, then Maddie.

"Dear Portia," Julia gushed, planting a kiss to the side of each cheek. "Darling Madelena," she cooed and clasped her hands. "So glad you could both come today." Behind her stood three other women under forty dressed in designer finery. Tall as a tree and thin as a twig was Tomasina Luino with her curly brunette tresses secured by a golden snood intended to bring out the gilded thread work in her maroon gown. The pudgy Isabella della Gazzada, her light brown hair worked into a sweeping updo, was the wife of a furnishing merchant. Standing behind the other two taking a sip from a fine crystal short-stemmed glass was Rose Bombello, a moonlit blonde with an infectious smile.

"Your home is truly lovely," Portia complimented as she glanced around the parlor decked out with vibrant, artful decorations for the season.

"Oh, thank you," Julia replied with pride beaming on her face. "You must try my new concoction," she invited, motioning toward glasses filled with an orangish liquid.

"It is the pinnacle!" declared Isabella, and she finished off her glass.

"Madelena, you will find this fascinating, I am certain," Julia stated. "I was in a wine shop a few weeks ago and came across a bottle of da Vinci wine and after we had discussed him and his relation to your tutor, I was curious, so I asked the shopkeeper and he told me it was the same da Vinci who did the painting. Apparently, Duke Sforza gave the artist a vineyard as part of his payment for that fresco, what did you call it?"

"The Last Supper," Maddie replied with interest as she considered, *perhaps today will not be a total waste of my time.*

"Yes, anyway, he bottled a couple of years' worth of the stuff before the French took over and da Vinci left Milan. The connoisseurs swear by its quality, so I bought one. It had an interesting, fruity flavor, so I thought to add citrus juices in keeping with the season, a few spices, and some honey. I think it turned out quite well."

Madelena lifted a glass from the table. "I should love to try it." After the first sip, she smiled at her hostess. "Julia, I believe you have developed a new skill as a vintner."

Portia took her own glass and sipped. Then the conversation shifted.

"Portia, wasn't the carol singing fabulous? All those instrumentalists playing along and the giant Il Ceppo burning in the Piazza Duomo?" Tomasina began.

Isabella picked up with, "Everyone was there… except for you." Everyone's focus turned to Maddie.

"It's end of the year audit," she explained with a casual air. "I must ensure the books are accurate. We don't want to be fined for not paying the correct amount of taxes the French have demanded, nor do we wish to pay them a single florin more than required."

"Which is why I take no part in my husband's business affairs," Tomasina said with a wave of her hand. "I wouldn't miss an important social occasion to play with numbers no matter how much it paid."

"We saw your children there with their tutor," Isabella noted with a dubious glint in her aspect.

"I must say," Julia commented, her face drawn into consternation. "Do you pay the woman enough? Can't she afford a suitable wardrobe?"

"So unfashionable," Tomasina added in a critical tone screwing up her nose as if there was a bad smell in the room.

Maddie was stunned. *How dare they criticize Florentina! I feared this would happen, these snooty busybodies. There is nothing wrong with how she dresses.* "My tutor is not employed to be fashionable," she said with as little disdain as she could present.

Portia placed a hand lightly on Madelena's arm and joined in the defense. "Florentina is a superb teacher and the children love her. I only wish I had been able to find someone so accomplished when mine were younger."

Maddie took a deep breath and glanced down at her sister-in-law. *I wonder if Ally told her about us, or maybe she figured it out by herself... Even if she doesn't know, she likes Florentina.* She smiled at Portia, appreciative of the support.

"She is strong, though," Julia asserted. "I saw her carry the littlest one home. Poor thing fell asleep on her shoulder, yet she walked as if she bore no load at all."

Madelena pictured Fiore cradling Betta on her shoulder, holding her baby close. It would have been no imposition. She harbored no doubt Florentina loved her children dearly. They were a family... if only she wasn't so afraid, so distraught and guilt ridden.

Then bashful Rose peeped into the conversation. "She is the most adorable little girl with those big blue eyes, as sweet as honey, and so tiny even I could most likely carry her with ease."

Maddie sent a grateful smile to Rose. "Thank you," she replied. "To me she is the most precious child in the whole world—along with her brother, of course."

Tomasina's high tinkling laugh sounded above the others as the tension was lightened. "Boys!" She declared. "I have two of them... or is it three? I lose track!" Laughter rang out again.

Julia said, "My Giovanni is an older man, but I am hoping for a child of my own. He has two sons already, but men never get too old and we are trying."

"I couldn't imagine not having my three," Portia replied.

"Well, I could certainly do without the pain of childbirth," Isabella stated. "And the weight gain which accompanies a pregnancy. Sometimes it just sticks to you."

A new thought thrust its way into Maddie's consciousness. *If Florentina stays with me, she will never be able to have a child of her own. She says Betta and Matteo are her dream children, but I have to wonder… she would miss out on the experience… but since I am of the mind she will get herself killed in the coming weeks, why am I contemplating this at all?*

* * *

IT WAS a lovely Saturday and Florentina knew Madelena was off to her women's circle brunch. It seemed she was always away somewhere of late, but it shouldn't spoil her day or the children's. Yet when she opened the door to Betta and Matteo's room, she found it empty. A stroll around the second floor turned up no little ones, however she did bump into Livia coming up the back stairway. "Where are the children?" she asked.

Livia, the young governess who was supposed to watch after Betta and Matteo when they were not in classes, shot her a look of surprise. "They aren't in their room?" She blinked.

Florentina assumed they were about the same age in years, but she had observed Livia's lack of responsibility on more than one occasion. "No," she replied flatly.

"I swear, I can just turn around and they have zipped off and away like rabbits! Betta," she called out. "Matteo!"

"Never mind," Florentina dismissed. "I'm taking them for an outing so you may do whatever you wish for a few hours."

"Are you certain you won't need me?" her tone brightened.

Florentina sighed and headed downstairs, saying over her shoulder, "We'll be back before dark."

When she didn't spot them in the courtyard, Florentina had an idea of where to search. With Night Flyer stealth, she opened a crack in the dining room door.

"Don't touch them, Matteo," Betta warned in a whisper. "If you break one, you'll be in such trouble!"

Matteo stood on the hearthstones, his hand reaching up toward the figures in the nativity scene. "I want a closer look at the tall wise man. I think he looks like Uncle Alessandro."

Biting back a smile, Florentina stepped into the hall, making her presence known. Matteo jumped and Betta sang, "See, I told you so."

"I didn't touch anything," he spouted out innocently. "I didn't break anything."

"I know," Florentina said with a wink as she walked over to the children. "Would you like to examine them up close?"

They both vigorously nodded their heads and Betta added, "Please!"

Florentina lifted the entire display from the mantle and set it on the dining table; then she took a seat in the nearest chair. Matteo climbed in on his knees beside her, and Betta crawled into her lap. Then she showed them each of the twenty pieces and let them hold them to study their faces. "This one does look like Uncle Ally, doesn't he?" Betta commented.

"He is certainly tall enough," Florentina agreed.

"He's carrying one of the jars," Matteo observed, "but I don't know if it's the frankincense or the myrrh?"

"Which one do you think it is?" his tutor prodded.

Matteo scrunched up a studious face and declared, "The frankincense."

"There you have it," Florentina commended him.

Betta held the donkey, stroking its wooden back. "The donkey is my favorite," she cooed, then quickly added, "and Mary and baby Jesus too."

Florentina's heart filled with joy to share the treasure with them. "I thought I would take you for an outing since the weather is so nice."

"Yeah!" they both cheered.

"Can we go see the castle, Castle Sforza?" suggested Matteo.

"I want to go to the sweets shop." Betta's big, round eyes as fathomless as the deepest ocean peered up at her.

"I don't see why we can't do both," Florentina admitted.

More cheers and hugs and then Matteo added, "And you can teach us about the castle and the Sforzas. Papa liked them."

"And you can tell us the stories of Christmas," Betta added, "about the wise men and La Befana. You tell the best stories, Florentina."

"We'll have a fabulous outing and if anyone asks, we shall tell them it was an educational trip and you two can then recite off everything you learned." All three beamed at each other. *I love them so much, Maddie! Please come back to me so we can be a family.*

CHAPTER 5

Wearing a summer weight day dress and straw sun hat on a balmy December morning, Florentina walked through the shopping district holding two small hands, one in each of hers. They were off to visit Castle Sforza first and then stop for a treat and lemonade before returning home. She encountered slight resistance from Matteo who declared himself too big to need his hand held, but because of the crowds of shoppers out on the Saturday before Christmas, Florentina had insisted.

"Tell us the story of La Befana," Betta requested, batting thick lashes at her from beneath a halo of golden hair.

"It all started when the Magi, three very learned scholars from the East, noticed a spectacular star suddenly appear in the sky," she began in her best story-telling rhythm and timbre. "They had studied the stars for years and were experts on all the constellations, so they knew this bright new star signaled some important event, like the birth of a king. They selected valuable gifts to take and set out on camels with a small escort."

"Did they know it was Jesus?" Matteo asked with acorn curls bounding in and out of his eyes.

"They didn't know his name or that he was the son of God, not until they arrived in Bethlehem, but they knew the new baby was someone very important. As they traveled west following the direction of the star, the wise men stopped along the way to spend the night. The journey would take them two weeks because they had to travel a long distance."

"I bet they got tired," Betta commented. "And hungry."

"I'm sure they did, but many kind people offered them hospitality as they traveled and one of those people was Befana." Florentina glanced down into eager faces. She knew they had heard the story before, but it didn't mean it wasn't enjoyable again. "When the Magi and their party arrived, Befana was busy cleaning her house. She was always sweeping and dusting and tidying up because she was obsessed with cleanliness. But, as is practiced by every civilized culture, she paused what she was doing to welcome them into her home and offer them refreshments."

"I'll bet she served them cakes and lemonade," Matteo suggested. "Those are what most people leave for her to eat on the night before Epiphany."

"I'm not sure," Florentina replied with speculation, "but you do make a very astute observation." Matteo beamed at her praise. "In fact, the wise men were so impressed with her hospitality and neat home, they invited her to come with them and bring her own gift for the newborn king. 'No, grazie,' she said. 'I am too busy cleaning. I couldn't possibly leave on a long journey.' So she returned to sweeping her floors while the Magi and their procession riding camels and donkeys, and some walking, proceeded out of sight."

"Who would like cleaning *that* much?" Betta exclaimed with distaste in her tone.

Florentina gripped their hands as a carriage whizzed by on the road at much too high of a speed for her liking. They were bumped by a couple avoiding being struck, but continued on unscathed. "Apparently Befana did. But the very next day she regretted her decision. She starting to think about how exciting it would be to meet a baby king and she felt remorseful about not at least sending a gift with the Magi. 'I know what I'll do!' she determined. 'I'll pack a big sack with treats and toys and strike out after them. I'm sure I'll catch up.'"

"But she didn't," Matteo grinned up at Florentina with two front teeth larger than all the rest.

"No, she didn't," his tutor confirmed. "She wandered all over while the wise men and those who had gone with them arrived in Bethlehem on Epiphany morning to present their gifts of gold, frankincense, and myrrh."

"Then what about Befana?" Betta asked.

"She was so sad she had missed her chance, an angel took pity on her and touched her broom with magic so she could use it to fly from village to town and house to house and continue her search. So, every year on the night before Epiphany morning, she does just that! When she arrives at a house, she whisks down the chimney looking for baby Jesus. If the dwelling has good children living there, she leaves sweets and toys in their stocking or hollowed out olive logs." Joy radiated from giggling faces.

"That's silly!" Betta bubbled with laughter. "People can't fly on brooms."

"No," Matteo said as he straightened up tall and in the most serious tone added, "but the Night Flyer can fly on big, black wings."

Florentina felt a tug on her right hand and glanced down at Betta who asked, "Is the Night Flyer an angel?"

A lump formed in Florentina's throat. "No, Cucciola, not an angel. I think he made mechanical wings like Daedalus constructed for his son Icarus, only his aren't made of feathers stuck on with wax and he doesn't ever fly too close to the sun." They had recently read the Greek myth in their studies, so the explanation had context and, she thought, reinforced a Classical Literature lesson. "And here we are—Castle Sforza."

Before them loomed the imposing fortress with high, thick stone walls topped with battlements and round turrets at each corner encircled by a manmade moat. At the front of the huge rectangular citadel stood a triangular shaped gate house one must pass through before crossing the drawbridge into the castle. Its door was closed and the raised drawbridge secured.

Matteo and Betta leaned their heads back as they peered up and up. "Wow," escaped from the little boy's lips. "It's so big!" Florentina studied the edifice and noted some unrepaired damage from the French assault on the castle a few years before, when Duke Ludovico Sforza had been ousted from power.

Betta reached her arms up and Florentina absently lifted her for a better view. "The gate is closed," Betta said, pointing. "How will we get in?"

"I don't think we will be getting in," Florentina sighed.

"Because the French rulers don't want to let us in," Matteo grumbled and crossed his arms over his chest with a frown.

"Matteo, I will not have you speaking ill of the city government," Florentina demanded. "Your Uncle Alessandro wouldn't like it."

"But Papa said the Sforzas always had the gate open, especially at Christmas, and they held grand celebrations," he protested.

"Yes, I remember," she replied. "I even attended one when I was a little girl. But look, Matteo, see those chips in the stone and up there at the hole? See the damage to the walls?" She pointed while jostling Betta on her hip with her other arm. "It may not be safe to allow visitors into the castle. Besides, the French authorities might be worried citizens will have the same ill will toward them as you, and they could be afraid to let in people they don't know."

"But we can't hurt them," Betta said as she lifted Florentina's hat off and placed it over her own head. It was much too large, and she giggled as it slid over her eyes.

"No, you can't." She took her hat back and smiled lovingly at the child in her arms. "But there are others who could and would if they had the chance." Then she returned her gaze to Matteo.

He peered up at her with an innocent expression. "I can't hurt them either. So, you've been inside? What is it like?"

"Let's walk around to get a better view." She set Betta down and took the children's hands again. "Construction was begun by Lord Visconti in the 1300s, back when it was called Castello di Porta Giova. The four corner towers were added in the 1400s. The ruling Visconti family lived here until 1447, when a coup overthrew the Viscontis and the castle was all but destroyed. But the group who took over, the Golden Ambrosian Republic, didn't last long and a few years later Francesco Sforza came to power and rebuilt the castle."

"Is he the Sforza our Papa liked?" Betta asked in curiosity as rounding a corner they got an unobstructed view of the length of the fortress.

"He may have, but Francesco died before your Papa was born. I suspect the Sforza he liked is the same one I met, Ludovico, also called Il Moro. He's the one who brought Master Leonardo to Milan," Florentina explained. "He was Francesco's youngest son and the fifth Sforza to rule."

"Who were the others?" Matteo asked, then pointed. "There's a hole in the wall."

Florentina nodded. "His first son, Galeazzo, continued the castle's construction after Francesco died; Ludovico was just a baby. But Galeazzo had a reputation as being a mean tyrant and people didn't like him—enough so, someone killed him in 1476."

Betta gasped. "Someone killed him? Because he was mean?"

"Well, it was a bit more complicated, and the assassins were caught," she confirmed. "But that led to Milan's first female ruler."

"A woman?" Matteo's eyes rounded in astonishment as he stared up at Florentina.

"Bona of Savoy, Galeazzo's wife, was the Duchess of Milan and regent until their son Gian was old enough; then he took over for a while. But Il Moro was clever and had great influence while both the Duchess and Gian held their titles. After Gian died, Ludovico became the official Duke."

"And he brought Master Leonardo!" Betta exclaimed with a big grin.

"Correct. He was a major patron of the arts and initiated many building projects, including extending the canal system. He also made policies which promoted business and trade."

"I'll bet that's why Papa liked him!" Matteo exclaimed. "He made it easier for the merchants to make money."

Florentina released his hand so she could ruffle it over his curly locks. "Are you the smartest seven-year-old in the whole word?" He beamed at her. "He commissioned Master Leonardo and other artists to paint frescos, create sculptures, and even paint a ceiling inside the castle. Leonardo was working on plans for a giant horse when the war started and—"

The thought struck her like an avalanche! *Leonardo's horse—the sign of the horse. I wonder if there's a connection; this could be a clue, a breakthrough! I'll have to explore this possibility. I'll need to study the sketches again and the Night Flyer must infiltrate the castle and find the clay model Leonardo delivered. Maybe it holds the answer!*

"And what?" Betta asked as Florentina was lost in her thoughts. The child's voice brought her back to the present.

"Oh, yes, the war required all the bronze for cannons and the horse statue was never completed. Sorry we can't get inside, but I see a few clouds rolling in from the west. If we're going to have sweets and lemonade, we'll have to hurry."

Betta's arms shot up. "We'll go faster if you carry me." Joy and excitement glowing on her face, Florentina whisked up the precious girl and they proceeded at a quick pace back toward the shopping district.

* * *

CLOUDS BLOTTED out the sun by the time Florentina and the children arrived at home that afternoon, however the air remained calm and warm. *No storm brewing,* she thought, *but mayhap a shower.* While Betta and Matteo raced to tell their mother, who had no doubt returned from her brunch by then, all about their exciting outing, Florentina slipped away up the servants' stairs to the small bedchamber she shared with young Angela. A tinge of regret tugged at her heart as she supposed she had fallen out of favor with her beloved, but there was no time to indulge such sentiments now.

Kneeling at the foot of her bed, Florentina opened the ornately carved wooden chest her father had made for her. In its secret compartment were hidden the Night Flyer costume and equipment, but the drawer remained sealed as she rummaged through undergarments and scarves to retrieve a leather binder. She brought it to her bed where she sat and untied the cord wound about it and began pulling out sketches and pages of notes which she arranged into piles. In one stack, she placed every sheet related to Leonardo da Vinci's horse. The master had left behind a sundry of writings, drawings, and observations when he departed Milan and Florentina had soaked them up like a thirsty sponge, not allowing a single pencil stroke to be lost to future generations.

An early illustration depicted a rearing horse with a fallen soldier at its feet while another rearing horse image held the soldier on its back, but these prototypes were abandoned. One sheet was part of his treatise on equine anatomy. Leonardo spent an impressive amount of time studying horses in preparation for his grand project. She and Cesare, da Vinci's student who was only a few years her elder, accompanied the master to pastures and stables so he could scrutinize them as they stood, frolicked, tensed, and relaxed. He made countless drawings of differing poses until her younger self wondered if he would ever actually cast a statue.

Then she examined the sketch Leonardo had deemed worthy, a magnificent representation of a regal steed prancing with one front leg raised and its opposite back hoof just leaving the ground. She marveled at the detail of musculature, the lifelike muzzle and jaw, the attentive ears and alertly lifted tail—every line and curve so exact it seemed the horse would at any moment trot off the page.

Duke Ludovico Sforza commissioned the monument in 1482 with the intent of it being the largest equestrian statue in the world; Leonardo desired it to also be the most splendid. But he didn't work with stone and chisel as many sculptors, so he had to create casts in which to pour molten bronze. Because of the enormity of the project, eight meters high, he had to fashion molds for each piece of the horse which were to be assembled into the completed masterpiece. However, before going to so much trouble, he needed to know the duke would be pleased with the final design, so he produced a full sized clay model which was delivered to Castle Sforza in 1493. *Yes, eleven years,* she thought, *but there were so many other demands on his time—especially weapons development and portraits for other wealthy patrons.*

Il Moro had been overjoyed with the model horse which he kept in a place of honor and exhibited at his wedding. He had assembled seventy tons of bronze with which to cast the statue that would make both he and his artist famous around the world… and then the war began and all the bronze had to go to produce cannons. As a consolation to Leonardo, who had devoted so much time and energy to the project, Duke Sforza hired him to paint a wall in the refectory of the Convent Santa Maria delle Grazie—the Last Supper.

Next, Florentina reached into the drawer of her small bedside stand and withdrew the leather-bound diary of a madman named Galeazzo Monetario which she had obtained from Don Benetto when the Night Flyer had confronted him, burned his mansion and warehouses, and spared his miserable life. She had tried to make sense of the scribbling on these pages for weeks and had inserted marks at every reference to the horse.

She turned to the first one and read to herself: *Beware the sign of the horse; they are as the months of the year or spokes on a wheel,* and there was a drawing of a wagon wheel with six spokes which created twelve points along the rim. Flipping a few pages she read, *Beware the sign of the horse; they are scattered as autumn leaves, and yet they are one.* "Too bad this Galeazzo fellow was so cryptic and incoherent," she muttered aloud.

Several sheets over, she came to another equestrian reference. *Beware the mighty steed, for he will trample the powerful under foot. He is relentless, unyielding, patient, and persistent. He craves freedom but would deny it to others. Beware the symbol of the horse, for they are undaunted and will in time prevail.*

"So," she said aloud, being alone in the room, "what can we deduce? The secret order carries the symbol of a horse, perhaps a mighty steed." She held up da Vinci's horse drawing and nodded. "This is a mighty steed. But…" Florentina wrinkled her brow and frowned. "Sforza commissioned the horse and was delighted with the model; though not part of his coat of arms, the horse symbol was important to him. Vergilio was an outspoken supporter of the Sforza family, so why would a clandestine league choose this symbol if they opposed the Duke, and what difference would it make now since he has been ousted from rule and France administers the city-state? And if they did not oppose Sforza, why kill one of his supporters? The French? But a group of French allies would not need to keep their associate hidden. Benetto said Vergilio wasn't important enough to kill, so what made him so significant? And why now attack his widow?" She sighed and began to put the papers back into their binder. The endeavor was frustrating, but one course was clear to her at this juncture—the Night Flyer had to sneak into the castle to examine da Vinci's horse and tonight was as good a time as any.

CHAPTER 6

A soft rain fell while fog rolled out of the canals and through the city streets as a figure in black drifted over buildings and small trees toward Castle Sforza. She glided silently, and with no effort as the breeze kept her aloft. The Night Flyer was invisible against the darkened sky and obscured by mist. There was the dim glow of street lamps and her knowledge of the city to guide her to light upon the southeast ramparts away from any gates.

The Night Flyer folded in her wings upon landing, securing them in her opaque backpack, and infiltrated the high outer walls. Taking vigilant steps, she crept along, peering over the edge to spy the interior castle grounds, but the same cover which hid her approach and landing also obstructed her view. She detected the noisy clomp of a watchman's boots making his rounds and crouched against the exterior stone wall and drew in a slow, deep breath to sustain her until he had passed. His gaze was away, if he was paying any attention at all, and he rambled by tapping his pike butt rhythmically with every other step of his right foot.

She continued searching for the best way to sneak inside and was just about to settle upon using her grappling hook and rope when she spotted something in the light of a trash fire. *It can't be*, she thought as orange and yellow flames illuminated a towering figure. Mixed in with a pile of rubble and skirted by old crates stood an eight-meter-high clay horse being washed in the gentle rain.

Perceiving no other guards in her vicinity, the Night Flyer raced around the top of the wall to get close to the statue. Once she reached the section of wall nearest to it, she determined she didn't even need to climb down. The horse's head did not stretch as high as the fortification, but was tall enough. She squatted down for a closer examination to determine what had become of it. The sculpture was riddled with divots and holes, had lost one nostril and part of its jaw. One ear was gone and half of its tail missing. The once majestic monument was now cracked and weathered, having been relegated to this junk heap, possibly for years.

Target practice! Bile and revulsion rose up from her gut into her chest, and Florentina clenched her jaw as fire ignited in her spirit. *They used this artistic treasure for target practice! Damn barbarians!* She seethed in quiet rage. *Wasn't it enough to capture the city, to bring it under their domain? Did they have to destroy our works of art as well? And Master Leonardo went to Paris! I wonder if he knows what they did.*

A knot tied tighter and tighter in the pit of her stomach and she roiled against the pain. *Alessandro hates war; he hates the waste of it and now I see why. War is a waste of lives, almost always young lives. It kills, steals, and destroys; it is utter devastation. War doesn't care about innocence or beauty; it just consumes whatever is in its path.*

Florentina rubbed at her stinging eyes and wiped gloved hands down her haunted face. This was not a clue. It was not the symbol of a secret society. It was a victim of war and a dead end in her search for answers. She wanted to pound something, preferably a French soldier. She craved to punish someone for this crime, but drawing attention to herself would be more than foolish. Feeling great remorse over something that had never even been alive, she stood, turned, and walked away.

* * *

MADELENA SAT behind Alessandro's office desk, swamped in a sea of papers. Several oil lamps lit the room along with the last of the day's sunlight waning through the windows facing the inner courtyard. The study was an awe-inspiring room brimming with bookshelves featuring rows of leather-bound volumes. The paneled walls were alive with painted arches showcasing suns, moons, and stars which curved up to a frescoed ceiling. Paintings adorned the room and an impressive weapons collection dominated the interior wall. A cherry cabinet displayed petite sculptures and vases behind glass, and a huge globe rested in its cradle, revealing the world as they understood it post-Columbus's voyage. The end of the room opposite the desk and nearest the doorway held a small sitting area with cushioned chairs and a rug. The chamber was Alessandro's retreat and intellectual fortress; tonight, it was her asylum.

She missed Florentina. She wished she had gone to the caroling and to see the castle with them but… she thought of how her heart would break when assassins take the joy of Fiore's presence away forever. It would be easier if there is distance between them, if she let go gradually. It was what Maddie had told herself, anyway.

As she tried to focus on debits and credits and calculating long columns of numbers, Alessandro opened the door and strode in. He walked right up to the opposite side of the desk and crossed his arms over his muscular chest. "It's Christmas Eve, Maddie; what are you doing in here?"

She raised an innocent expression to him. "The end of the year audit."

"And I repeat," he said with some irritation, "what are you doing in here?"

She signed and put her pencil down. "I want everything to be correct, 'tis all."

"And I have no doubt it will be, but you've been engaged in this for weeks and it never took you so long before. In a few minutes we are gathering for the *cenone della Vigilia di Natale,* our traditional family feast the night before Christmas. Bianca has prepared *bollito misto* and apple mousse for dessert, and we are going to say a special prayer for Antonio. You are not allowed to hide in here and miss dinner."

"I'm not hiding," she lied. "I can manage half an hour I suppose."

"Maddie…" Alessandro relaxed his posture and leaned forward placing his palms on the desk. In a kind voice he asked, "What's wrong?"

Madelena expelled a nervous giggle and waved a hand. "Nothing's wrong; I've just been busy."

But he would not let it go. "I know you too well for you to lie to me. Something is off between you and Florentina. No one has said anything, but they don't have to. The whole atmosphere of the household is tense and uncertain. Whatever it is Maddie, she deeply loves you. It is as clear as a bluebird summer sky."

She had dreaded this moment. She suspected he would notice and confront her, but she had hoped to stave it off. Alas, brothers. "I know she does," she admitted in dismay. "And I love her so very much, more than... And there's the trouble, you see?"

"No," Alessandro replied. He picked up a wooden chair in one hand, carried it around to her side of the desk, and sat beside her. "Explain please."

She fudged and rearranged herself in her seat, then caught his gaze, determined to hold back any threatening tears. "Oh, Ally, don't you understand? I love her more than I ever thought was possible, and we have such a deep connection. With Florentina I can be myself, I'm so very happy and complete in a way I never was with Vergilio." He contemplated her attentively, still bearing a confused expression. "Then one day it hit me—if Vergilio hadn't died, I wouldn't have this, wouldn't have her in my life. I know extraordinary bliss because my lawful husband died!"

Madelena could hold back the tears no longer and began to weep. "It's almost like I'm glad he died so I can be happy, and such thoughts make me a horrible person."

"Oh, sweet Maddie," he sighed and placed a comforting hand on the back of her neck. "Do you think you are the first widow to ever find someone again, or to even enjoy a better relationship the second time around? Every day widows remarry or move on with their lives in successful ways; are they all horrible people?" She lowered her head and mopped at her tears. "If I were to meet with an untimely death, I would expect Portia to mourn me for a while, but I would want her to be happy. I wouldn't want her to live out her days alone and unfulfilled."

"I understand, but—"

"But nothing." He pinned her with his fathomless brown eyes and lifted her chin with an index finger. "Answer me this: did you wish for his death before it happened?"

Insult flashed across her visage, and she sucked in a breath. "Certainly not!"

"And did you even meet Florentina until months after Vergilio passed away?"

"No." Madelena's mouth drew in and her tears dried up.

"Did you ever engage in a passionate relationship with someone else while married to him?"

"Absolutely not," she swore. "You know I didn't."

"Then you have nothing to feel guilty about. You were a good wife to Vergilio, but he is gone. You have the right to be happy, Madelena. I don't completely understand it, but you have found a brilliant and resourceful individual who loves you, and I bear witness you have never been happier in your entire life than you are with her—at least until a few weeks ago. Please, stop tormenting yourself and come rejoin the family."

She sniffed and took his hand. "My brain knows you're right, but it may take my emotions a while to catch up. I don't mean to disrupt the household," she said with regret.

"And don't start piling on guilt over that too," he instructed with a smile. But as he studied her face, the smile faded. "There's more."

"Just…" Maddie hesitated. Fear swept through her, but she couldn't tell him. "Nothing I can talk about." But he saw it. Damnation if he didn't catch every little nuance of body language, pick up on every inflection in the voice. She was convinced at times the man could read minds.

"Are you afraid?" he asked, knowing the answer full well, she imagined. "Afraid people will find out? I assure you, our business can easily weather any scandal—not that there would be a scandal. There certainly shouldn't be and—"

"That's not it," she mumbled, lowering her head once more before jerking it up with wide eyes. "Unless you are afraid of a scandal! Ally, I would never—"

"No, darling sister; I fear no such thing." He smiled at her reassuringly. He licked his lips, took in a breath and proceeded as a sage. "Maddie, there are no guarantees of anything in life. Any of us can lose a spouse, a child, a sibling, or a best friend at any moment. I could step out into the street tomorrow and be struck by a speeding carriage; Pollonia could contract a dread disease. Of course I worry about Antonio being in a war zone, but he could outlive us all. In truth, we don't ever know, and just because my oldest son is the one who appears to be in the most danger doesn't mean he will be the one death finds. We are never guaranteed tomorrow or the day after; all we have is today." He returned a sturdy hand to the back of her neck and rubbed it gently. "Don't miss out on all the wonders of today because you fear the future."

This time the tears streamed for a different reason and she turned into his shoulder, putting her arms around him. "How did you become so wise?"

"Because I'm the big brother!" He laughed and embraced her. "Fear and guilt are powerful enemies, ones I have had occasion to face myself."

"You?" Maddie sniffed, and he produced a handkerchief. She laughed and took it to wipe her eyes and nose. "You aren't afraid of anything!"

"Perhaps not now," he smiled and winked at her. "Come. It is time for our big dinner before Christmas."

Madelena nodded and stuffed the damp linen square into her dress pocket. "Thank you. I shall try to pull myself together." *But, she thought, it will not be quick or easy.*

* * *

FLORENTINA WAS ALREADY SEATED at the table along with everyone else when Maddie and Alessandro entered the dining room. They had brought in an extra chair so Antonio's customary seat left of his father's could remain open for this occasion. A place was set for him and a glass of wine poured as if he may walk in the door at any moment. He wouldn't, they all knew, but it was often done when a loved one was absent for the traditional family meal. The night was so warm in the hall all the windows had been opened to offset the heat from Il Ceppo, the Yule log.

Florentina's gaze drifted to Madelena as she watched her take her seat. "Finally!" Matteo exhaled. "We couldn't start until you got here."

"Matteo." Florentina spoke his name in warning and pinned him with a serious stare. He shrank back into his chair.

"I apologize for being late," Maddie said. "I lost track of the time and Ally had to come get me."

"You have been working harder than usual on the audit this year," Portia noted. "Why?"

Bernardo offered a suggestion before Maddie could speak. "Because we made so much more money this year, right Papa?"

Alessandro smiled at his son. "Never mind about it. Let us say our Christmas Eve blessing."

"I want to say the prayer, Papa," Bernardo declared in earnest as he sat up tall in his seat. "I want to say a special blessing for Antonio for Christmas. He's my brother."

"Yes, he is," the head of the House acknowledged as he inclined his chin toward his youngest child. Pollonia and Portia bowed their heads, and everyone around the table joined hands. Florentina felt an instant jolt as Madelena took her hand for the first time since they had made love.

The spark was definitely still there, and the realization shot fresh hope through her heart.

"Dear God our Father," Bernardo began in the most adult voice he could muster. "We thank you for all our blessings, but particularly on this night we thank you for the gift of your Son, Jesus Christ, who was born of the Virgin Mary. We thank you for our family, friends, and loved ones and for Your grace and protection. We especially pray You will keep my brother Antonio safe, that You will watch over and protect him and bring him home to us safe after the war. And come to think of it God, we pray the war will be over soon and people will stop having wars altogether. Such would be a good thing, I think, something You would like. So, bless this bountiful meal and those who prepared it. In the name of the Father, Son, and Holy Ghost; Amen."

"Amen," they all echoed. Florentina noted the pride on both Portia and Alessandro's faces at their child's prayer; she was impressed as well.

Betta had to blurt out what everyone was thinking. "That was good Bernardo," she said grinning. "You didn't squeak a single time!"

Maddie's cheeks turned as red as ripe apples, and she whispered a correction into Betta's ear. The others all laughed, taking the five-year-old's comment in stride. "It was a very eloquent and fitting prayer, Bernardo," Florentina praised. His mouth full of food, he just beamed back at her.

The *bollito misto,* a traditional Milanese meal, was loaded with chicken, pork, veal, and sausage all slow boiled to a tender, silky texture in a flavorful broth. Added in were onions, garlic, carrots, celery, an assortment of spices, herbs, and peppers, and a bottle of dry white wine. Served with Italian bread slices drizzled with olive oil, it was a special feast.

Conversation at dinner was more fluid and less stilted than it had been in weeks, and the air felt less tense. Florentina didn't want to raise her hopes too much, but maybe there was a crack in the ice and with any luck Maddie would at least tell her what the problem was. But as everyone excused themselves from the room and began to drift their separate ways, Madelena turned away from her. "Please, Maddie," she asked, touching a finger to her sleeve. "Talk to me," she pleaded.

Maddie's eyes were nervous and fearful. "I–I can't, not yet. Don't worry. I'm alright; it will be alright. Just do what you have to do, and I'll do what I have to do, and it will all be over soon." She sighed and placed a sisterly kiss on her cheek. "Merry Christmas, Fiore." And then she was gone, leaving a baffled Florentina standing in the hallway.

Well, I'm not alright. And what does she mean by, "it will all be over soon?" Is she planning to dismiss me? Our relationship will be over soon? It seems to me it already is. Then why preface by saying "it will be alright"? Oh, Maddie, why can't you tell me what's wrong? I really need to know where I stand.

Then an extraordinarily tall man with broad shoulders and the face of an angel stood right behind her. Alessandro placed a hand on her shoulder. "All will be well," he said in a confident voice. "She just needs time to adjust, to get her thoughts and emotions all sorted out. Merry Christmas, Florentina."

"Merry Christmas," she replied with patient hope.

CHAPTER 7

Sandwiched between Christmas and Epiphany, the Gilda dei Maestri Mercanti, the Master Merchants' Guild, gathered for their bimonthly meeting. Don Giovanni Sacchi, the current guild leader, adjusted his round-rimmed spectacles over green and gold emblazoned eyes as he surveyed his membership as they arrived. A sudden cold snap drove the colorfully silk and velvet clad lot inside the hall to socialize before the day's session began. Guilds were of paramount importance to the economy and governing of the city-states and Giovanni was head of the richest and most elite guild of them all.

Giovanni smiled and nodded as his associates strolled past to gather around one of the two prominent stone hearths on either side of the high-ceilinged hall whose walls were adorned with elegant tapestries. The middle-aged arms merchant smoothed a hand over his silver hair, which he kept cut shorter than the prevailing fashion. He lifted his smooth, cleft chin upon spotting Don Alessandro Torelli and waved to him with the grace of a nobleman despite his common birth. A smile lit his countenance as the tall man moved in his direction.

"Good day, Don Giovanni," Alessandro greeted amiably. "And a happy Christmas!"

"Blessed Christmas to you as well, my friend," said Giovanni.

"Are you wearing a new suit?" Alessandro asked.

He has always had a sharp eye, Giovanni thought. "Sì," he replied extending his arms to show off the stylish black velvet giornea with white silk lining the pleats and slashes in its puffy mutton sleeves. Red hose added color to the monochrome ensemble. "How good of you to notice. My adorable wife Julia had it made for me. She is such a gem, as I am sure is your Portia. So glad they are friends."

"Indeed. Portia told me all about the lovely decorations Julia has up at your home. Are you ready for the Miracle Play tomorrow evening?" he asked.

"Ah, yes." Giovanni scratched his head and turned a bewildered look up to Alessandro. "Julia talked me into agreeing to portray one of the Magi. The Church asks me every year, but I feel a bit nervous to perform in front of people. What about you?"

The tall merchant drew in a breath and returned Giovanni's uncertain expression. "Portia said it was an honor to be a wise man in the play. In truth, I know it is. You and I are precisely the kind of men who are chosen for these pageants. Normally I prefer a more subtle, behind-the-scenes role, but damn if they didn't bring in a live camel this year! I can't turn down the chance to act opposite a real camel, and my children would never let me hear the end of it if I refused."

Giovanni exhaled a quick laugh. "Julia wanted the part of Mary, but they gave it to Magistrate Girard Delafosse's daughter. Can't blame the Bishop for that. And mayhap our wives are correct; it is our civic and spiritual duty to participate in such events."

"You are right, no doubt," Alessandro acquiesced with an incline of his head.

"Oh, there he is," Giovanni motioned to Alessandro and drew his attention to a short, rotund fellow draped in a rainbow of silks. "Don Strozza da Caprio," he called and waved the man over. Then aside he said, "He is next in line and will be taking Benetto's seat on the guild council."

Strozza beamed a joyous smile and waddled his way toward them as hurriedly as he could. "Don Giovanni, Don Alessandro," he greeted and vigorously shook each man's hand. "I am thrilled to join your ranks on the council and finally sit on the dais. This is such an honor!" Oozing enthusiasm, his round face glowed.

"You have earned the position," Giovanni declared. "Why don't you tell Alessandro about your product which has become the new sensation?"

"Oh, yes!"

Giovanni raised his bushy brows, almost afraid Strozza would burst like a bubble, which would be unfortunate, as then he would have to be replaced. The guild leader had more essential duties than sifting through members' bank accounts to determine who was eligible to move up a rank.

"My new pasta maker!" Giovanni found the egg-shaped man comical as he expounded with exaggerated animation. "Every café in the city has purchased one as well as many of the great houses. Oh, Alessandro, you need one of these! You see, my pasta maker is unique, with interchangeable heads to form any and all types of pasta fresh in your kitchen, and from a single device. There are ten different disks that screw on and off so when you press the dough through it may come out as vermicelli, fettuccini, regular spaghetti, or with various size holes for rigatoni, macaroni, manicotti, or whatever size pasta you desire. Just attach a new head and you get a new pasta. And it cleans like a jewel, so easy your cook will love you for it!"

Alessandro smiled in amusement. "I'll take one, Strozza. Please have it delivered to my home along with a bill. Bianca will be thrilled, and if it is as fun and amazing as you say, Portia will want to play with it as well."

"You see?" Strozza said, pointing a pudgy finger at Giovanni. "All a man needs is one great idea and the determination to see it through, and like magic, here he is on the dais sharing the light with you two wonderful fellows!"

Giovanni had to laugh. The invention was all the rage and propelled Strozza right into the upper circle of wealth, despite his being younger than the other council members. As Giovanni recalled, he was about the age Alessandro had been when he ascended. The guild council was comprised of the seven wealthiest and most successful merchants in Milan, and they served in rotation as chairman. When his term was up, it would be Alessandro's turn at leadership. He deduced the composed, steady man would perform well in the role, even if he had merely inherited the business and fortune from his capable father.

* * *

FLORENTINA HAD SEEN little of Madelena since Christmas Mass. They had both been busy with the events of the season, preparing gifts for the children, and pursuing their individual projects. *I refuse to worry about the state of our relationship*, Florentina had determined while she carved, painted, stitched, and sewed. And she may not have felt so alone and defeated if she had been able to make any headway interpreting pages of the journal or found any viable clue concerning the secret society. *At least there have been no more attempts on her life,* she consoled herself.

"It was the most wonderful Christmas!" Angela gushed as she threw herself on her bed and beamed up at the ceiling. The girl chattered on incessantly and Florentina managed to nod and smile at what she hoped were appropriate times as she wasn't listening to a word of the babble. *I want to give her the gift I have acquired, but I wonder if it is still fitting? Will she even want a gift from me? Whatever will I do if she is disappointed with it? Why is this so hard? I know I am a gifted intellectual and talented, but when it comes to this—to people... to love... I am at a complete loss. I don't know what I did wrong or how to repair it... or even if it can be repaired.*

"What are you making?"

Silence. Florentina was suddenly aware Angela had stopped talking and looked up at the pretty blonde. *Did she ask me a question?* With a brilliant smile still shining from her youthful face, Angela gestured toward her crafting.

"Gifts for the children," she replied. "For tomorrow morning."

"I just love Epiphany!" Angela cooed and launched into another rambling recollection of holidays past.

* * *

Florentina heard footsteps in the hallway before dawn on the highly anticipated morning, followed by loud whispers outside her door. "Don't knock on the door!" the little girl's voice strained.

"Would you rather wake up Mama first?" the boy asked.

Florentina rolled over with a sigh and a smile. "I hear you," she sang out.

"See!" Betta scolded. "I told you!"

"I'll be right out," Florentina said as she slid from her bed and put on a robe and slippers. The verbose Angela was snoring. She heard the shuffle of feet, a giggle, and a squeal. *They are such a joy!* She opened the door and joined Betta and Matteo in the hallway. "Do you know what time it is?"

"It's Epiphany morning!" Matteo rang out.

"Shhhh!" Betta put a finger to her lips. "You'll wake everybody!"

"I want them to wake up so we can open our presents," Matteo explained. "Only Mama's been working so hard, I wasn't sure if she'd be angry with us for knocking on her door when it's still dark out."

"But we just couldn't sleep," Betta expounded in an excited hush.

"Why don't we go downstairs and wait for the others to come and join us," Florentina suggested. "It won't be long now. I'll bet La Befana stopped to visit at our house."

She led the bubbly children downstairs and entertained them until the first light began to peek in the windows and family members started to stir.

Presently, they were joined in the ladies' parlor by Madelena, Portia, Pollonia, and Bernardo all wrapped in their wool robes with sleep tousled hair. Bernardo rubbed his hands up and down his arms. "I'll start the fire," he said in his new, almost completely acquired male voice.

"Thank you, Cucciolo," Portia said. "Ally will be right along."

"And here I am," he said with a smile crossing his unshaven face. "Shouldn't we have breakfast before presents?"

All four children turned incredulous expressions to him and shuddered. "Papa!" Pollonia cried. "Don't tease us like that!"

The adults all laughed, and any lingering tensions were swept away. "Go ahead then," he gestured, and they all rushed to stockings hung from the mantle and packages wrapped in fir boughs and tied with string.

Florentina thought of the book tucked inside her robe while excited children opened gifts. "Look Mama!" Betta exclaimed and ran to her mother. She held up a doll dressed in mint green and white silk. "It's you!" Madelena picked up her daughter, doll and all, for a closer examination. "See, she has red hair and green eyes just like you. She is so pretty and soft to hug. I'll call her Lena since everyone calls you Maddie—that way we won't get confused. How did Befana know which doll to bring me?"

Madelena lifted her gaze to Florentina and smiled warmly. "I think she had a little help."

"Wow!" whooped Matteo as he held up one of his presents. "It's Antonio!" While most toy soldiers were cast in lead or tin, this one was carved out of wood and painted in the colors of the Milanese attachment to the French artillery. He was about six inches tall with a rapier in his right hand and pointing with his left, the red cap covering brown hair the length and style Antonio wore.

"Papa, I have one too!" Bernardo held up his soldier with reverence and awe. It was fashioned and painted like Matteo's but in a different pose holding a ramming rod in his left hand and a wheel-lock firearm in his right.

"La Befana knows Alessandro does not approve of toys which imitate war or its weapons," Florentina said in a knowing tone. "But she thought this exception would be acceptable to him."

"Indeed," Alessandro replied with a misty countenance. The head of the House stepped forward and held out his hands. Both boys relinquished their prizes for his inspection. "I agree your soldiers look like Antonio." He returned them to their owners. "You can show them to him when he gets home." Then he turned to Florentina, blinking back tears. "I believe Befana chose well. Can you tell her thank you when you see her?"

Bernardo exchanged a knowing glance with Florentina and inclined his head to her. "Yes, please tell her thank you very much."

"Florentina, do you *know* La Befana?" Betta asked in amazement. "Do you really talk to her?"

She knelt down as Betta brought Lena over for her inspection. Florentina stroked the doll she had fashioned out of scraps from the silk production house and stuffed with cotton balls. "Oh, I know a great many important people, but none more important than you." Her heart fluttered as the little girl wrapped arms around her neck for a hug. She felt the gentle peck on her cheek and blinked back her own threatening tear.

There were other gifts to open—toys, clothes, games, and treats for the children. Florentina had noticed a new piece of furniture in the parlor draped with a sheet. She had supposed it was a finely crafted piece, maybe an import, for Portia. Then Alessandro stepped over to it for the grand unveiling. "You may have wondered what this is," he began mysteriously being sure to catch every eye in the room before proceeding. Observing the knowing sparkle in Portia's expression, Florentina determined she already knew what it was, and she felt anticipation growing. "Pollonia," he said in a reserved tone as his daughter danced to his side. "You have been after me for several years about wanting to learn an instrument and I concur such a skill is desirable for a young lady. So..."

With the whole family gathered around, he snatched the white sheet up and away, revealing an elegant harpsichord. "Oh Papa, it's the pinnacle!" The girl, who was perhaps a year younger than Angela, flung herself into Alessandro's arms with a face glowing behind tears of joy. Florentina was so thrilled to see the very instrument she had played for years and had to sell along with most of her possessions upon her father's death standing right in front of her, she longed to do the same. She was as giddy as a schoolgirl and for the first time in ages, felt young. The hours spent learning and perfecting her music flooded over her, inducing the same sensations of delight they had then. As she raised astonished eyes to Alessandro, she decided he must have read her mind. Beaming, he opened his other arm to her, and she fell into his encompassing embrace.

"I started looking for one after Florentina joined us. Her references said she is skilled on the harpsichord and I thought she could teach you."

"I would be honored," Florentina cooed. "I saved some of my music and can buy more."

He unwound himself from female hugs to open the top. "See the exquisite artwork?"

Florentina rubbed a hand over the cherry wood embossed with delicate carvings and painted in oils. She wondered if he knew this had been hers. Now it would be Pollonia's, which made her happy. It would be in the Torelli house and she would teach the girl to play. Pollonia would likely take it with her when she married and moved away, but it was also possible her new husband would move in here; Madelena's had. Either way, she had assumed she would never see it again, and yet here it was. Her heart swelled with delight.

"Can you play something for us now, Florentina?" Pollonia asked in anticipation as she, too, stroked the instrument, caressing its smooth surface.

"Certainly, if you like." Florentina's face lit as she settled herself on the bench and stretched her fingers over the ebony and ivory keys. "How about a Josquin piece? He is so popular, I'm sure you have all heard this chanson."

Although it had been many months since she had played, Florentina's fingers found their places on the keys with ease and the long-memorized notes practically bypassed conscious thought as they sprang to life. Each keystroke caused a mechanism to pluck a string housed in the body of the instrument; thus, the harpsichord married the percussion family to the string family.

Everyone gathered around to listen and when the piece was concluded Pollonia asked, "Will I be able to play like you someday?"

Florentina grinned. "If you are dedicated and practice your lessons every day, you may well play better than I do in a few short years. No

SECRETS OF MILAN

doubt you will be entertaining your father and mother with real songs quite soon."

Florentina rose from the bench, allowing Pollonia to sit and press the keys, delighting herself by immediately creating sounds. She walked past Madelena and then turned to her with hesitation. Relief poured through her when Maddie spoke. "Thank you so much for Matteo and Betta's presents." She said it with such emotion, Florentina was encouraged.

"I have something for you, too." Taking a deep breath and steeling herself, Florentina withdrew the book and handed it to Madelena.

As Maddie read the cover and then opened to the first few pages, Florentina saw the light wash over her face and was flooded with joy. "Wherever did you find this?" Maddie asked with a renewed spark of life. "I have been wanting to read Sappho's poetry for years but could never find an Italian translation. I never learned Greek as numbers were my proficiency, not languages. Oh, Florentina, it's wonderful!" The words were true music to her ears. "And I have something for you."

Florentina blinked, fixed in breathless anticipation. Maddie withdrew a small box from her robe pocket and handed it to her while Portia's laugh tinkled and little fingers tried to help Pollonia strike the keys. When she opened the box, it took her a moment to register what lay within it. She carefully retrieved a golden heart pendant on a woven chain. It was etched with fine lines and swirls with a tiny ruby affixed to the upper left quadrant of the heart. "It's a locket," Madelena said. "See, it opens up for something to go inside. It was my mother's and one of my favorites. I noticed you never wear jewelry, and I didn't know if you even owned any. There may be an occasion—"

Florentina raised her gaze to Maddie's and interrupted. "If it was your mother's it should go to Betta. I couldn't—"

"I have plenty of heirlooms to pass to her, ones more costly. I want to give this one to you."

Florentina pressed the latch, and the small heart popped open. She smiled in wonder at what lay inside. "It's a lock of your hair."

Maddie blushed. "I forgot she had put that in there. You can remove it if you want."

Florentina beamed radiantly. "It is staying right where it is." She closed the heart and fastened the chain around her neck. "I'll wear it to Mass this morning. Thank you, Maddie. This means the world to me."

"It's just a necklace."

Oh no; it's a lot more, she thought.

Bianca's voice sounded from the hallway. "Breakfast is served. You best all come and eat while it is hot."

"On our way," Alessandro answered.

"We're going to the Duomo for services," Portia said to Maddie as the children rushed out first toward the food. "Special day, special cathedral. Do you want to join us?"

"I prefer the small chapel down the street," Madelena replied. "The Duomo will be too crowded."

"I'll go with Maddie and the children," Florentina said.

"Wherever you are most comfortable." Portia's radiant eyes moved from Maddie to Florentina, and her smile broadened as she bounced out of the parlor beside her husband. *She thinks we are getting back to normal,* Florentina thought. *I hope she is right.*

CHAPTER 8

Madelena found it difficult to keep her attention on the Mass. She spouted off the correct words by rote, going through the motions of worship while her mind was fixed on Florentina and how she might explain her avoidance of the woman she truly did love. How had she ever thought putting distance between them would serve to soften the blow when... if something tragic was to occur? All she had succeeded in doing was to hurt Fiore and herself in the process. Her bed was woefully empty as her weeks keeping to herself had been.

In an attempt to bring herself back to the moment and the occasion, Maddie cast her gaze around the quaint chapel.

The Holy Name Church was Franciscan by affiliation and had first been constructed in the thirteen hundreds. The interior of even an intimate sanctuary in Milan boasted magnificent frescos and intricately carved woodwork. Silver and gold gleamed in crosses, candlesticks, and fixtures, while stone and bronze statuary occupied their various stations. The congregation's benches had no cushions for comfort, however the brick Lombard style Romanesque facade incorporated uninterrupted rows of tall windows which were opened in summer to release heat. Mid and lower-level windows may be smaller than the newer Gothic style but still featured translucent stained glass that transformed sunlight into prisms of color. Transverse arches crossing the nave were more than ornamental as they served as firebreaks in the construction of the ceiling. As was typical, the building was laid out in the shape of a cross, this one situated diagonally on a corner lot. In front was a small piazza, a freestanding *campanile*, its bell chiming the time for Mass, and an arched entryway. The roof was vaulted and supported by thick walls.

Madelena had taken an aisle seat, Betta and Matteo to her right with Florentina to their right, closer to one of the vibrant windows. The priest led in the singing of the Gloria in a Gregorian chant style. *Florentina always comments about how beautifully I sing,* she thought and almost missed noticing the man passing her down the aisle toward the exit. She may have considered it rude or odd had she not been absorbed in her thoughts.

After the Collect Prayer, all stood for the scripture readings, one from the Old Testament followed by the singing of a Psalm, then the New Testament reading. While another hymn was sung, a second priest and his acolytes processed up the aisle carrying an illuminated copy of the Latin Vulgate Bible, a tall cross at the top of a pole, and a swinging canister of incense leading to the climactic reading of the Gospel account of the Magi presenting their gifts to baby Jesus. When she glanced to her right, she noticed Florentina was keeping the children quiet and focused on the ceremony. Her heart leapt into her throat as the thought formed within her: *my family!*

Turning her attention back to the pulpit, Maddie determined to listen to the homily. When they returned home, she would invite Fiore to her room to try to explain the emotions she had been struggling with and to reassure her and ask forgiveness. It was time to put everything right and stop letting fear rule over her life.

Madelena had just cleared away the mental replays to concentrate on the service when a most unusual occurrence diverted her complete attention. Florentina had scooped up Betta and Matteo and was pushing her out of her seat toward the aisle. "Run," she commanded fiercely as she jerked her chin at the door.

For an instant Maddie was too stunned and confused to move, but for only the blink of an eye. Florentina—the Night Flyer—had the most excellent instincts and if she was bolting out of Epiphany Mass, imminent danger surrounded them. "Get out now!" Florentina shouted as she continued to push Maddie down the center walkway.

There were likely murmurs and stirring among the congregation members at the outburst, but Madelena, heart racing, dashed ahead with a glance over her shoulder to see her tutor with one child under each arm a mere step behind her. The sudden noise was deafening, but it was the shock wave from the blast that sent them all flying. Maddie hit the floor hard amid screams and the sounds of breaking glass and crashing bricks. Smoke began to fill the chapel, and someone stepped on her hand in their haste to evacuate.

"Remain calm!" a tenuous voice intoned as panic broke out in earnest.

"Mama!" Maddie pushed up to her scraped hands and bruised knees and turned toward Betta. The wide-eyed, frantic child clutched her arms around her mother's neck.

"I'm here, baby; I've got you," she comforted and reached a hand to Matteo. "Are you both alright?"

"Florentina saved us," Matteo said in astonishment. "We aren't hurt; don't be afraid, Mama."

"Keep moving," Florentina insisted as she stumbled up to the trio. "Out the door, now."

Maddie did not argue, but with a somber expression fixed on Fiore, gave her a nod. Carrying Betta in her arms, she forged on through wreckage and stampeding parishioners toward the open doorway. Florentina followed, holding tight to Matteo's hand. Once past the archway, they collapsed on the steps.

"Are you injured?" Florentina's voice was drowned in concern. They were all covered in pink brick dust with small scraps of debris having showered over their hair and clothing.

"No, just some bruises from falling. What about you?" Maddie turned her attention to Fiore who sat an arm's length away leaning against the exterior wall of the church.

"I'll live," she replied queasily. "My back feels as if it's on fire and my head is pounding like a chorus of drums."

"My children," Maddie uttered in disbelief. "You saved them, and me."

With smudged face and disheveled hair, Florentina raised a sincere gaze to hers. "Sì. You may not love me anymore, but I am still devoted to you and to them. I would lay down my life to save any of you without hesitation."

Panic of a different sort grabbed hold of Madelena's soul, threatening to undo her. "Is that what you think?" Grief clouded her soul, and her mouth fell into a gape of horror.

"What am I supposed to think?"

"I am so sorry!" Tears swam in Maddie's eyes. "That is not the problem; it never was." *Quite the opposite,* she thought.

"We love you, Florentina!" Betta declared and left her mother's lap to hug her tutor. "How did you know the church was going to fall down?"

"It didn't just fall down," Matteo stated as he took his turn to embrace his mother.

"No, it didn't," Florentina confirmed exchanging a glance with Madelena and then it clicked.

Even greater shock swept over Maddie's features, turning them pale as death. "A bomb? Someone bombed the church?"

"Someone did indeed, and I need to go back and help. People are injured and some may even be dead." Florentina started to push to her feet but collapsed on the step again with her head in her hands. "Seems I'm a bit dizzy still."

"You don't have to do everything," Maddie said and reached a hand to tenderly stroke her head. "Look, some city watchmen have arrived and the fire brigade will be here any minute. You alerted everyone and saved lives, including ours. How did you know?"

"Paying attention," she answered with difficulty. "Knew something wasn't right, then glass breaking, saw the bomb… was on our row… two of them."

"Fiore, don't try to talk now," she instructed. "I'll secure a carriage to drive us home and then I'm going to inspect you for injuries."

"It's only a few blocks," Florentina dismissed. "I can walk."

"That may be, but we aren't sitting here waiting for tomorrow, which is about when you'd be able to walk home," Maddie declared.

"I'm scared," Betta said in a small voice as she snuggled back against her mother again. "Church is supposed to be a safe place."

Matteo took her hand in his as he settled on the spot between Florentina and Madelena. "Don't be scared, Betta," he said with assurance. "I'm right here." Then with his other hand he patted Florentina's shoulder. "Thank you. I'm glad you are the smartest person in Milan and that you're with us."

"I'm glad I'm with you, too, Matteo," she replied and offered him a weak smile.

Maddie could tell by her pained appearance and weakness Florentina had absorbed some measure of shock from the blast. She was also certain without Fiore's lightning reflexes they would all be seriously wounded or dead. Feet rushed past the spot where they sat; men called out, women screamed, children cried. She looked around, between those coming and going, to see a gigantic hole in the side of the brick facade, broken windows with smoke trailing out, and a body lying on the ground. She closed her eyes and swallowed hard.

"Make way for the fire brigade!" a man shouted.

Madelena pushed to her feet and reached a hand for Fiore. "Come now," she instructed. "We have to move out of the way. Let's get you in the carriage and home."

*　*　*

FLORENTINA'S HEAD had felt like the clapper inside a church bell, but it had subsided to a constant throb. She couldn't see her back but was aware it bore burns and lacerations; hence she had stopped by her room to collect a bottle of salve. Nevertheless, love, hope, and excitement overshadowed any pain. *She does still love me!* was all she could think. Madelena had invited her to her bedchamber and told her to wait while she settled the children down for a nap on account of the disaster. Florentina sat on the rose velvet cushioned settee across from the bed in the spacious chamber decorated with a feminine touch. Her thoughts were inundated with memories of the nights spent in this room, especially of the night Maddie had shown her another way to fly.

She stood when the door opened, anticipation sucking her breath away. Madelena gave it a shove to close and whisked across the floor like a sprite, caught Florentina's face in her hands, and proceeded to kiss her mouth long, hard, and deep. Eventually she broke for air, searched Fiore's expression, then dove in for another as if the intimate contact was as necessary for her survival as the air had been. Link established, Maddie finally spoke. "Holy Mary, how I have missed you!"

Florentina's world sprung back into life as her heart brimmed with joy, releasing and forgetting all previous anxiety like a puff of mist struck by sunlight. With soft honey eyes making love to Madelena's luminescent gaze, she caressed an alabaster cheek with one hand while reaching the other around her slender waist. "I should almost get blown up more often," she said with a flirtatious wink.

"Nonsense! I never meant for you to think... it wasn't you, and no, I have no regrets about our night together," Maddie struggled to explain.

She sighed and combed her fingers gently through Florentina's long brunette strands. "It turns out I am so in love with you I didn't know how to process it, and I was afraid—scared of what it would do to me if you got yourself killed chasing these madmen."

Florentina could feel Maddie begin to tremble and she pulled her into a tight embrace. "Neither of us can control the future, my love."

"Exactly what Alessandro said." Then Maddie drew back with a frown, stepped to the side, and inspected Florentina's back. "Oh my God, Fiore, your dress is slashed and bloody!"

"I suspected as much," she replied with a sigh. "Which is why I picked up my salve."

"Why didn't I notice before? You are hurt; we should call a physician immediately!"

"No, no," Florentina corrected with a sly smile. "I know how to treat it, but I'll need your help. Besides, you were a little busy consoling children and overcoming the shock of the attack to detect torn clothing."

"We should get you into a warm bath and you will need new clothes. When I take a better look, we can decide about the physician," Madelena said with motherly authority.

"I agree with the bath and fresh clothes, but this ointment should be sufficient. I don't believe the cuts are very deep."

"I'll ask Livia and Angela to bring in some buckets of hot water," Maddie said, "and explain to Angela you are too injured to climb another flight of stairs and sleep in a small, uncomfortable bed, and you have to stay in my room tonight." The insistence in her words brought a smile to Florentina's lips. "Here," Maddie said, removing a plush robe from its hook near her bed. "Take this and meet me in the bathing room. I am going to take care of you."

Madelena paused to give her another kiss. "You saved us, my children… our children."

And that did it, turned Florentina's knees to jelly, overwhelming her with emotion. The kiss she brought to Maddie's lips was as tender as it was erotic, as if all the love in the universe had been condensed into a few drops to be passed from her mouth to Maddie's. "I love you, and them, with all I am… and always will."

CHAPTER 9

❦

Madelena thanked the servants for bringing the warm water, closed the bathing room door, and turned to rake her gaze over Florentina as she sat in the comfort of water neither too hot nor too cold. For a moment, desire almost overtook her as she soaked in those long legs, toned muscles, firm youthful breasts which had never filled to nurse an infant, and the nest of dark hair nestled between the base of her thighs. Maddie sucked in a breath, swallowed, and deliberately walked around the tub; Florentina's injuries took priority at the present.

When she observed Fiore's bare back, her mouth dropped and eyes flew wide in concern rather than passion. "Sweet Jesus, Fiore!" She knelt at the side of the bathtub for a closer examination. "It looks like you've been beaten with a cat-o'-nine-tails!" She shuddered, raising a hand to her chest.

"I've never been struck with one of those," Florentina replied, "but I imagine this is how it would feel. Can you wash it for me?"

"But there are slivers of glass, bits of crushed brick, and splinters sticking out of the cuts." The sight of the bloody wounds made Maddie's heart hurt.

"Do you have a pair of tiny tongs?"

"Like you use for plucking eyebrows?" Madelena asked.

"Like *you* use for plucking eyebrows," Florentina corrected humorously.

"Yes, yes," Maddie affirmed, understanding where Fiore was leading. "I'll run get them to pluck out the foreign objects."

When Madelena returned, she found Florentina had dunked herself and was lathering soap in her hair. "Got them!" she announced and pulled around a small stool to sit behind the alluring woman and perform the minor surgery. *And she has no idea how beautiful she is,* she thought in amazement. "How is your head feeling?"

"Better," she mused. "I'm not nauseated anymore."

"Good." As gently as she could manage, Maddie began to pull out the debris lodged in Florentina's flesh by the power of the blast. "Who do you suppose threw the bombs into the church, anyway? Such a horrible thing to do, and on Epiphany morning! It was probably anarchists or anti-papists." Florentina turned her head over her shoulder and gave her a flat look, indicating she thought not. "What?" she questioned. "Who then?" Fiore continued to stare at her with a knowing expression. "No," Maddie declared, rejecting the alternative. "Absolutely not."

"Let us consider the facts," Florentina began as she relaxed her neck and returned her attention to her bath. "I agree anarchists or anti-papists may attack a church, even on a high holy day, but why *that* church? They would want to make a grand statement at the Duomo. The cathedral is the symbol of Catholicism in Milan and the grandest example of church architecture in the world, saving the opinion of some claiming St. Peter's in Rome is the grandest. Thousands of parishioners were there, not the fewer than a hundred at Holy Name neighborhood chapel. And if they were after political targets, all the important people were at the Duomo. If the purpose was to generate terror and chaos, once again—"

"The Duomo," Maddie concluded in resignation. She held out a triangle of sharp blood-dipped glass the diameter of a coin for Fiore to see. "This is one of the bigger ones."

Fiore cringed. "You are doing an admirable job of it, my sweet. Then there is the placement of the bombs—two of them, round like small cannonballs, like the ones I have in my trunk."

"You what!" she exclaimed in horrified shock as she whisked the tongs away and stared at Florentina. "You have bombs in our house?"

"Calm yourself," Florentina soothed. "They can't explode all by themselves." She said it in a tone like every lady kept bombs in her hope chest. "The thing is they both were thrown through the window on our row, not in two separate locations to maximize damage."

"But how would a potential assassin know where we were and on which row we sat?"

"How indeed?" she echoed. "Perhaps we were followed, or he had a cohort inside the chapel who informed him."

Something awakened in Maddie's hazy memory of the sequence of events. "A man walked out during the service, while we were singing. I thought it was rude. But if you're thinking—"

"I'm sorry Maddie, but it's the only logical deduction to be made. This morning was another attempt on your life." A hint of fear tinged Fiore's voice as she stated what was becoming increasingly clear.

Madelena huffed out a breath and swallowed a lump in her throat. "That would mean... if what you say is true... Betta, Matteo, you, all the people sitting near us." She fought to hold panic at bay. "We would have all been killed." Anger erupted to choke down horror, and she held the tiny tongs still lest she hurt her lover on accident. "They tried to kill my children! It's one thing to come after me, but they don't care who they kill to do it."

Florentina sighed and twisted around in the tub to face her. "So it would seem."

Her eyes were fierce when they met Fiore's. "I have gone about this all wrong," she admitted. "Instead of avoiding you and expecting the worst to happen, I should have been assisting you. I never thought..."

"And before your mind veers off in a misguided direction, it is not your fault some murderous underworld assassins damaged the chapel, or that others were injured."

"You are damned right—it is their fault, and I am going to stop being stupid and start helping you find them," she declared with determination.

"Good!" Florentina smiled. "Have you removed all the pieces?"

"Oh." Maddie returned to the moment and passed a gaze over Fiore's back again. "I think so."

Florentina dunked her head under the water and swished out all the soap. When she resurfaced, she asked, "Now, you see the brown bottle on the table beside the towels and jar of salve?" Maddie nodded. "I need you to pour it over all the cuts."

Madelena moved to retrieve the bottle but stopped short when she opened it. "This is really strong alcohol. Fiore, my love, this will burn like fire."

"Yes, well, the lovely healing balm contains juice from the aloe vera plant among other soothing ingredients," she explained.

"But why?"

"Master Leonardo never does anything halfway," Florentina explained. "When he started the project to produce anatomy books for the medical schools, it was not enough for him to merely draw the organs in their proper arrangement within the body. He took the liberty to observe various treatments as they were tested on patients. He told me once that sometimes on the battlefield, there was no clean water to wash victim's wounds and so wine was used instead. He observed in the cases where the injury was washed with alcohol instead of water, the soldiers did not suffer an infection, or if so, it was much milder than those where only water was used. If the wound was not washed at all, the soldier almost always developed a nasty puss or gangrene. His deduction was to always wash a cut with alcohol."

Maddie was impressed, as she invariably was with Florentina's knowledge. "You're right; you don't need a physician. Here goes." She poured a generous portion of the potent liquid over the slashes in Florentina's skin and cringed as she witnessed the discomfort it caused. "Now for this nice, soothing salve." She felt much better smoothing the cream over the cuts and abrasions. "When you leave the bath, you can put on the robe and when we get you to my bed, I'll apply bandages and you shall lie quietly on your stomach."

Her proposal was met with an incredulous stare. "I'll have you know I have been waiting over a month to be invited back into your bed and have no intention of lying quietly."

Maddie's breath caught in her throat as once again the sight of such an exquisite body filled her with desire. "But you are in no condition… I don't want to hurt you."

A sly smile pulled at the corner of Fiore's mouth as she rose from the water. She stepped out, turning toward Madelena as droplets pushed their way into trickles across her tight, tan skin. "I'm willing to compromise." She reached for a towel. "When we are done making up for lost time and are too spent from our passion for more, then you can apply bandages and I'll lie quietly on my stomach."

It was a suggestion Madelena found impossible to refuse.

* * *

BENETTO'S MOOD was as gloomy as the weather. It was January, wet, foggy, cloudy, occasionally cold and snowy, and he was banished to a rickety old manor house on a useless vineyard, but after the altercation with his son, he tried to get out of his room more. He had been a grouch through Epiphany, yet somehow his irrational wife and daughter had smiled, laughed, even sang carols and exchanged silly homemade gifts. He sat in the great hall reading a broadsheet from Milan so he could at least keep up with some of the happenings he missed out on.

Stefano, Benetto's younger brother and previous strong-arm, strolled through, munching on a piece of bread smothered in soft cheese and slathered with herbs. He was a bull of a man with short coal hair brushed with ash at his temples who had loyally served Benetto for years. "I'll be leaving tomorrow," he stated in a casual tone, and took another bite of his snack.

Looking up from his paper, Benetto inquired, "For how long? A couple of days again?"

Stefano shook his head and answered while still chewing. "I'm moving out for good."

"You're what?" Benetto stormed to his feet to face his shorter, but much stronger, brother.

"I have been awarded the position of chief of security at the city canal docks by the Port Authority," he relayed with pride. "Well, there is this brainy fellow who handles administration and such, but I am in charge of seeing the imports and exports are kept secure while they are there. I'll deter any thieving knaves who get a bright idea about pilfering goods. Every merchant in Milan will count on me to keep their products safe— me, Stefano Viscardi!" He beamed with a wide grin at his brother.

Benetto was not amused. "You can't leave me!" he bellowed. "I need you here."

Stefano's pleasure wilted in an instant, replaced by a mask of disappointment and confusion. "You don't need me for anything," he said, taking a step back. "There's nothing here that needs protecting. And you can't expect me to wither and die in this God-forsaken middle of nowhere. I'm not ready for retirement; I'm younger than you, remember?" His tone heated as he continued. "I miss the gaming halls, the taverns, and the women."

"Yes, yes," Benetto waved impatiently. "You can still go into town a couple of times a month to satisfy your urges. But you can't move away, Stefano. You owe me; I'm the head of House Viscardi."

"I served you for twenty years," a stern-faced Stefano declared. "I don't owe you anything. Besides, there is no more House Viscardi."

"But who will I talk to?" Benetto moaned. "Who will I play cards and shoot dice with?"

"There is a saying: If you want to have a friend, be a friend. I stayed here with you for a month and you only locked yourself away upstairs brooding. You don't need me," Stefano stated. "You need to find a new purpose. It's what I did. I went and applied for a position and was selected to perform an important job, but is my brother happy for me? Did you congratulate me and say, 'what a fine opportunity; I'm proud of you'? No," he snapped and slammed his cheesy bread onto the nearby dining table. "All you can think of is yourself. All you ever think of is yourself. You can just sit here and rot—it's time for me to live my life!" Stefano turned on his heel, stomped out of the great hall, and up the stairs.

Benetto felt as if someone had kicked him in the gut. *First my business, my wealth, then my mansion gone. The guild dismissed me, my friends turned their backs on me, Niccolo will have nothing to do with me, and now my own brother has abandoned me!* He balled his hands into fists at his sides and ground his teeth together behind a miserable frown.

He pivoted when he heard Daniella enter the hall bringing in a plate with hard salami sliced and arranged in a neat semicircle with cheese wedges, olives, and small wafers. "I brought you something to eat," she said, then quickly set down the dish and shied away upon seeing his expression.

"Even your own wife and daughter are terrified of you." The words of the Night Flyer shot threw his mind like a poisoned arrow. "Stefano is moving out," he snarled. "Are you going to leave me, too?"

Daniella blinked, her face displaying bewildered surprise. "No. You are my husband; where would I go?"

"But I'm not the rich man you married," he said, taking slow steps in her direction. "There will be no more designer dresses, no fine jewelry, or high society events to attend for you."

"I may have coveted those things at one time, but not anymore."

"Is that so?" He stopped when he reached her and peered down into blue eyes which seemed to fire with something he rarely observed in his meek wife.

Daniella raised her chin and spoke in a voice laced with both desperation and defiance. "I just want us to be a family and to enjoy some measure of happiness in this life."

He could see the shimmer of tears she held back in an uncharacteristic strength of will. Her words drove into him like the blade of a rapier, as if to sever his soul from his body, but he would not allow her view their effect. Don Benetto Viscardi was not defeated yet. "When you find out how to be happy with no money, then you let me know," he snarled and strode away.

Benetto did not want to accept what either she or Stefano had said, but their words stayed with him, dancing an odd ballet through his consciousness as he stepped out into the drizzle. *Do I only ever think of myself? Have I neglected my family? Have I ever truly been happy? What does it all mean?* He reached a hand to brush the scar on his chin. *The Night Flyer said he was giving me a second chance—a second chance for what? The bank denied my loan, and the vineyard's soil has been salted. I'll never have wealth, power, and influence again. I'll never be anyone of importance ever again, so what is this second chance?* He took in a deep breath and let it out slowly. Raising his gaze, he surveyed dormant grape vines clinging to their trestles draping rolling hills, with forests and majestic snowcapped peaks beyond. It was quiet here, he noticed, and lifted his eyes to the gray expanse of sky to see a small "V" of geese fly overhead. When he was under the Night Flyer's blade, he was certain he would die, and then what? Hell, centuries in Purgatory, or simply cease to exist? He knew he would not be welcomed into Heaven by angels and saints. "A second chance at life," he asserted aloud, but how to accomplish it was the great mystery.

CHAPTER 10

Madelena marched into the family's silk production house with a folded copy of the *Milan Gazette* news sheet gripped in a gloved hand. She was dressed for business from her braided hair cradled in its golden netting secured with a gold band, to her fur-lined houppelande, a floor length winter outer garment, lavish jewelry, and high heeled Pianelle shoes. Madelena radiated all the fire one associates with a red-head as she breezed past the shop foreman and several customers as well as busy employees straight into Don Alessandro's office and shut the door. "Have you seen this news report?" she demanded and slammed the paper down on his desk.

Alessandro looked up from a manifest sheet with a bewildered expression. "No," he offered. "But I gather you are not pleased with it."

"These idiots are claiming the Night Flyer bombed the Holy Name Church!"

Seeing she shook with rage, he put his paperwork aside, rose to step over to her, and picked up the broadsheet. He narrowed his eyes on the report as she continued. "And I know for certain he had nothing to do with it. In fact—" She stopped mid-sentence as if an invisible hand had just clamped over her mouth.

"How do you know this for a fact?" he inquired.

"Because." Maddie frowned and starting wringing her hands together. "It would make no sense at all for the Night Flyer to risk his life battling an assassin on my balcony a few weeks ago saving me and then to try and blow me to kingdom come on Epiphany. And besides, it is entirely unlike him. The Night Flyer doesn't hurt women and children and has never perpetrated any crime toward the Church."

"Hmmm," he mused and set the paper aside. "Your points do have merit. But the article says witnesses saw a man dressed all in black wearing a mask throw the bombs through the chapel window and then run away."

"Exactly!" she exclaimed and poked a finger into his chest. "*Run* away, not fly away. I tell you this villain is an imposter, someone who copied the Night Flyer's garb to hide his own vile identity." She paused for a moment, temper waning from her face. "Florentina thinks…" She sighed and then raised a concerned gaze to his. "We both think I was the target. The secret society behind all this is getting bolder and doesn't care if others are hurt or killed."

He stroked fingers affectionately up and down his sister's arm. "Two fatalities and ten more sent to the Policlinico for treatment." He shook his head and rubbed the back of his neck with his other hand. "If you were the target, those deaths and injuries are not your fault."

"I understand that," she replied and leaned into him. After a brief moment she stood apart, her righteous indignation returning. "So, what are you going to do about it?"

Alessandro widened his eyes. "Do about what?"

"About this false report being spread around the city!"

"I don't see what I can do about it," he admitted, lifting his palms innocently.

Then she shot a brilliant, gleaming expression up at him in sudden inspiration. "You can buy the publication."

Alessandro laughed and leaned back to sit on the edge of his desk.

But Madelena began to expound upon the benefits of such a move. "Think of it, Ally." Her voice took on a dreamy quality edged with excitement as she moved about in animation. "If you owned the *Gazette*, you would guide the whole direction of the publication, decide what stories were printed, make certain they were *fact* and not conjecture," she stressed, pinning him with a shining gaze. "Consider the influence you would have over the people of the city. True," she mused as she paced back and forth, "fewer than half of the residents can read, but they are the educated half, the policy makers, the ones with money, power, and authority. You could infuse the minds of Milan with our values, give them stories to read which we deem important."

Alessandro had stopped laughing, having been swept up in Maddie's vision. "I see the potential in this. Why didn't I think of it before?" A grin stretched across his face, and his aura lit with enthusiasm. "Maddie, you are a genius!" He grabbed her up in an enormous hug. After setting her feet back on the floor, he began to emote along the same lines she had. "Certainly, we will keep the financial and war reports, but we could also include cultural headlines about art, music, and theater. We could inform the public about charitable opportunities and report acts of heroism and good deeds as well as crimes and tragedies. This is huge!"

She embraced him again, placing a kiss to his cheek. "And you can dispel these rumors of the Night Flyer bombing a church."

"Indeed!" With a smile and a wink, he replied, "I'm off to make the owner of the *Milan Gazette* an offer he can't refuse."

* * *

SALVADOR SFONDRATI, a city watchman and friend of the Torelli family, stood with a dozen other constables, watchmen, and municipal guards in the foyer of the French magistrate's administrative building. A red watch cap covered the bald spot in his short, graying hair. The atmosphere was solemn as feet scuffed over the fine woven carpet bearing its fleurs-de-lis. Heads displaying frowns shook as the men exchanged details in hushed tones, but all stilled and dropped silent when the magistrate entered the hall.

Girard Delafosse was in his early forties with smooth black hair, a French style pencil mustache and goatee, and sharp eyes. Today his high ruffled white collar offset a royal blue velvet jerkin, black hose, and a prominent codpiece which despite French influence had failed to rise to fashion in Milan. Being short of statue required Delafosse to raise his chin to catch the eye of most law enforcers present. "I have called you here," he began in his native tongue, "because of the outrageous attack on Holy Name Church a few days past. We cannot allow such activities to go unpunished."

There were nods of agreement among the assembly. Salvador was not fluent in French, but he could to make out the tone and content of the magistrate's speech. He was not the only native Milanese official to be displeased with Delafosse's assumption that all the world should speak French, but he was wise enough to never mention it.

"Witnesses have described a perpetrator dressed all in black and wearing a mask," he continued. "We can logically conclude the Night Flyer is the attacker."

"But Monsieur Delafosse, one witness clearly stated the bomber wore a beard and the Night Flyer does not," interjected a constable.

"And he has never carried out an attack as violent as this," Salvador added with concern.

"He used bombs before, no?" asked Delafosse. "Didn't he blow up Don Benetto's warehouses?" Others nodded, murmuring among themselves. "And can a man not grow a beard if he chooses? So." The dandy, as Salvador thought of the Frenchman, clicked his heels together and raised his aristocratic chin. "You shall search for this Night Flyer. I want him captured and brought in for questioning. You are authorized to use deadly force if necessary as it is my belief he is the bomber."

Salvador's mouth twisted, and he lowered his gaze to the floor with a sigh. "I understand he is admired by many of the commoners, so I prefer he is taken alive," Delafosse explained. "Also, it is quite possible he is but a hireling. This would explain his change in behavior. If so, we must discover who hired him to throw a bomb into a church. Finding the Night Flyer is your first priority, yes?" The assembly of lawmen nodded, some affirming aloud, a few even enthusiastically. "Well, what are you waiting for?" Delafosse asked. "Go and arrest the man!"

The various constables and city watchmen filed out with Salvador in their midst. This directive troubled him, and he didn't want to believe the Night Flyer had executed such a detestable act. He was aware this same masked man had saved his friend Alessandro's sister from an assassin, and he had tossed Don Benetto's coins out to the citizens of Milan rather than keep them for himself. To think this same creative thief, for loss of a better term, had attacked a church filled with women and children was inconceivable. *I need to let Don Alessandro know about this*, he thought. *But I can do some investigating as well.*

Salvador turned down streets as he moved into his regular patrol sector, which happened to include the neighborhood where Holy Name was located. There were a few men down on their luck who would inform him of crimes in the area occasionally and he headed straight to one Bruno Bacci, who he was sure to find in the cheapest tavern the quadrant offered. Upon spotting the scruffy, gimpy Bruno, he chose the barstool beside him. "A drink for my friend," he called to the bar keep.

"Salvador!" Bruno's lazy eyes perked up. "Are you keeping the city safe?"

"Doing my best," Salvador replied and laid out a coin for the wine. "Hey, were you around when the church was attacked the other day?"

Bruno took a deep swallow from his fresh glass of burgundy liquid before returning his gaze to Salvador. "Sì," he said grimly. "Nasty business."

"What can you tell me about it?" Salvador laid a few more coins on the bar, these aimed at Bruno. The thin man rubbed his bad knee, then scooped the money into his pocket.

"What are they telling you?" he asked and sipped more of his wine.

"Word is the Night Flyer did it." Bruno laughed and shook his head. "Tell me what you know," implored Salvador.

"I was outside the chapel that morning, you know," he said motioning to his crutch propped against the bar. "Epiphany morning is an excellent time to collect alms from all those generous church-goers." Then he leaned in close to speak in a hush. "There were two of them."

"Two?"

Bruno nodded. "One fellow dressed in black was across the way when this fine fellow strolled right out of Holy Name and crossed the street to him. They exchanged words, and the fine fellow went on his way. Then the other one—which weren't no Night Flyer, I can assure you—puts on his coif and mask and skips over toward the chapel. I didn't know he was going to throw bombs in there!" he exclaimed. "I would have tried to stop him. Then he just dances around like he wants someone to see him before he runs off. The man had a beard and was too stout and old to be the Night Flyer."

"Excellent, Bruno," Salvador said, placing a friendly hand on his shoulder. "You may have a bum leg, but you still have the sharpest eyes in the city. Would you be willing to testify to what you saw if it comes to it?"

"No reason I shouldn't," Bruno replied, then downed the last of his glass. "But I never seen the one who tossed in the bombs, nor the fancy fellow. I couldn't tell you who they are, just they aren't from this neighborhood."

"Not a problem," Salvador assured him with another pat.

"Hey, Watchman." Bruno caught his arm before Salvador could leave. "Don't let them pin this on the Night Flyer. That nice boy gives out coins to folks like me; he gave me a handful once upon a time."

"I'll do my best," he confirmed, then headed to House Torelli to inform Alessandro.

CHAPTER 11

"*B*onjour, Mademoiselle Florentina," Matteo recited as he sat up straight in a child-sized chair in front of the student desk in his and Betta's chamber. Sunlight flooded the second-floor room from the wide windows overlooking an inner courtyard and the pair of prized twin olive trees. The garden was dormant save for some evergreen shrubs and a patch of pansies. Hanging on the walls to either side of the desk were two maps of the Italian city-states, painted and labeled by little hands, and other displayed samples of writing and drawing to showcase the children's accomplishments. Matteo's soldier stood on a shelf beside a model sailboat carved from wood and adorned with canvass sails and tiny cord rigging Antonio had made for him last Christmas. Betta's new doll rested on her bed, surrounded by yellow silk pillows.

"Bonjour, Monsieur Matteo," she said in response as she set two books on the desk. "Quelle heure est-il?"

Matteo glanced at the clock set on a shelf across from the foot of his bed and counted the hands. "Huit heures et demie, I think," he said and scrunched up his nose.

"Tu es jolie ce matin," Betta declared and beamed at her tutor as she sat up straight in her little chair with her hands folded neatly in her lap. Florentina was relieved and pleased the child thought nothing strange or inappropriate about her presence in Maddie's bed the night after the bombing when she had come in crying from a nightmare of loud noises, falling buildings, and screaming people. She had nestled in-between her and her mother, welcoming comfort from both of them.

"Merci," Florentina said with a smile, "and you look pretty this morning, too." Betta giggled.

Then with bright eyes and an eager grin Matteo asked, "How do you say, 'may we go outside and play' in French?"

"After reading and mathematics, is how," Florentina answered with a wink. "And you both need to practice your—"

"A-choo!" Matteo sneezed and wiped his nose on his shirt sleeve.

Florentina scowled at him. "Use a handkerchief, Matteo, not your sleeve."

"Sorry," he begged pardon and sniffed. Florentina fished a linen cloth out of her pocket and handed it to him.

Then Betta got up and took the few steps required to stand right beside where Florentina sat. She peered up at her with an expression conveying distress. "My throat hurts." She rubbed at her neck. Matteo sniffed again, but after a commanding stare from Florentina blew his nose on the handkerchief.

"It looks like the two of you are coming down with a cold," Florentina noted. "Little wonder since one day it is as hot as summer and the next it's freezing. Nothing to worry about," she added with optimism. "If it is a cold, then I know just how to take care of you. Either way, we should be able to get through a full day of lessons before you start to feel the effects in earnest. Now, I brought new books for you to read from today. Then after our practice at adding and taking away, we can all go downstairs and continue our French lesson by singing O Rosa Bella while I accompany on the harpsichord."

"Yeah!" they both cheered, then Matteo coughed. "Then we get to go outside and play," he chanted.

Florentina narrowed her brows at him. "The fresh air and sunshine may do you good, but no running around."

Betta reminded her, "My sore throat."

Florentina patted her head and retrieved two lemon drop candies from her pocket, handing one to each child. "Suck on it; don't bite down. It will help your throat and I have plenty of recipes for cold remedies should we need them."

"No medicine!" Matteo groaned as his fingers folded into fists.

"Why not?" Florentina asked as she handed a small book to each child. "Medicine will make you feel better."

Matteo drew his face into a sour contortion. "It tastes like bear grease."

"Bear grease?" she asked and blinked, feigning disbelief. "Have you ever had bear grease?"

"No," he giggled and Betta joined him. "It's an expression. It means it tastes awful."

"Ah, well, not the medicine I have. Does your lemon drop taste like bear grease?" They both grinned and vigorously shook their heads. "We'll wait and see if you need it tonight or tomorrow, but I promise no bear grease. Now, who wants to read first?" Betta's hand shot into the air.

* * *

MADELENA WAS in a pleasant mood when she strode into her bedchamber that afternoon to change out of her business clothes into something more comfortable. Her face lit with unexpected joy to find Florentina sitting at her writing desk with a pencil and paper, taking notes from the worn journal she studied. "Well, well, what have we here?" she greeted and tossed her warm houppelande on the bed.

"You said you wanted to help," Fiore answered without looking up. "I have to keep the book secret so it was either here or in my room; Angela doesn't read so I can tell her anything and she won't know the difference."

"No, no, I am glad to have you," Maddie assured as she removed her hairnet and unwound the braids to free her long, crimson strands. She sat to pull off the shoes. "Any progress?"

Florentina sighed, set down her pencil, and turned a frustrated expression toward Maddie. "Sadly, no. So much of this makes no sense to me, and one page appears to contradict another. Take this passage, for example," Fiore vexed, then read aloud. "On the Appian Way, Quo Vadis? Look to the left; the dead cannot answer. Or this one," she continued flipping a few pages. "Deep beneath Good King Wenceslas' heart there beats a drum; the River Vitava splits asunder." She shook her head and closed the small leather-bound volume. "When my cuts heal enough, the Night Flyer needs to patrol the streets. Somebody saw who threw those bombs and their testimony will likely be my best lead."

"Speaking of…" Madelena padded over to Florentina and brushed her lips across hers, lighting her lover's eyes. "Everyone is blaming the Night Flyer."

"What? That's crazy!"

"It seems the bomber dressed all in black and wore a mask, but Salvador Sfondrati, the watchman—you remember him?" Fiore nodded. "He said the French Magistrate has all the city guards on the lookout for the Night Flyer, and the *Gazette* reports witnesses described the Night Flyer." Then Maddie beamed and changed tacks for a moment. "I convinced Alessandro to buy the Gazette—isn't it marvelous!"

She radiated joy, inspiring Fiore to reciprocate with a congratulatory hug and kiss. "It truly is!" she beamed in agreement. "But I'll have to be careful of all the extra attention."

"Yes, you will," Madelena commanded. "Anyway, Salvador found a witness who said it was *not* the Night Flyer, but a heavier, older man with a beard who spoke with the stranger who left church early before he threw the bombs."

Florentina snapped into strategy mode. "I wonder if we could bring an artist to the witness and have him describe the man as the artist sketches him." She thought about the talented friend she had known since childhood. "Cesare would do it for me without requiring an explanation. Then the Night Flyer could prowl the city searching for him."

"It wouldn't hurt to try." Maddie positioned herself behind and to one side of Florentina's chair and peered over her shoulder at the odd handwritten book.

Florentina turned back to it and started to flip pages. "There are several references to a horse or symbol bearing a horse and I explored the possibility of Master Leonardo's horse statue, but it was a dead end. The French occupiers—"

"Wait," Madelena said, laying a hand on the desk and leaning in closer. "Go back a few pages." Florentina turned the sheets until Maddie declared, "Yes, there!"

But Florentina was dismissive. "Those are just pages full of numbers. I checked them for patterns or codes, but to no avail."

A satisfied smile formed on Maddie's sunny face. "Dear, sweet, silly Fiore," she chided lovingly and placed a kiss to Florentina's cheek. "These are financial ledger sheets," she explained. "See the numbers at the top? Those are the dates. These columns of numbers are assets, debits, and balances and each row is from a different contributor, these cities listed at

77

the left-hand side. At the bottom are the totals. This is very important information!"

"Oh," she answered with a sound of embarrassed confusion. "I'm sorry, but what does it tell us?"

Maddie squeezed herself into the chair with Florentina, sharing the intimate space so for once she could play the tutor. "A great deal. First, we know this in an international organization and each member contributes and spends some of the funds, and they are well funded indeed. See here how Venice and Milan have much larger amounts in the asset and balance columns than Lisbon and Prague? That's because Venice and Milan are wealthy cities and their members can contribute more to the treasury. It also tells us the society members are very rich men or have the ability to produce huge sums of money, whether legally or through theft. Look at these figures," she instructed as she pointed to the bottom line. "This is where their power lies. With these enormous resources they can bribe officials, hire assassins—or entire armies of mercenaries for that matter." She raised her gaze to Florentina's seeing the information register in those sharp, intelligent eyes. "It is clear they have been doing whatever they are doing for a very long time, are well organized, and have more money than many small countries. You must tread very carefully, my love."

However, the gleam forming in Florentina's aspect was far from an expression of concern. "Having you instruct me arouses my passions," she said in a smooth, husky tone. "You are so amazing, Madelena Torelli Carcano. To think, I only saw a jumble of numbers." With mere inches between them, Fiore caught Maddie's bottom lip between hers and nibbled her way into a full kiss.

Partly to draw closer and also to keep from falling out of the chair, Madelena wrapped her arms around Florentina. "You know so many things," she offered with a sense of wonder. "It is only fair there is one arena in which I excel more." Then she seconded the kiss with one of her own.

"Which is why we are going to make an excellent team," Florentina mouthed against her throat as she trailed kisses down to the hollow at its base.

The moment was interrupted by coughs in the hallway. Maddie leaped up in alarm. "Are the children sick?"

Florentina remained calm and dreamy. "They are coming down with colds. I'll prepare them a special tea before bed."

"It frightens me when they are sick," she said as a flood of fears dating back to her childhood and the whooping cough which took the lives of two siblings many years ago. The sounds of the whoops and gasping for air along with the terror, tension, and sorrow within the household were among her earliest memories.

Florentina closed the journal, stood, and wrapped steady arms around her as if to hold back the sea of rising dread. "Let's go see to them now," she suggested. "There's no fever, no whooping, just ordinary childhood sniffles."

Maddie nodded. "Yes, please. I don't mean to be so anxious, it's just—"

"I understand," Fiore consoled. "If it gets bad I will tell you, but for now you have nothing to worry about. Remember the adage, 'don't borrow trouble.'"

"Yes, you are right." Maddie opened the door and called out. "Betta, Matteo, come here little ones!" She gave them hugs and put a hand on each of their heads, which were as cool as they should be, and her heart began to settle.

"We have colds," Betta said in a wee voice.

"And Florentina is going to pour bear grease down our throats," Matteo predicted with a mischievous grin and a wink toward his tutor.

"Bear grease?" Maddie repeated skeptically. "I doubt it. But let's all go get something to eat and then back to your room for medicine and an early bedtime."

"Ohhh…" a disappointed Matteo moaned.

Then Betta's countenance lit up, and she rattled off her French. "Tu es jolie ce matin."

Fear was overcome by love in an instant as Maddie's heart swelled. "You look pretty today, too, Cucciola."

* * *

FLORENTINA HAD ASKED Bianca to prepare a special soup for the children loaded with onion juice, garlics, petite diced chicken, and a few lentils. They were further required to eat two oranges each, which almost proved too much with the annoying illness dampening their appetites. Next, she made a specific herbal tea for them and spiked it with honey and lemon juice. Matteo was suspicious, but when he sipped it, his expression brightened. "Not bear grease after all!" he announced and finished his tea.

Livia started the fire in their bedchamber hearth early to warm the room before they arrived, and Maddie insisted on extra blankets for their beds. Since Betta's nasal passages had become stuffy, Florentina prepared a steaming bowl of menthol water with a towel draped over it. She instructed Betta to hold her head under the towel and allow the vapor to rise into her nose. After a few minutes, her precious head peeped out with blond curls drooping from the humidity. "I can breathe a little now," she announced and brightened.

"One last thing," Florentina said and produced two small glasses each holding two ounces of warm wine infused with celery seeds, parsley, anise, pepper, and honey. "Your cough medicine."

They each drank down their remedies and were tucked into bed. "Good night, my sweet ones," Madelena cooed and kissed each little cheek.

As they closed the door, Florentina said, "You know a cold has to run its course. It will be a few days, maybe a week before they are completely over it, but these treatments along with staying warm will help them feel better and prevent them from getting worse."

"Yes, I know," she replied. "I will try not to worry."

"I should be going upstairs to my room too, soon," Florentina spoke quietly. "I am not so injured to use that excuse anymore."

Madelena's chin dropped. "I suppose not." Then she raised sultry green eyes to Florentina. "I wish… there must be a way, somehow."

With a knowing smile Fiore replied, "I am grateful each day for every moment I have with you, dearest. If there is a way, we will find it. For now…"

Maddie nodded and whispered, "I will dream of you, and of us."

CHAPTER 12

The weather would not have felt so cold in Barletta if not for the high humidity. Warmed from the Adriatic, the Kingdom of Napoli enjoyed very mild winters, but January 1503 was proving to be wet and uncomfortable for Antonio. He was glad for the company of his new friends, especially the straw-haired Papi. Antonio considered himself of average height and weight, somewhat typical in his abilities, and no less attractive than his comrades, but Papi was so twiggy the army had not been able to provide a uniform that fit well, and the knee-length green tunic hung on his bones like a tent.

The four Milanese artillery standard-bearers used barrels and crates as stools to sit around their campfire, being entertained by Papi's animated storytelling. Their camp was large and spread out with thousands of soldiers, most French, some Milanese, and other mercenaries from Switzerland or one of the German states, occupying land to the west of Barletta as the sea bordered the east. A handful of French hulks, carracks, and caravels armed with cannons and arquebuses formed a loose blockade of the coastline while the army encircled the rest of the port city. At the time, the French forces outnumbered the besieged Spanish defenders, and yet the Duke of Nemours who was in charge indicated no hurry to press their advantage.

The land was moderately flat, composed of fields, pastures, and small clumps of trees; none were producing food for Barletta as they were currently occupied by French troops. A damp breeze blew from the south as Papi danced about describing what Antonio considered an improbable, if not impossible, encounter with a certain young woman. The quartet of junior officers laughed at his narrative as they sipped broth from tin cups.

"Papi, who believes these tales?" Roberto asked, his red curls flopping and bouncing as he shook his head.

"If you want to hear a genuine story of conquest, then let me tell you about the time," Conte began as he caught their ears. The fourth of the Milanese standard-bearers was a compact, stocky young third son of a lesser nobleman, sporting a dark complexion, short brown hair, and a French style mustache and goatee. Before he could relay his tale, Sergeant Beaufort strode up with a snappy captain. Antonio and his peers jumped to their feet and assumed the posture of attention, formally saluting the captain.

"As you were," the captain spoke in French after returning the salute.

"This is Captain Marseille," the sturdy Beaufort introduced. Although he technically held a rank lower than the young Milanese standard-bearers, he had served as their instructor and still advised the lads. Beaufort stood erect, his large feet at a forty-five-degree angle, and Antonio noticed he had groomed his broad russet-tinged beard. The sergeant motioned toward a man younger than himself and older than the junior officers.

Captain Marseille surveyed the four Italians with reserved suspicion. "The general has decided it is time we gave the Spanish a Parisian Bonjour," he said. "He has placed me in charge of the artillery and I further wish to see how you perform. So, we will position your twelve cannons in range of the Castello Svevo walls and see if you can hit them."

Excitement flashed in the youthful men's eyes, and Antonio began to tingle with the anticipation of doing something at last. "But you must be accurate with your shots," he continued firmly. "The general does not want any building of cultural significance damaged. You must not hit the Basilica of the Holy Sepulcher, nor damage the famous Colosso. Understood?"

"Understood," Antonio replied as the others also agreed.

"Very well." The dark-haired captain raised his chin in an air of authority. "I am timing you starting now. Get your crews and weapons set and await my signal to commence."

All four dashed away, calling for their crews. It took over an hour to move the culverins into position. Teams of horses had to be hitched to the big guns to pull them into their row at the prescribed distance. Then the artillery carts drove in, bringing the shot and powder. Measurements had to be calculated, and the barrels raised to the correct angle. The French culverins were an important improvement over medieval cannons as they were lighter and more mobile and the long barrel afforded them more range. They fired round iron balls propelled by gunpowder. The velocity and mass of the projectiles could reduce stone walls to rubble with continuous bombardment. Even with the innovations, they were weighty, cumbersome, and tedious to maneuver.

Captain Marseille tsked and clucked and shook his head. "Too slow!" he shouted in obvious disapproval. "We must practice this every day. By now the Spanish arquebuses would have cut you to ribbons, their cavalry overrun your position, and you would all be bloody smudges in the mud."

At last Antonio stood at attention between the first and second of the three culverin cannons under this charge. His fifteen enlisted soldiers remained at the ready at their assigned positions, two manning the artillery cart near the big gun's barrel, another beside them holding the long ramrod, and a fourth at the breech end waiting to pull the firing mechanism for each cannon, and the others were primarily there for muscle. He was almost lightheaded with anxious anticipation. This would be their first actual experience, the first time to fire at a real enemy.

"You Milanese volunteers, you are now French soldiers, and I expect nothing less than superior performance from you," the captain called out, unaware or unconcerned with the fact the uneducated enlisted ranks did not understand a word of French. Antonio turned to his squad and repeated a translation, only to be rebuked. "Shush!" Marseille glared at him. "You rude, impudent hireling!" Roberto, Papi, and Conte closed their mouths before repeating the mistake.

Sergeant Beaufort tried to catch the captain's attention to explain, but the officer never glanced his way. He finally shrugged and offered Antonio an apologetic look. The verbal slap for doing what he had always done before caused Antonio even more nervousness, and he grew eager to prove his worth.

"When I say to fire," Captain Marseille drilled, "you will fire off down the row, one after the next, at precise five count intervals; no sooner, no later. Is that clear?"

Antonio answered snappily, "À vos ordres!" and his comrades echoed the reply.

"Your squads will immediately reload and be ready to fire again when the last cannon has fired its shot. If your projectile falls short of the wall, you must adjust your angle so the next one will land. If your missile by some strange occurrence flies over the wall, then you are in deep shit." He eyed them all with a serious gaze. "The general does not want to produce casualties which might anger our foe. He simply wants to let them know we are still here. Understood?"

"À vos ordres!" the four standard-bearers shouted while their crews looked at each other with shrugged shoulders.

"On the ready!" Marseille lifted his sword as all focus turned to him. "Fire!"

Antonio signaled his first cannoneers; the fuse was lit, and with a loud report the shot was away. The excited men of the second crew were focused on watching the cannonball fly toward the wall and he had to run in front of them, waving and shouting to press them into getting their fuse lit. By the time he signaled his third crew, the first ball made its landing short of the castle's stone wall. He rushed back across the grass, yelling as they were just standing like spectators to see if the second shot landed.

"This is not a calcio game! Reload this gun!" The bite of his tone snapped their attention back to duty while Antonio turned a crank to lower the barrel one degree. "You can't just stand about," he continued to scold them in their native Italian. "The captain said to keep firing down the row." A beefy man at the first cannon lifted the dense iron ball into the barrel after his partner had poured in the powder. A lanky young buck rammed in the pole with its cushioned cylinder at one end to pack the shot.

"Wait," Antonio called to his triggerman. "When the last cannon on the row fires, I'll count five and give you the signal." Then he dashed to his other crews to make sure they were readying their shots. The second two culverins had landed their shot on the wall and chipped away chunks of stone. The excited, inexperienced soldiers were cheering and waving their arms. "Get your culverin reloaded, men!" he commanded, but in truth he wanted to cheer as well. He could feel the adrenaline pumping through his blood, sending him into a kind of battle-high which he imagined fueled the Norse berserkers about whom he had read.

They continued for three rounds down the row before the captain called for them to cease firing. Smoke was thick in the air, and Antonio's ears rang from the blasts of the guns. He determined next time he would insert wax in his ears and instruct his squad to do so as well. Surveying the castle wall, he could make out the damage with dozens of chips and a few deep craters. Defenders had surged to the top of the ramparts and fired arquebuses at them, but they were out of the handheld firearms' range.

"Now they are awake!" the captain chanted with glee. Hearing the tone of his voice relaxed the Milanese soldiers, and they all began to cheer, slapping each other on their backs in congratulations, pushed to the pinnacle of exhilaration. "Sergeant Beaufort, once the barrels have cooled, have the crews take the cannons and artillery carts back to where they were being kept. Tomorrow we will practice at another section of wall, and I want to see a quicker setup, more shots landed, better performance all around, understood? These boys are fresh and unproven. How are we to win a battle, much less a war with this rabble?"

"Yes, sir, Captain," Beaufort saluted. "We shall execute faster and more proficiently tomorrow."

"See that you do," Marseille warned and strode from the field toward his sector of the sprawling camp.

Sergeant Beaufort turned a stern eye to the young officers who had been placed under his charge. "Standard-bearers," he called, and Antonio and his cohorts trotted over, enthusiasm bright on each youthful face.

"Did you see that?" Papi grinned. "We blasted that wall! Stone was flying, and their men were running about not knowing what was happening!"

"Tamp down your zeal, boy," Beaufort scowled. Then he winked. "Not bad for a first volley," he allowed, then resumed a serious note. "But Captain Marseille is correct; you need practice for speed and accuracy. What we are doing here is nothing more than harassing a foe, but real battles are coming—ones where the enemy returns fire. Your crews must be able to do their jobs in their sleep, in the dark and rain and storm, with bullets and arrows whizzing by, when the man to their left or right is struck down."

Beaufort's solemn reminder war is not a sporting event brought Antonio's fevered emotions back to the solid, wet earth beneath his feet. The day had produced a good experience, and he was certain he would share drinks with his friends as they recounted their success that evening, but Antonio understood both he and his squad still had much to learn and much to prepare before they would truly be ready. The young cannoneers had not paid attention to his instructions as they were distracted by things going boom around them. Would they be able to stand under pressure? Such would rest upon his leadership, or the lack thereof.

CHAPTER 13

The Night Flyer glided over a sleeping city, hoping against hope to get a glimpse of the man in the drawing she had folded into a pouch on her belt. Cesare was happy to accompany Madelena and Salvador to visit Bruno. The sketch came out rather generic, but at least displayed a few particulars. Bruno was certain the man was older and heavier than the Night Flyer, maybe in his late thirties or early forties. His dark hair and beard eliminated men with light coloring. Even though the witness had seen the perpetrator before he slipped on the mask, he was too far away for eye color or facial details. Bruno estimated his height at between Madelena's and Salvador's. *Height is close to mine and dressed all in black with a mask, easy for people to draw assumptions,* she thought. *Even if I see someone who resembles the drawing, how should I approach him?*

Pulling a handle and tilting to the left, the Night Flyer headed for a high warehouse rooftop to land on. This quadrant of Milan was dark and quiet under a cool, starry night. Every now and then a gust would sweep in from the south, which helped to keep her human kite aloft. Once her feet touched the roof, Florentina folded in her wings. She was grateful for Maddie's attentiveness to the injuries on her back. She had even made a thin pillow for her to wear as padding between her backpack and new skin to protect from reopening the cuts. Florentina smiled as she considered how well it actually worked. She was glad Maddie knew her secret now, the pillow being only one of many reasons why. She still had to sneak around to hide her identity from everyone else, but no more keeping secrets from the woman she cherished.

After determining there were no midnight lurkers below, Florentina pulled a cord to unfurl her wings once more. Taking a running start, she leapt off the north side of the warehouse allowing the southerly wind to catch the silk and lift her into the sky. After a few more minutes of scanning the shadowy streets below, the Night Flyer's keen eyes spotted light and movement. She arced around and came to rest on a low roof overlooking the occupied alley. After retracting her wings and securing them into her pack, she peered over the edge to spy a small group circling a fire in a brazier at the other end of the narrow passage between buildings.

She secured her grappling hook on a smoke pipe near the street-side of the house, tossed the coil of rope over the edge, and slid to the ground. She left it there as it would be simple enough to use it to climb back up after questioning them. Employing practiced stealth, the Night Flyer stole right up to the edge of their circle, then stepped into the glow of their fire. "It is a nice, clear night, is it not?"

The small group of three older men and two younger shot alarmed expressions to the masked vigilante. With knee-jerk instinct they backed away, holding up hands with either tattered or no gloves. "Do not be afraid." The Night Flyer slipped into her ambiguous Venetian tenor. She held empty hands before them in a nonthreatening gesture. They regarded the interloper warily.

"We're not looking for any trouble from the likes of you," growled a dirty man with bushy gray brows drawn together.

"Nor do I seek to give you any," she confirmed. "I seek the man who bombed the Holy Name Church last week. Look at this drawing of the rogue."

As she reached into her pouch to retrieve the sketch, a slighter, pale fellow asked, "You mean 'twern't you? Everyone is sayin'—"

"No!" sliced the deliberate reply. "People should not believe such a thing. I do not attack women and children." At her affirmation, a few heads nodded, and the group began to relax. "Examine the image and tell me if you have seen this man."

The drawing prompted head scratches, chin rubs, and negative shakes. "It could be Leo or Piero, from the docks, but it's hard to tell," one mused.

"I saw a fellow with this general appearance at Getti's Gaming Hall earlier tonight, but…" The older man shook his head. "I never caught his name, and I can't be sure t'was him."

"This man might have a military background or work as an enforcer for a Great House, may keep to himself a lot. He probably doesn't have a wife and family," she suggested, hoping the added clues would help. "Getti's Gaming Hall you say?"

With hands clad in brown gloves whose fingers had raveled away long ago, he passed the paper back to her. "You think it was this man?"

The Night Flyer nodded. "Coins for your time," she said and handed several to each man in the circle. "Eat hearty and stay warm. If you see this man, please tell Watchman Salvador Sfondrati. He took the witness' statement and had this drawing done of the real bomber."

As she glanced about the small gathering, she noticed one was missing. "Where is the boy?" she asked as her senses burst into full alert. "There were five of you."

The others looked around and shrugged, but she suspected he had snuck away to report a Night Flyer sighting. In a flash, she turned and darted down the alley where her grappling rope still hung. No sooner than she had started to scale the wall, a constable accompanied by two city watchmen all wearing the standard colors and hats of their positions arrived where the men encircled their fire.

"There he is!" one shouted pointing, and the constable raised a handgun rattling off a shot in her direction. It ricocheted off the brick wall as she quickened her pace.

She heard a deep voice scold, "Giorgio, why did you do that?" and the sound of stampeding boots. Reaching the top, she rolled onto the roof and yanked the rope up after her. With an agile dash to the smoke pipe, she unhooked her grappling device and recoiled the cable, tucking it into her belt.

She could hear the clamber of someone attempting to climb up the drainpipe and a French accent predict, "You are going to fall and crash to the ground!"

Florentina did not wish to fight city watchmen so as not to hurt one of the "good guys", so wasting no time she deployed her wings and with a running start leapt off the far side of the roof. The noise had rousted some residents of the neighborhood who peered from their doors or windows at the commotion. A few amazed tenants likely caught a glimpse of the mysterious Night Flyer as she soared out of sight.

The next few hours reflected her first interrogation. Few sober people were out, those who were feared the masked crusader, and no one could positively identify the man in her sketch. The gaming hall connection was the best she had been able to get, and the Night Flyer couldn't just waltz into such an establishment and start placing bets. She would return to watch from the shadows another evening when the enterprise would be brimming with patrons. It was time to return home for a couple of hours sleep.

* * *

Two days passed and the children's colds were much better to both women's relief. In the meantime, Florentina had formulated her plan and laid it out to Maddie. "I'm just going to loiter around the gaming hall in my black attire with a cloak and hood covering it and my hair," she had told her partner. "I'll keep the mask and coif tucked away and only put them on if necessary. My goal is not to engage the murderous lout, but to ascertain who he is and follow him to where he lives. Such a course may provide a clue as to who he works for or is associated with."

"I wish there was a better way," Madelena had bemoaned. "Without weapons and wings you are as vulnerable as any woman."

"Not any woman," Florentina corrected her. "I'll still have a few tricks should they be necessary. It's not like Donna Madelena or her children's tutor could enter such a gaming hall without turning heads and creating a whirlwind of gossip. The city guards are searching for the Night Flyer, not a lad in a cloak." The kiss Maddie had laid upon her mouth was enough in itself to lift her feet from the ground, and she recalled it with promise and affection.

She sat in a corner with an unobstructed view of the door, nursing a pint of cheap wine. The gambling house was loud and boisterous with laughs, cheers, and shouts bitter in their defeat. Zealous women served drinks or worked the crowd for a man with more money than sobriety, while rough men who uttered curses easier than a monk offers prayers packed the room. They played dice and cards and assorted games of chance. Smoke from a single hearth and inferior oil in the lamps permeated the air, as did the aroma of alcohol, sweat, and bad perfume. It was the kind of place her father had always warned her to avoid. "A new way to pick one's pocket is invented every day," he had sagely instructed.

It appeared Milan was at no loss for men who were happy to have their pockets picked. Despite common knowledge the advantage went to the house, young bucks and bored older men ever wanted to try their luck. Some did win, and the rare man walked out richer than he had been when he walked in, but most called it a good night if they broke even. She figured it was the activity, the rush, and the excitement which acted as the lure as much as the chance to strike payday. Adoring young ladies in low-cut off the shoulder gowns offered to blow on a man's dice for luck in hopes she may share in the profits. Twice during the evening fights had broken out as one accused another of cheating or a drunk had to be thrown out for abusive behavior.

Around ten at night, when the early crowd was shuffling out and the late nighters filing in, Florentina, obscured beneath a gray hood, spotted a man who could be the one from the picture. Her keen gaze followed him as she observed every nuance and mannerism, listened attentively to every word. He strode to the bar without speaking to patrons along the way, and when a fellow draped an arm on his shoulder and invited him to join them, he brushed it off and banished him with a dangerous glare.

In a slow and casual manner, Florentina positioned herself closer to the suspect as he ordered his drink. Then she watched as he bypassed all the lively, colorful games to a back corner to meet three other men whom she had not previously detected. He shook hands with an older gentleman whom she noted wore a prime quality of clothing and then took his seat. When the barmaid approached to ask if she wanted another mug of wine, Florentina asked in her disguised voice, "What are those fellows in the back doing?"

"Oh, that is the primero table," she explained. "It is a high-stakes card game and new to Getti's. It brings in a more prosperous clientele and has quickly gained popularity."

"What does the house take?"

"We often have a player in the game, but if not, the house gets five percent," she replied.

Florentina scoffed. "Five percent is not much compared to what you make from these other games."

"Not so!" The barmaid appeared insulted by the lad's rudeness. "Five percent of a thousand is more than the take from all the dice tables."

Florentina's lips parted, and her brows raised. "Indeed. And the bets are always so high?"

"The players set their own stakes, but when these four play it is for serious money. Another wine?"

"Sì, grazie," she replied and let the girl take her empty mug away. *He must have much money to play in this game; therefore, he is being paid well. The ledger page showed this cadre has plenty to pay the likes of him. He looks enough like the drawing, displays anti-social behavior, has a heavy coin purse, and enjoys the thrill of a high-stakes game. This could be the one.*

Florentina declined two invitations to dice and one sexual proposition before the crowds thinned out. Not wishing to draw attention milling around all alone, she left to stand in the shadows across from Getti's main door to await the suspect's exit. The night was cold, foggy, and damp and excessively dark with the moon obscured. But the glowing orb of a streetlight just outside the popular gambling hall would allow her to detect the gambler.

It was well after midnight when the four men departed Getti's Gaming Hall to go their separate ways. Now the challenge was to pad silently behind the bearded man at an ample distance to remain hidden, yet close enough to not lose him in mist as thick as sauce. Hearing his footsteps became more important than keeping eyes on him. Her gray cloak blended with the fog and her soft-soled boots made no sound as she took careful steps down deserted passages. She could feel tension rise into her throat as she steered with unease through swirls of murky vapor oscillating between impenetrable and imperceptible. Whenever a breeze would push away the fog, she could see clearly and catch a glimpse of him.

Florentina had shadowed her suspect for several blocks and completely lost orientation of where she was in the unfamiliar neighborhood when she no longer perceived his footsteps. She stopped and waited, listening for a door to open or close, but heard nothing save the lap of water against a pier. *We're near a canal,* she thought and tried to reorient her position but was unable to so much as see across the street. She stood as still as marble, not even venturing to take a breath lest her presence be detected.

As sudden as a change in fortune, the wind shifted directions, driving out the heavy fogbank. And there he was, directly opposite her, poised in a fighting stance with his rapier drawn and a stern visage of determination on his grizzled face. "Fool, to think you could steal my winnings," he growled in a Spanish accent.

Florentina fought to stamp down panic; it would not serve her. "No, señor," she retorted. "I have no interest in your florins, only your whereabouts on Epiphany morning."

He had already begun a steady march toward her when he stopped, his bearded, tan face swept with astonishment, and she knew. He recovered swiftly, tossing her a reply. "Opening my stocking like a good little boy."

He raised his sword and quickened his pace with even more determination reading in his expression. All Florentina brought with her was a dagger and a few vials of noxious potion, but they would be sufficient for defense. Retrieving a stoppered glass tube from her pouch, she smashed it on the cobblestones in front of his feet. Smoke rose up halting his advance, and he fell into a coughing fit. "I will find you again," she promised, and used the precious seconds to escape back into the misty lanes away from the canal and toward more familiar avenues.

He rained curses and swears at her, but his voice faded to a distant echo while she eluded danger, more frustrated than relieved because he had escaped without her learning his name or where he lived. But she had a lead at last!

CHAPTER 14

Julia Sacchi all but floated down the sunny boulevard after Sunday Mass at the Duomo, so overwhelmed with glee she wasn't indeed certain her tiny feet touched the pavement at all. The third Sunday since Epiphany fell in late January and was a notoriously slow week for church attendance. The lull between the Christmas rush and Ash Wednesday, marking the beginning of the season of Lent leading up to Easter, was a time when even the most faithful would take a break from services with the more well-to-do Milanese making their way to a seaside resort to enjoy a winter holiday away from the city. Julia had wanted to take just such a vacation, but her dotard husband insisted upon business before pleasure. His schedule was too full of scooping up Benetto's old clients and making sure to fill their weapons orders on schedule. He explained the war was good for trade and that by this time next year he would be in a position to buy her the seaside villa she had her heart set on. It was worth the wait, she had supposed.

Prominent citizens waved and greeted her as she danced along oblivious to their existence, although it is quite possible each believed the radiant smile she boasted was meant for them. It was not uncommon for a young socialite to marry a much older man, particularly if he was rich, which is precisely what Julia had done. Giovanni had not been in the market for a new bride after the mother of his two sons passed, but Julia had set her sights on him. While she would have preferred one of his handsome sons, Giovanni was the man with money, power, and influence. His eldest son, Ambroso, was away at the University of Bologna while his athletic younger son, Pietro, was a calcio player who occupied the mansion with them causing her a great deal of temptation and erotic dreams. For three years she had been his faithful, doting wife, a jewel on his arm at social events, and a cause for envy among his peers.

She was uncertain if the fault lay in his seed or her womb, but she had yet to conceive a child, which was acceptable in Julia's mind. Women deteriorated after having babies with the weight gain, the stretching of their bodies, and her breasts were full enough as it was. Most society women such as herself were little bothered by the baby after its birth; like Tomasina, they had servants to tend to the needs of the child. *Maddie was always peculiar that way,* she contemplated. *Nursed those babies herself, carried them around town, and she said she even sang lullabies to them at night. What a bother? Why would she do such a thing? Just another reason why I consider her odd.*

If it was possible, her glow expanded more as she began to think about Madelena. Since the little chapel the widow preferred was closed until repairs could be completed, she had attended Mass with her family at the Duomo that morning and Julia's watchful eye had not missed a single expression or nuance which passed between Maddie and Florentina. The show was lost to Portia and her children sitting on the row in front of them, but Julia's seat afforded her an excellent view. Rather than sit with the children between them as was proper, Maddie was squeezed up against her tutor so not a hair could pass between them, and the little boy and girl were set on either side of them. The sensual attraction between the women was so obvious, their ardent devotion to one another so tangible, the amorous glances and incidental touches so fluid, Julia was flabbergasted nobody else noticed. Then again, most people pay no attention to anyone other than themselves. She, however, had long ago devised a game with which to entertain herself. Julia collected secrets. She made it her business to be acquainted with everyone else's and when the time was right, she would spin a web to trap some hapless social fly. Then she could extort from them whatever she wanted, be it money or favors, or sometimes she would merely spread the news around town for amusement. In fact, she held several important citizens under her thumb at this very moment.

This is simply too rich! she gloated to herself as she glided through the Sunday strollers and church patrons on the gorgeous day. *If there is one thing I can spot quicker than flies spy honey at a picnic, it's illicit passion. Don Alessandro Torelli's sister and a female member of the household staff—I couldn't make this story up! This is far better than Donna Dolce Bella and the gardener or even Father Joseph and the altar boy. But how to use the information is the real question,* she pondered as she patted her honey updo and waved to an eager admirer.

I likely have more money than she does, so perhaps I should go straight to Don Alessandro, she schemed. *Money may not be the angle I want to pursue, however. He has influence and...* A light flashed in Julia's brain as she remembered something Portia had said at their last circle meeting. *Alessandro bought the Gazette! I could have him print favorable articles about me and my husband and unfavorable ones about our adversaries. Yes, an excellent possibility. Then again,* she mused as she turned a corner into her own neighborhood. *I may wish to hold this one and spring it when I desire a favor. There's no rush. I need to think and plan. Oh, this is going to be so much fun! I just love when I am privy to other people's secrets—it gives me tremendous power over them. And to hold power over the wealthiest family in Milan... well, maybe not anymore. With Giovanni's new clients and orders, we will soon surpass the Torellis. Every man will want me, and every woman will want to be me. To imagine, at twenty-four years old, I have reached the pinnacle!*

Julia simply radiated elation when she whisked in the front door of her mansion. She hummed as she slipped out of her wrap and hung it on a cloak tree in the entry hall. The sound of unfamiliar voices woke her from her dream-state.

"Giovanni, Dear?" she called absently, her thoughts still whirling with possibilities.

Giovanni appeared at the doorway to the men's parlor with his jaw set and glare piercing from behind his spectacles. Her meek, doting husband seemed like a different man, one chiseled from granite. "What are you doing home?" he asked in a dangerously low tone. "You said you were going out to lunch with your friends after Mass."

Julia was startled and off-set by his interrogation. This was so unlike him. Perplexed, she took a step back. "I'm sorry," she apologized. "I didn't know you were meeting a client. My plans changed at the last minute." She mustered a smile but curiosity getting the best of her, she peered past her husband to observe the man in the parlor. He appeared rough and uncultured, dressed in common clothing, his black hair in an unfashionable cut and his beard—well, fine gentlemen simply did not wear beards. *But then, Giovanni is an arms dealer,* she told herself. *I suppose he makes sales to all kinds of unsavory characters and likely acquires low cost goods from the same sort. It's none of my business.*

He stared through her with impenetrable eyes of green and gold which bore into her like an icy blade. "I won't disturb your meeting, dear," she mustered with a smile. "I'll just stay upstairs in my room and be no trouble at all." She brushed an apologetic kiss to his lips and skipped up the steps without looking back.

In a wink, her mind was again ablaze with the possibilities lying before her. *How to proceed with the juiciest secret of them all?* she gleamed as she flopped down upon her satin comforter and piles of pillows.

* * *

THE TORELLI FAMILY sat around the breakfast table Monday morning as was their custom before venturing their separate ways for the bulk of the day. Bianca had prepared scrambled eggs with cheese and ciabatta rolls with a side of sliced oranges, citrus from Sicily being the main source of winter fruit in Milan. Alessandro had come to anticipate Florentina's "morning lessons" in which she employed the Socratic Method to induce the family members to produce correct responses to questions she would pose, the current subject being oranges.

"What is the purpose of fruit?" she asked. He passed an interested gaze around the table, expecting the initial response.

"For us to eat!" *Matteo beat Bernardo to it,* he thought, *or my boy has gotten wise to how this works.*

"But..." Florentina responded with a considering expression. "What if the fruit falls in an untended orchard and there are no little boys or girls to eat it? Is it wasted?" she prodded gently.

"An animal or bird will come along to eat it," Bernardo ventured, causing Alessandro to smile in amusement.

"But what if no animal eats it either?" Betta chimed in, guessing what her teacher would ask next.

She was rewarded with a grin and a wink from Florentina. Young faces skewed as they shoveled in bites of their breakfasts. Alessandro threw them a bone. "What is inside the oranges?"

"Seeds," replied Pollonia in a tinkling, feminine tone.

"I was about to say that," Bernardo declared. "The fruit protects the seeds so they can grow new trees."

"And if the birds and animals eat the orange, they may swallow the seeds and poop them out somewhere else to start new trees," Matteo added with a silly grin.

Betta turned to her mother. "Matteo said 'poop.'"

Maddie stroked her bouncy blond strands and was about to reply when a sudden knock hammered at the front door. The dining room had its own door but was close enough to the entry hall they could hear so loud a rap. Everyone stopped what they were doing and grew concerned at the unusual interruption. Only one tense moment passed before Geppetto, the new head of staff Alessandro had chosen to replace the ill-fated Iseppo, opened the heavy oak double-doors.

"I apologize for the intrusion, but the watchman Salvador Sfondrati is at the door with important news." Geppetto was younger than his predecessor but had come with excellent references. He was a sharp, stylish man with a barren wife. Alessandro felt it was good to have her share his room, and she brought her own skills to the household as a seamstress. He had been pleased with the impeccable grooming and punctuality displayed by the somewhat portly chestnut-haired majordomo during these first few weeks of his employ, but after Iseppo it would take much longer for Alessandro to trust him.

"Show him in," he instructed from his seat at the head of the table. The vibrations in the room had transformed from cheerful to anxious at the interruption, and all attention shifted to the door.

Salvador's expression did nothing to calm their fears. "Don Alessandro, Donna Portia, and family, I am so sorry to interrupt your morning meal, but I was certain you would want to be informed right away." He held his hat in a shaky hand and appeared as if he may burst into tears at any moment. "Don Alessandro, if we could talk in private, it would be best."

Portia clutched Pollonia's hand, and Maddie grabbed Florentina's. Alessandro nodded and excused himself from the table, stepping into the hallway with Salvador. *Not Antonio; oh, please God, not my boy!*

"I didn't want to speak of it in front of the children," Salvador explained as he shifted his weight from one foot to the other. "Early this morning a woman's body was found behind a row of gaming halls in a sordid district of the city; it was Donna Julia Sacchi."

Alessandro was simultaneously relieved and stunned. He raised a hand to rub the back of his neck. "Are they sure? I know Julia; she is my wife's friend. She doesn't frequent that part of town."

"Her body was positively identified. There were marks around her neck and her eyes bulged, indicating she had been strangled. The constable has gone to inform Don Giovanni."

"When did it happen? Who, why?" The questions flew from his lips as fast as his mind conceived them.

Salvador explained. "Don Giovanni came in late last evening to report his wife had gone out and was expected to return before dark, but she never made it home. He was worried and wanted us to mount a search. The constable assured him she was likely having such a delightful time at a party she had lost track of time or had too much wine and fallen asleep but said he would ask the night watchmen to be on the lookout for her. Just before dawn..." he sighed and slumped his shoulders. "They found her. All I know is she had been dead for some time as her body was cold and stiff."

"Did it appear... were there signs that..." Alessandro wasn't sure how to ask the question.

"Her clothing did not appear to have been disturbed," he answered in a hush. "People always want to know."

"Salvador, you did right to come to me with this news. Giovanni is my guild leader and my friend. Julia is—was—friends with both my wife and sister. This is such grim tidings. We must go to Giovanni and offer what solace we may. The city will certainly make finding her killer a priority."

The watchman raised a hopeless visage. "We will do what we can, but if there were no witnesses I'm not certain anything can be done. You know, if you count the mysterious death of Countess Anna Marie last summer and the attempt on Madelena's life last month, I count three prominent women of the city who have fallen victim to violence or violent intent."

Alessandro found himself stunned once again. He had not even thought to make a connection until Salvador suggested it. He merely nodded his head with a blank stare. "Something to consider. Thank you, old friend."

After showing Salvador out, he trailed back into the dining room. They would all need to be told, he realized. Alessandro met frantic eyes and Portia burst out with, "Is it—"

"No," he said definitively. "No ill news of Antonio. But Julia Sacchi is dead."

CHAPTER 15

Madelena, Alessandro, and Portia were ushered into Don Giovanni's mansion while Luca, a young man in their employ, stayed with their carriage out front. Each was dressed appropriately in subdued colors and unadorned styles. Wanting to do something herself, Portia had assisted Bianca with baking a lasagna while Ally had escorted Maddie to the florist to select a bouquet for her to bring.

Madelena had some experience with this sort of thing and recollected Julia had been among those who had called on her to convey their condolences after her husband Vergilio had been killed. She understood Giovanni did not need weepers but would appreciate knowing others expressed empathy and compassion for his loss.

The middle-aged maid who showed them in was as solemn and gloomy as the house itself. She took the dish holding the lasagna with a nod and a "Grazie." Maddie noticed how quiet the halls were. She glanced around, picturing in her mind where various Christmas decorations had been only a month ago, recalling the delicious beverage Julia had created, and her heart grew heavy.

She and the bouncy, buxom, honey blonde had never been close friends, despite the nearness of their ages, but they had spent a few hours together almost every Saturday for years. Julia was… familiar. She was a peer, beyond an acquaintance, and too young to die. Maddie thought the woman could be shallow and was certain she had married Giovanni for his money, but she didn't deserve to be killed. After all, none of them were saints. It occurred to her, *She won't be at our circle meeting for brunch this Saturday.* She considered they most likely wouldn't meet at all under the circumstances.

The trio turned to the left and trudged into a darkened parlor with drapes pulled closed, lit only by a few candles. Giovanni lifted haunted eyes to them. Maddie was struck by how old he appeared, the lines in his wan face more pronounced. She set the flower decanter on a small lamp table, hoping they would convey the appropriate message. Signs of life flickered in Giovanni's face when he recognized his guests. He started to push up on the arms of his chair to stand, but Alessandro moved in swiftly. "You don't have to get up, Giovanni," he said in a sympathetic tone.

"Yes, I do," he replied with determination as he rose. He extended his hand to Ally who received it with a firm shake. "Thank you so much for coming."

Portia and Madelena took their turns to give him a hug and kiss on the cheek. Alessandro answered saying, "Certainly we would come, my friend. We only wish the visit was under happier circumstances. I am so very sorry." His gaze met Giovanni's, conveying his honest sadness.

"Sorry indeed," the widower echoed and plopped back into his seat. "My Julia," he uttered, his voice cracking, and he motioned for them to all sit. There were several armchairs and two settees, all crafted of walnut with matching crimson cushions. The three sat in the ones closest to the grieving man. Then he let out a desolate sob. "My beautiful young wife! What am I going to do now?"

"There, there, Giovanni," Portia tried to console. "Julia was my friend and it would break her heart to see you like this." She reached over and stroked a hand on his upper arm as he buried his face in his hands.

Maddie had been in his position, so struck with shock and disbelief, so fearful of the unknown tomorrow without a familiar partner. She could not perceive if he had truly loved the young socialite, although she was convinced he had enjoyed her company. Even with her personal experience, she didn't quite know what to say to him. But when he wiped shaky hands down his face and returned them to his knees, she simply reached over and took one between her palms giving it a squeeze.

His hollow expression turned to her. "You understand," he said. She nodded and made an effort to connect to him through emotion alone. "I remember thinking when your husband died how I was sorry for your loss but so glad it wasn't me. And I know I bore my first wife's death," he continued, "but this is different. She was older and had been ill. Julia…" This time he lifted those damp, hazel eyes to Alessandro and croaked out, "was taken from me—murdered! Why?" He looked from one of them to the next like a lost child. "Why would someone kill my Julia?"

Alessandro shook his head, dropping his gaze to the floor. "I couldn't say," he uttered in despair. "It is hard to comprehend."

Giovanni retrieved his hand from Madelena to ball fists on the arms of his chair, and Portia drew her comforting touch back as well. This time when he spoke, his misery had doubled. "I had been cross with her. It's one thing to utter words of love as the last you say, but I snapped at her. She came home early, I wasn't expecting her, and I had a client over. We were in here discussing a business deal and, you know, arms buyers aren't always the highest class of clientele. She waltzed in just as happy as a bluebird in springtime, and I growled at her about interrupting my meeting. It was so thoughtless!"

Portia spoke in a soothing tone. "You didn't know. There was no way to predict what would transpire. We all utter words in the anger of the moment, remarks we don't really mean. I'm sure she understood."

He lowered his head and attempted a nod. With a sigh, he continued. "Later on, after the client had left, she returned downstairs, collected her wrap and hat, and said she was off to see a man about a horse and would be home before dark. I thought it was an odd thing to say as Julia didn't ride. Then it dawned on me my birthday is coming soon, and mayhap she was selecting a gift for me. She knows I enjoy the races." He stopped, mouth slightly agape, staring at a spot on the wall. "My birthday… I dreamed of my birthday and a present and now… she won't be there with me." He turned a haunted aspect back to Alessandro. "I am twice her age; I never assumed to outlive her."

Maddie thought of her brother's son and how young Antonio's life was in danger daily. She realized Ally feared the possibility of outliving his son. Then the awesome dread, that sea of apprehension she had harbored about losing Florentina, washed through her soul like a torrent. People do die, and not always who you expect nor when you expect them to, but Ally had been right; we don't know and can't predict, therefore must find our joy in the moments we do have rather than waste them fearing a future which may never come.

"She spoke of you often," Maddie said at last. "Julia, she was so spontaneous, so full of life. Every day was a party for her, each outing an adventure." She recalled it had helped her when people retold pleasant memories, said kind things about her husband. "And she spoke very fondly of you. She would say, 'Giovanni bought me this,' and 'Giovanni is taking me on a trip there,' and 'My Giovanni spoils me silly'. She appreciated you, and no single spat can cancel out years of doting."

He nodded his head and lifted his chin, his moist gaze meeting hers. "Thank you," he voiced. "She was one of a kind."

"Listen, we do not wish to intrude on you or make you feel you must entertain," Alessandro said as he stood. "We just wanted to come by, to pay our respects, and to let you know if there is anything you need, please call on me. I have no matter more pressing than to be a comfort and aid to a friend. I remember when I was a lad of about twelve or so when my younger sisters died from the whooping cough and baby Maddie was very sick, you came to see us, to offer sympathy to my mother, to provide whatever you could for my father. You were a mere journeyman merchant then, not yet a wealthy man, but took time for us. My father never forgot that; neither have I."

Giovanni stood, and the women followed suit. He grasped Ally's hand again. "Thank you, Alessandro, Portia, Madelena. It means a lot to me you care enough to come."

* * *

THE TORELLI FAMILY exited the oppressive atmosphere of gloom and heartbreak into a bleak, cloudy day. Alessandro helped his wife and sister into the carriage and instructed the lanky, sandy haired Luca to drive them home. "That was so sad," Portia sighed as she snuggled against Ally's warm side. "Poor Giovanni."

"Yes," he agreed. "And it is not happening to me." He looked first at Maddie who sat across from him, then at Portia tucked under his arm, pinning them both with a serious visage. "From now until this matter is solved, neither of you are allowed to leave the house alone for any reason, nor you are to go anywhere after dark unless I am with you, and that is a direct order from the Head of your House. Do I make myself clear?"

"I have been being careful," Madelena began.

"Especially you," Ally pronounced. "We know someone is trying to kill *you*. The question is, did the same malefactor kill poor Julia? And if someone is out to get prominent women of Milan, Portia dear, few are more prominent than you."

Maddie bit her lip and peered anxiously at her brother. "Come now, speak up," he decreed. "Whatever you are thinking is about to spill out anyway."

"It's just... the Night Flyer found the church bomber... sort of," she admitted.

"What do you mean by 'sort of'?" he demanded, turning full attention to her.

"Well, you see, I took Florentina's artist friend, Cesare, along with Salvador to meet with his witness, and Cesare made a drawing based on the witness' description. Salvador is passing copies among the other watchmen, but I left one for the Night Flyer. He found the man at a gaming hall and followed him for a time but lost him in this thick fogbank somewhere near the docks. He is going to continue searching for the fellow to determine if he is in fact the one who threw the bombs and it could be he killed Julia too, but..." she trailed off. Maddie turned a flabbergasted look to Ally and Portia. "Why would anyone kill Julia, and why is someone trying to kill me?"

Alessandro shook his head and rubbed the back of his neck. "I have tried to wrap my brain around the same questions. At first, I suspected an enemy of attacking you to get to me, but it doesn't fit. Why not try to kill me, or Portia, if such was the case? And I am barely acquainted with Julia."

"Oh, Ally," Portia purred. "It's not you; you are not to blame for any of it."

But Alessandro was not so certain, at least where Maddie was concerned. He gritted his teeth and frowned. "It could also be Julia's murder is completely unrelated to the attacks on Maddie. Regardless, we are taking no chances, either of you; is that clear?" His women nodded in agreement. "I have no travel plans until spring and can postpone those if necessary. I'll not have either of you shot with crossbows, blown up, or strangled, or whatever devious method he concocts next."

Ally was confident the Night Flyer would do everything possible to solve the mystery and see to the fate of this villain who attempted to impersonate the vigilante while perpetrating a most heinous crime. But the Night Flyer was just one person and could only be in one place at a time. Alessandro determined to increase his household security and keep a very keen eye on his family members.

CHAPTER 16

～

Florentina rested on a stool to Pollonia's left as the young lady sat on the bench seat designed to match the harpsichord it accompanied. An instructional book of manuscript paper bearing clear, handwritten notes was propped against the music stand built onto the instrument whose top was opened displaying the exquisite artwork as well as releasing the sound. Pollonia pushed the keys in turn, producing the unique plucked string tone quality with a studious visage of concentration, her long, coppery hair falling loose around her shoulders.

"Very good!" Florentina praised her student. "You have learned all of your notes and are progressing nicely in five-finger position. As your fingers get stronger, the chords will be easier to play."

"Thank you," came her bashful reply. "I've been practicing."

"I can tell." Florentina flipped a page in the music book. Hearing a squeal, she peered out the parlor windows into the courtyard. A wet February snow covered the yard and Betta and Matteo, completely recovered from their colds, were running around throwing snowballs at each other in the waning twilight. She turned back to Pollonia and continued the lesson. "Next we will proceed to full scales and arpeggios, the building blocks of music. I want you to keep playing your simple chanson as well, you'll just need to spend more time on these. Here, let me demonstrate how to move out of five-finger position to complete the scale."

Pollonia slid to one edge of the bench, allowing room for Florentina beside her. The teacher demonstrated how to fold the thumb up past the little finger going up the scale and then reset each finger where it had been before on the way down. "See? Now you try."

She did so correctly, just not with even timing, her fingers hesitating as she changed positions. Pollonia grimaced and raised a questioning gaze Florentina.

Florentina nodded. "Keep doing it until it feels fluid and natural. Count to yourself to make sure you don't slow down on the transition. This week we'll practice hands separately. Next time we'll try putting them together. You'll find the arpeggios are easier." Florentina demonstrated, and Pollonia repeated the movement. She smiled when she was able to maintain proper timing.

A snowball splatted against the windowpane, and Florentina rolled her eyes. "I'd better calm them down before dinner. You are progressing beautifully, Pollonia," she congratulated before taking her leave from the keyboard. She heard the ascent of the scale as she crossed to the door and out onto the patio.

"Matteo, Betta!" Florentina called, a disapproving look on her face.

"We're sorry!" Matteo called as he raced around the fountain. "A snowball can't break the window."

"That is not the point. It's time for you both to come inside and wash up for dinner."

"Yes, Florentina," Betta replied and skipped through the snow, now smashed down from dozens of little boot prints.

Matteo started to throw another one but had the good instinct to glance up at Florentina first. Her expression had him opening his hand and letting the icy ball plop to the ground. "I'm coming too," he said and followed his sister in.

* * *

MADELENA HAD ARRIVED home in time to witness the exchange and after greeting the children and sending them on their way, moved closer to Florentina. She could hear the distinct sound of the harpsichord from the parlor and asked, "Aren't you supposed to be conducting Pollonia's music lesson?"

"We were almost finished when snowballs started their assault on the parlor windows," Florentina explained. Maddie drew her brows together and began to glance around as though searching for something. "What is it?"

"Where is Livia? It is her task… oh, never mind," Madelena dismissed in disgust. "I need to find the careless girl. This incompetence, or total disregard for responsibility, has gone on long enough."

"Are you planning to dismiss her?" Florentina's voice was tinged with sympathy.

"I should," Maddie replied, "but there is one thing I can try first. Either way, she will no longer be my concern." Softening her resolve, she turned an affectionate mien to Fiore. "Are you… going anywhere tonight?"

"I have some reading and studying which I need to focus on," Florentina answered, meeting her gaze with sensual heat.

"Mayhap you can bring your book up to my room, say around ten o'clock when everyone will be retired for the evening?" Maddie's eyes darkened as the thrill of anticipation leapt into her throat.

"I could indeed. But remember, Portia and Pollonia want to play us in a card game of Trappola after dinner."

"Ah, yes," Maddie recalled. "After we win a few hands, Pollonia will probably ask you to play some songs for us to sing. It would not be a surprise if Ally joins us. I'll be waiting for you afterward."

"I look forward to it," she said with a seductive smile.

"Now, to find Livia." Maddie marched off in search of the wayward governess and found her on the third floor exiting the kitchen giggling like a child with the lanky Luca grinning like a cat who just caught a mouse. They both froze upon noticing her. "Luca, go see if Geppetto needs anything else tonight."

"Sì, Donna Madelena." The youthful man bowed politely, shot Livia an expression of apology, and scampered away.

Maddie crossed her arms over her chest while Livia lowered her head, obviously aware she had been shirking her duties again.

"I am so sorry, Donna," she began, but Maddie cut her off.

"No doubt," she stated, all business. "I have concluded my children no longer require a governess. Florentina is instructing them in their studies, they are old enough to bathe and dress themselves, and you are never watching after them anyway."

The girl's eyes rounded like saucers, her mouth fell agape, and she began to quiver. She wrapped her arms around herself in comfort and fought to hold back tears.

Maddie continued in formal authority. "In the morning you are to report to Geppetto to be reassigned to another duty. From now on you shall be under his direction, do you understand?"

Livia nodded and swallowed a considerable lump from her throat. Then Madelena spoke to her in a more motherly tone. "Livia, if you do not perform better for Geppetto, he will dismiss you from this household. This flirtation between you and Luca is normal for young people, but you have allowed it to interfere with your work, which cannot be tolerated. If it is just a game, then don't let the distraction of a handsome smile and charming personality cost you a good position. And if the two of you are more seriously involved, then ask Luca to speak with Don Alessandro. Provisions can be made for a couple, should you both wish to remain in domestic service as careers. Honestly, you should give more thought to your future—both of you. However, I warn you: if you continue to ignore your responsibilities, you will be seeking employment elsewhere. Is that clear?"

Livia sniffed, her visage conveying both shame and gratitude. "Yes, Donna; I am sorry. You're right. Thank you for giving me another chance."

"You are welcome," Maddie replied with a nod. "Now don't waste it."

* * *

FLORENTINA MADE a light tap on Madelena's door around ten p.m. "I have the book you asked for," she said just loud enough for any lingering servants to perceive her words.

Maddie opened the door, having already changed into her nightgown and robe for bed. "Please be so kind as to bring it in. I may need you to point out the important parts."

Once inside, Florentina fell into Madelena's warm embrace, a surge of arousal coursing through her veins. She actually heard herself purr as she pressed into Maddie's bosom, soft and heated, unencumbered by weighty garments. Florentina placed a kiss to her cheek at almost the same moment Madelena's lips brushed hers. Then their lips met, pleasure and anticipation building as she tasted her strawberry mouth, which never failed to leave her weak in the knees.

"Fiore," Maddie breathed against her neck as they held the embrace.

Florentina found the rhythm of her lover's heartbeat against her chest and closed her eyes to linger in the moment. She didn't want it to end, ever, but… they could concern themselves with how to carry on their relationship after assassins had been caught and dealt with. Of paramount importance was solving the mystery and keeping Maddie safe.

"I brought the diary," Florentina said as she loosened her hold. "There are still passages I have not been able to decipher."

Madelena met her gaze, then brushed moist lips lightly over hers. "Come, sit with me on the settee and we can work together. I have an idea," she suggested. "What if we give the assassin what he seeks? I could go out and about alone, make myself an easy target—with the Night Flyer observing from a distance, of course. That will lure him from his hiding and—"

"And it isn't going to happen!" Florentina declared definitively. "I am aware Alessandro has forbidden you and Portia from leaving the house unescorted."

"But you would be right there, in your disguise with all your weapons," Maddie explained.

"There are too many variables. I can't watch every direction at once. Listen to me, Maddie," Fiore implored. "A crossbow and a bomb are distance weapons. He could strike before I even detected his presence. There is no way in heaven or hell I would allow you to dangle yourself in front of him like a worm on a hook!"

Maddie sighed, a discouraged frown twisting her face as she plopped onto the settee. "Well, the Night Flyer has had no luck finding the Spaniard who bombed the church. I only wanted to help."

Relief overtook Florentina's features as she settled beside Maddie. "I understand, but I did discover this Saturday night Getti's Gaming Hall is sponsoring a primero championship tournament, extremely high stakes, and all the best players are sure to attend. I suspect our enemy will not be able to resist; therefore, the Night Flyer shall be watching and waiting for him. This time I will be ready."

A look of concern crossed Maddie's face, and she intertwined her fingers with Fiore's. "Why not alert the watchmen and constables? You don't even own a sword."

Fiore smiled at her and gave her hand a squeeze. "I have what I need. Besides, most of the authorities still think the Night Flyer committed the crime."

"All the more reason—"

Florentina cut her off by placing a finger to her lips. "I will be careful. Now, back to our mystery. What do you know about this countess who died under mysterious circumstances last summer?"

"Countess Anna Marie, wife to the Count of Como," she said playfully catching Fiore's finger between her teeth and drawing her lips around it before letting go.

Florentina's eyes sparkled as she tried to contain a grin. "Business before pleasure, good Donna," she teased. "How did she die?"

"I was there, in fact." Madelena's tone dropped its flirtatious charm and became more serious. "It was at the May Day Gala, a magnificent ball attended by anyone who's anyone. I was still in official mourning at the time so did not dance or join in the games, but I felt obliged to attend. It was late in the evening and guests were beginning to leave, when we heard a crashing noise coming from the direction of the back staircase, one typically only used by servants. A few of the men rushed to see what happened only to come running back frantic, calling for physicians and a constable and the count."

"She fell down a set of stairs she normally would not use?" Florentina asked as she caressed Maddie's fingers in her hand.

"It's what everyone assumed. There was an official inquest because she was nobility, but no signs of foul play were uncovered. Mayhap she had too much wine and was unsteady on her heels, but she could have been pushed. No one saw her fall."

"Was she old, young?"

"Not so old, perhaps her mid-thirties, and not heavy or known to overindulge. The heels of her shoes were not broken, but her neck certainly was." Maddie sighed. "There have been murmurings about it—why was she using those stairs? Was it for a clandestine rendezvous with a lover? Did her husband catch her? Or had she been the initial victim in a series of attacks on prominent women?"

"Hum." Florentina gathered her thoughts. "She was noble, whereas you and Julia are simply rich, and Vergilio... he doesn't fit."

"What do you mean?" she asked.

"Something Benetto said has stuck with me, needling my mind ever since: Vergilio wasn't important enough to kill." Florentina looked her in the eye. "I don't think he was ever an intended target. I suspect your husband was in the wrong place at the wrong time and witnessed something or someone he shouldn't have."

Maddie furrowed her brow and inhaled introspectively. "I hadn't thought of that. He was quite curious and would sometimes be rebuked for trying to concern himself with other people's affairs. Alessandro was even annoyed with him for it. Add in his penchant for talking too much." She raised her gaze to Fiore's again. "You could be right. He may have witnessed a crime."

"Or a gathering of criminals," Florentina added. "Maybe he overheard them planning a murder and was not covert enough to escape undetected. All we know for certain is two prominent women have been killed and two attempts have been made on your life thus far. But we have no actual evidence they are connected. Perhaps Countess Anna Marie fell, or was murdered by her husband or lover; perhaps Julia was the unfortunate victim of a robbery gone wrong. But twice professional assassins have tried to kill you and we are no closer to finding a reason or who has hired them."

"But we are closer to catching the man who bombed the church," Maddie added. "You will be very careful, won't you?" She raised a hand to caress Fiore's cheek.

"Now that I have found you, I shan't take any risks with my life. I love you, and I wish nothing more than to grow old with you." Florentina drew her into a deep kiss, reveling in the touch and taste of this extraordinary woman who actually loved her. It exceeded anything Florentina had imagined possible, and yet here she was, enthralled and entranced, more excited to be alive than she had ever dreamed. No, she had no intention of allowing herself to be killed.

"I love you," Madelena echoed as she moved a hand to caress Fiore's breast through the cloth of her dress. "Can you stay with me tonight?"

I desire nothing more than to stay with you every night! "Dare I?" she breathed. "Someone may notice I haven't left, and—" A wee knock sounded, and the two women froze.

"Mama," whimpered a small girl's voice. "I had a nightmare," she said wiggling the handle.

Maddie crossed the room, opened the door, and picked up her daughter, cradling her against her shoulder. "It's alright now," she soothed as she pushed the door closed with a toe.

"The roof was crashing down," Betta recounted, brushing tears from her cheek.

"I'll see you in the morning," Florentina said as she stood.

"No, you stay too," Betta insisted as her arms clung around Maddie's neck. "If something happens, you can save us."

"Nothing will happen, Sweetheart," Fiore promised as she joined mother and daughter. She stroked Betta's hair and placed a kiss to her forehead. "Your Uncle Alessandro will keep us all safe."

"But what if they throw a bomb through the window?" Panic began to rise in her voice as her eyes widened with fear.

"Uncle Alessandro has guards all around the house," Maddie explained. "No one can get close."

"You will be safe, Betta," Florentina repeated and hugged them both.

"But can you stay?" she begged. Florentina's gaze met Maddie's. She wanted to stay more than anything and the fact Betta wished it too tugged at her heartstrings.

"Florentina will be right upstairs," Madelena assured her. "You come get in bed with me now. It was just a dream. Our house is a safe place."

Florentina slipped out, praying Maddie was right.

CHAPTER 17

Sunshine melted the residual snow Saturday morning. Florentina started her day in the Torelli Silk production house repairing two looms, one with a faulty foot pedal and the other needing a harness replaced. Those would take no time at all to refurbish, but becoming entangled in the procedure, her creative brain kicked into full inventive mode as she began experimenting with the broken loom. *What could aid the weaver in increasing the speed of the process? Is there a better way to design this reed so it battens the threads more uniformly with each pass?*

House Torelli specialized in silk, although they kept a few other sidelines such as wool just in case ships from China did not arrive as expected. Raw silk was imported from China, primarily to merchants in Venice, Napoli, and Milan, except Napoli was being bypassed now because of the war. Alessandro acquired large quantities of the material which was woven into traditional silk cloth and velvet in his weaving production houses. Then it was dyed, cut, and rolled onto bolts which were sold to tailors and dressmakers, or exported throughout Europe. It was premium fabric, warm but light, strong and tear resistant while pleasant to the touch, and Torelli Silk had gained a reputation as one of the best money could buy.

Normally dozens of workers would be busy weaving on these looms even on a Saturday, but this was a Church proclaimed holiday: February 14, St. Valentine's Day. A glow overtook Florentina's face, rousting her from any mechanical musings as she thought of the special occasion. *Invention will have to wait; I want to craft the perfect card for Maddie.*

While the old Roman festival of Lupercalia had been outlawed by the Church, St. Valentine's Day had been celebrated by lovers and close friends for ages. Everyone was familiar with the third century Christian priest who defied Emperor Claudius' decree soldiers were not allowed to marry by performing their weddings in secret. Once discovered, Valentine was thrown into prison and sentenced to death. There, he fell in love with the jailer's daughter, and when he was taken to be killed on the fourteenth of February, he sent her a love letter signed "from your Valentine". The day become one of the first saints' days to grace a Christian calendar and the practice of writing cards and letters with proclamations of affection had survived the centuries.

Satisfied the machines were functioning properly, Florentina started for the door then remembered it was also the day of the primero tournament and she would be hunting a killer that night. With a careful glance around the vast, warehouse sized room, Florentina determined she was indeed alone in the space. She walked back to her tool box, a trunk in a corner where she kept implements for repairing equipment, knelt down, and opened it. She lifted out a substantial tray to reveal a few items hidden beneath it. The first was a bola, the Spanish name for a weapon they reported the Natives used in the New World to bring down large animals or geese; she had originally read of it as a type of flail employed by the Chinese. She held the three weighted balls connected by braided leather cords in her left hand while extending the length of the cord to its thick, twined end in her right. The iron balls were each a little smaller than a billiard ball, with one weighing more than the other two. The object was to throw the flail such that the twine wrapped around the legs or feet of whatever, or whoever, one was attempting to catch. It had been months since she had last practiced with the device, but deemed it could be quite useful should her quarry decide to flee. She knew a man in prime fitness could outrun her.

Seeing no one around, Florentina decided to take this opportunity to reacquaint herself with the bola. Holding the end of the braided leather lead, she swung it around her head several times, getting used to the feel and balance once more. Then, setting her sights on a support pole in the center of the room, she let it fly, aiming low toward the floor. It made a slight whir as the iron ball apparatus spun through the space between looms and struck the post, wrapping itself around the beam tightly. Florentina's heart raced at the thought of tripping up her foe with this, but realized he would not be standing still. Unfortunately, she had no chance to practice on a moving target. It wasn't like she could go home and say, "Hey Luca, can you run down the street and let me try to trip you with this contraption I've devised based on reports from foreign lands?" With a sigh, she retrieved the bola and practiced a few more times with the post.

Content it was all she could do, Florentina placed the bola into her shoulder bag and returned to the toolbox. Next, she removed a Spanish bullwhip. Whips of this kind had been in use since at least the second or third century as their likeness appeared in Roman mosaics and painted earthenware, but the Spanish seemed to have perfected the craft. And while its primary purpose was to drive cattle and horses, the lash had been used as an instrument of punishment and even as a weapon for centuries. Florentina did not own a sword, nor would she be proficient in its use if she acquired one. Knowing the Spaniard carried a rapier, she would need a way to defend against it. She recalled finding the whip in a pile of assorted junk in a corner of Master Leonardo's work room and being fascinated with it. He told her he had no use for it, but to be careful because a bullwhip was famous for biting the one who snapped it. She had been bitten more than once, which only caused her to be more determined to master its use. At age twelve, Florentina could flick a horsefly off a steed's haunches without causing the animal to flinch. But her father made her put it away and keep it hidden when people rebuked him for allowing his daughter to engage in such unladylike activities. She had taken it out from time to time since then, but she was aware her precision had waned.

Florentina gripped the handle in her right hand and let the fine twined leather lay flat. She took a deep breath, remembering the proper technique. She lifted her arm, then flicked her wrist so fast the whip's crack sang through the air. But could she hit anything with it? Florentina glanced around again, making sure the sound did not alert a passerby. When no one entered, she found a tin cup by the drinking barrel and set it on the edge of a worktable. Stepping back about ten feet, she focused, bearing intense concentration on her task at hand. Her first snap missed altogether, the second struck the table shaking it enough to cause the tin cup to topple off. Florentina groaned and replaced it. She returned to position and tried again, this time popping the cup with the whip's fall. "Yes!" she cheered herself.

After a few more successful strikes, she decided it best not to press her luck. Someone was bound to hear and come in to investigate. Florentina rolled up the whip and tucked it into her shoulder bag with the bola. It was time to return home and make ready for her Valentine's Day outing.

* * *

FLORENTINA HAD ALREADY HELPED Matteo and Betta create cards for their mother; as she sat at the desk in the children's room with all her art supplies spread out before her, it was now her turn. Her curious, talkative helpers bounced to her left and right. She may have preferred to have her own space to work, but there was no desk in the Spartan servants' room she shared with Angela. It would be inappropriate for her to use Alessandro's office, so the student desk it was.

"Look, Matteo," Betta chimed, attracting his attention as he marched his wooden soldier around the desk. "Florentina is painting flowers. Yours look better than mine do."

Florentina flashed a loving smile at the little girl who peered over her shoulder. "Your flowers were beautiful," she complemented. "And when you have been drawing and painting for fifteen more years, I have no doubt the quality of your work will surpass mine." Florentina was well aware art was not her greatest talent, but she hoped at least the proper sentiment would show through in her attempt.

Betta giggled and Matteo glanced down with a shrug. "They're nice," he conceded. "But Florentina, can you paint me a picture of Castle Sforza? It would look really good hanging..." he paused to glance around the spacious chamber he and his sister shared. "There!" he pronounced, pointing to an empty spot on the wall near his bed.

"I will put it on my list of things to do," she replied as she cleaned violet from her brush and dipped it into the green pigment.

"Betta, it's sunny. Come outside and play with me," Matteo urged, noticeably bored with watching his tutor paint.

"But I want to stay and watch Florentina," she insisted. "If we both leave, she will be all alone."

"I can't play tag or hide and seek by myself, now can I?"

Betta turned big blue eyes up to Florentina. "Go on out and play in the courtyard," Florentina suggested. "It is a pleasant day, and it is a safe place to play. I won't get lonely; besides, I'm almost done. But don't tire yourselves out—we have our trip to the park."

Betta grinned and hugged the woman she saw as her protector since the church incident, then took two slow steps, tapped Matteo's shoulder and cried, "You are it!" The two disappeared from the room, leaving the door open behind them.

Now, what verse to write inside... Fiore pondered as she blew gently to dry the paint. They had planned an outing to the park to fly kites that afternoon and she only had about an hour left to finish. Inspiration struck, and she scrawled down the poem, hoping it would hit just the perfect note.

* * *

MADELENA SAT beside Florentina on a plaza bench in the spacious piazza on a sunny Saturday marking the midpoint of February. A cool breeze pulled a few red hairs loose from under her hat, but it also lifted her children's kites into the air. Several other mothers or caretakers had brought children out, and she was glad Betta and Matteo had playmates. Maddie recognized some of them from church or around the neighborhood. One mother waved at her from across the square, but neither woman got up to move.

Daffodils and mimosas burst into cascades of yellow and pink while deciduous trees adorning the common space pushed forth tiny chartreuse buds from tender branches. A lively fountain gurgled as water flowed over three marble tiers into a round pool at its base, the central column featuring the Three Graces who appeared to be holding the bowl of the second tier aloft. She was aware there would likely be a first of March cold snap, but it was clear spring was in the air.

As Madelena watched her children play, laughing and dancing about as they tried not to tangle their kite strings, feeling vibrations of love from Fiore's intimate presence, the warmth of sunshine and cooling balance of air, she thought to herself, *This is what it is all for—the joy of the moment, a piece of Heaven on earth.* Soaking it all in, she determined to commit every detail to her memory where she could draw it forth to be relived.

"I made sure the staff knows you will be away for the evening,"

Maddie said to Florentina, "something about spending the night at your cousin's."

"Clever," Florentina responded in an admiring tone. "You'll leave the balcony unlocked?"

"Sì, and I will have clothes for you to change into for tomorrow morning for when you 'return home,'" Maddie added with a subtle wink. Then her eyes darkened to near emerald as she pinned Florentina with a serious gaze. "You will return home safely." It was not a question.

"I shall do my best," she smiled in reply. "I am looking forward to my Valentine gift tonight. By the way, the children and I made cards for you. We'll give them to you when we get to the sweets shop, which they don't know about yet, but I thought it would be a good time for it."

"I planned to surprise them with a special treat for the occasion," Maddie said. "*You* will be my special treat." Her heart warmed with laughter at Florentina's blush, even as she tried to settle her nerves.

"I may be quite late," Fiore stated. "I have no idea how long a primero tournament lasts. There is no reason to wait up for me."

"As if I could sleep anyway knowing you will be facing down a killer." Madelena sighed and glanced back at Betta and Matteo. "I trust the Night Flyer knows how to take care of herself."

"Your trust is well placed," Florentina assured her.

Every instinct in Madelena's body and soul shouted to embrace Fiore in her arms and kiss her right then and there, but her mind discerned better. It was not easy having to be casual everywhere they went; even within the walls of the home Maddie grew up in she had to keep her hands to herself, guard the words from her mouth, and try not to radiate when Fiore entered the room. She was a woman in love with no one to tell about it. Yes, Alessandro knew, but it wasn't like she could discuss details with him. *It's alright*, she thought, *having a secret can be fun.*

The moment of introspection was shattered when Matteo called in an anxious tone, "Betta got her kite all wrapped up with mine and now they are both caught in a tree!"

"It wasn't my fault! It was the wind," Betta countered.

Madelena turned toward Florentina, but her agile lover was already standing. "I'll get it, Maddie," she said with a smile and scampered to the distraught pair. *I am truly blessed! Has there ever been a woman with more to be thankful for? Has anyone ever known the joy that fills my heart?*

CHAPTER 18

Florentina was glad the sunny, windy day had worked to inhibit fog formation that night, leaving the air crisp and clear. Dressed in opaque costume, the Night Flyer watched the gaming establishment from a perch on the roof across the street with an unobstructed view of the front door and windows. Lights gleamed through the panes, revealing the boisterous activity inside. Getti's Gaming House was filled to capacity as those of high and low station turned out to compete or watch and bet on who would win. Side bets were placed on who would win each hand, each round, or the championship, but the big winners would be the players who advanced to the final round. Tavern girls in their off-the-shoulder white blouses and burgundy corsets hustled back and forth with trays laden with mugs and glasses to quench the thirst or lower the inhibitions of the patrons. Florentina could hear shouts, cheers, and jeers reverberate into the avenue below.

It would be a long while, so she checked all her Night Flyer gear to be sure everything was in its place and at the ready. Then she settled down as comfortable as possible to wait for the Spaniard to emerge. Earlier in the evening, she had seen him arrive—at least she thought it was him. The man had tried to change his appearance by cutting his hair and shaving his beard leaving only a mustache, but the gait with which he moved, his toned physique, his stony face, and dark, dangerous eyes all remained the same. Yes, he must be the same man she faced in the street a month ago.

To pass the hours, Florentina rehearsed moves in her mind and how she would respond to any perceived attack, but from time to time her awareness strayed to amorous thoughts of Madelena. *She so completely trusts I will keep her safe,* she mused in amazement. *I could never have imagined a year ago that tonight I would have a Valentine rendezvous with the most beautiful, kindhearted, sensual woman—an upper-class woman from one of the Great Houses who, despite my humble origins and plain appearance has found something in me to love. Mayhap I am not destined to spinsterhood. But even if we can't stay together forever, right now, at this chapter in my life I have everything I could dream of in her and her dear, sweet children. No twist of fate can ever rip those memories from my heart!*

As the hours passed, the moon and stars marched across the sky and Florentina gazed up to study them. *Arab and Indian astronomers have long claimed the moon and planets do not create their own light but reflect the light of the sun, which is still shining somewhere on the other side of the world where we can't see it. A few have even proposed the idea it is the sun the celestial bodies revolve around rather than the earth as Ptolemy wrote and has been accepted without question for centuries. But there's also a young Polish student of professor Domenico Maria Novara da Ferrara at the University of Bologna who is convinced they are correct, that it is the sun, not the earth, at the center. Wouldn't it be astonishing, to discover the universe doesn't revolve around us after all? And what would such a discovery signify for philosophy and religion? The Church teaches the geocentric theory as fact, that the entire universe was painted across the sky just for man's sake, and our planet was the first thing in creation. But...* she mused, *Genesis states in the beginning God created the heavens and the earth, so wouldn't that order denote either they were created at the same time or at least some heavenly bodies came first?*

Florentina returned her focus to Getti's so she would not become lost in mental exploration and miss seeing her target leave. Luckily, she had brought a small bag of water along to take a sip as her mouth and throat had gone dry.

Hours after arriving, she heard a louder uproar and snapped to attention, hoping it signaled the end. Within minutes people began streaming through the exit and into the street, speaking with each other about how exciting it was down to the last hand, who had won what and who had lost. Poised at the ready, the masked avenger scanned each face as men and women strolled off in all directions. She spotted her quarry shaking hands with another man just outside the open door. A tavern waitress beamed up at the Spaniard and placed a promising kiss on his cheek. He brushed her aside, and her hopeful smile fell into disappointment. *He must have won a fair amount,* Florentina supposed. Then she perceived someone else familiar in the crowd. *Stefano Viscardi! You appear happy,* she considered as she watched him receive pats on the back from his fellows. It was not so long ago she had dropped a chandelier on his head, rendering him unconscious before engaging in a battle to the death with Viscardi's hired guard, Zuane. The Night Flyer made certain Stefano would be able to get out of the mansion before she lit it on fire; he may have beaten and killed people, but it would have been on Benetto's orders.

However, there was no time to wonder about what Stefano was doing in town nor how Don Benetto faired at his worthless vineyard in the countryside; she had a new enemy, and he warranted her full concentration. The Night Flyer crept along the roof following the Spaniard, making the five-foot jump to the next. She needed to stay out of sight until they were alone and there were still too many primero fans in the vicinity. The next few rooftops were crammed together, but when she came to a cross street she would either have to deploy wings and glide across or climb down; she decided the latter was less likely to draw attention, so she trotted to the far side of the building, slid down a drainpipe, and raced back to the lane to spot her man make a right turn at the next intersection.

With the speed and agility of a cheetah, she closed the distance to peer around the corner. He was walking alone, and she didn't see anyone else on this street. She could call him out now, but they were still near the gaming district, and she really wanted to discover where he lived. To tail him all the way to his doorstep would be ideal.

The Night Flyer continued along the edges of buildings on the side of the lane which fell into shadow, keeping to the balls of her feet in light steps; it worked for two more blocks, but the assassin possessed keen senses, glancing over his shoulder several times. At once, the Spaniard leapt into the middle of the road facing her and drew his sword. "Who's there?" he called, and she recognized the voice. She was right—he was the one.

The Night Flyer stepped out of obscurity into the center of the cobblestone street. "Who hired you to throw bombs into the church?" she demanded in a deep tone tinted with a Venetian accent.

"Who said I did?" he retorted. "Everyone says it was you, Night Flyer."

"And why would they think so, Spaniard? Do you have a name?"

"Not one I will share with the likes of you," he replied in disgust. "You hide behind a mask."

"So did you on Epiphany," Florentina countered.

The assassin shrugged. "A mask works both ways. It may conceal your face, but it also makes it easy to imitate you. Anyone can pretend to be the Night Flyer—just don black clothing and a mask."

The Night Flyer initiated a resolute pace toward her foe. She could simply shoot him with her special crossbow; he wouldn't be able to dodge so many bolts, but she needed to discover who was behind the plot. "I am not here to play games; this is not primero, and I am not bluffing. If you do not tell me what I want to know, I will kill you."

He took one step back to set himself into a fencing stance, extending his rapier in his right hand. "Is that so?" His voice was steady, but she could detect anxiety beneath the surface. He squeezed the hilt of his weapon tighter than he ought. "Will you stand and fight me like a man this time? Or throw smoke at me and run away like a scared rabbit?"

As she approached, the Night Flyer took hold of her whip and lifted it from a hook on her belt. "Tell me who wants Donna Madelena Carcano dead and why," she commanded.

The man laughed. "A whip against a sword?" But Florentina saw his eyes widen as she deftly handled the length of braided leather like a seasoned vaquero.

Florentina snapped her lash toward his face and he raised his sword to strike at it, but as he dodged to the side both efforts missed. Then the Spaniard executed a quick lunge to work his way in close before she could slash at him again. He winced when her whip caught the outside of his left shoulder, tearing his clothing and his skin.

With her quarry dancing to her left and holding out his sword more as a shield than a weapon, the Night Flyer set her jaw, her focus penetrating her foe with steel determination. She snapped the bullwhip to his right to stop his motion, and he sidestepped to the left with haste. He was clearly becoming frustrated as he slashed his blade at her whip, which flew with much greater speed.

"See, you do not fight fair," he spat between clenched teeth. "You, you, in your mask, flying around, snapping whips at people, using smoke and mirrors—smoke and mirrors! Take up a sword and face me like a man!"

The Night Flyer flashed teeth at him. "I have no sword. And tell me what is fair about tossing a bomb into a church filled with unsuspecting women and children? Your predecessor attempted to shoot a sleeping woman in her bed with a crossbow. Did your employer inform you of his fate?"

She popped the whip, catching him in the right side as she came close to disarming her foe. He backed away to his left, favoring his stinging side. He started to move his off hand to the injured region, but stopped himself in mid-motion. "You think I am this assassin you seek?"

"I can see he did not," she continued without answering his question. "I tossed that villain from the lady's balcony to his death on the stone paving below. His head split open and blood and brains poured out. Those who hired you do not care if you live or die, only that you carry out whatever insane orders they issue. Would you die for them?" she asked as unremitting they circled each other.

The Spaniard grit his teeth and burst forth in a sprint toward her, his steel poised to run her through. The Night Flyer back stepped to her right, aimed her strike, and wrapped the whip's tail around his sword yanking it free from his hand. Another crack of her lash sent the rapier flying down the street behind him, where it clanged across paving stones a block away.

The startled aggressor skidded to a halt and gripped his stinging sword hand with his other. He stared at her in pain and astonishment, an anxious expression meeting the icy glare she pinned him with. "Tell me what I want to know and you shall live," Florentina stated with authority.

He bolted. The man turned in the direction of his blade and ran, presumably to retrieve it. *There's the flaw in only being proficient with one weapon,* she considered. *Lose it, and then what?*

Unconcerned, the Night Flyer replaced her whip on her belt and pulled the bola from a pouch. She gave it a few good whirls around her head, then threw it at the fleeing Spaniard. As soon as it left her hand, she sprinted after him, watching for him to fall. He did, but her aim and distance were off just enough that the leather twine and balls only trapped one leg, not both. The impact sent him crashing to the street, but he was able to scramble to his feet before she overtook him; fortunately, the sword was still out of his reach.

Florentina drew her dagger and watched as if in a mirror as her enemy did the same. Then the unthinkable occurred; a woman dressed as one of the tavern maids rounded the corner, doubtless on her way home from a late night's work. The Spaniard grabbed her, thrust her body in front of his, and raised his blade to her throat. Panic stricken, she screamed, but he pressed the knife closer, just pricking her skin, and growled, "Quiet, wench!"

The Night Flyer stopped dead still and lowered her weapon, holding out her open left palm in an unthreatening gesture. She could see the frantic look of terror on the woman's face as it paled, and tears began to stream. "This is between you and me, Spaniard. May I call you Spaniard, as I do not know your name?"

"Come any closer and I'll cut her throat," he avowed with labored breath, the fingers of his left hand digging into his captive's arm.

"I'm standing still, you see?" Florentina demonstrated, holding her arms out away from her body. "You have a knife, and I have a knife," she pointed out in a calm voice. "It's fair, isn't it? Or does one as strong and brave as you feel he needs hide behind a woman?"

She watched a humiliated rage envelope the man's tan face, turning it red hot. He shoved the barmaid to the ground and leapt toward the taunting Night Flyer. Florentina crouched into her stance, thankful to see the woman speeding away without serious injury. However, she was not skilled at knife fighting either. She had an instant to prepare as her adversary shook the bola from his leg.

"Now we'll learn who is better," he jeered behind his black mustache.

As the two combatants circled each other trading incidental swipes, Florentina tried to relax, even as tension wormed its way into her taut muscles. She had promised Maddie she would return home unharmed and supposed getting herself stabbed would not fulfill her promise. She trained her eyes on his, keeping secondary focus on the movement of his feet and hands, responding quickly to avoid his blade while attempting to get a cut in with her own. Her opponent was older and heavier than she, a skilled cutthroat, and she suspected this would not end well unless she could break the current rhythm.

A part of her wanted to kill him as punishment for those slain and injured in the church bombing, but then she would lose any chance of discovering who was behind the violence. She knew he wasn't working alone and given his behavior and responses, she did not believe he was the man in charge. No, he was indeed who he appeared to be—a hired assassin.

She winced as one of his swipes cut her forearm, tearing the silk sleeve of her tunic. It would be bleeding, she could ascertain, but didn't hit the bone. Then she got a slice of her own in on the same shoulder she had nipped with her whip. This would require a quick change in tactics.

Florentina feigned to her right, leaving an opening on her left side. When he lurched forward with the jab, she spun around on her right foot, back to her attacker, and donkey-kicked him in the gut with a strong left foot. She completed the rotation, arcing around with the same left foot in a round house kick to his knife hand. The move was executed in an instant and was followed up by a powerful punch to his nose with her right fist which still gripped its dagger. Both of her feet now planted on the ground, she watched him stumble back doubled over, his blade bouncing on cobblestones, as he reached for his bleeding nose and tried to stay on his feet. The Night Flyer ripped the whip from her belt and in three swift strides stood behind the Spaniard with its braided leather coiled around his neck.

Her grip strength pulled the man back against her chest and he instinctively grasped the ligature to pull it free, but it was too snug. The plats pressed so tight he could scarcely draw breath, let alone slip fingers beneath it. "Answer me, Spaniard, or I will squeeze the words out of your throat one syllable at a time," she huffed through gritted teeth. She had to know; Maddie's life was at stake.

Florentina felt his leg tense and rise and jerked her foot back before he could stomp on it. She twisted her wrist pulling the whip even tighter, causing him to gasp and flail. "Tell me who they are, where to find them," she commanded.

Allowing his neck to be drawn toward her, he rasped out, "You wouldn't believe me if I did." He attempted reaching over his shoulder to grab at her to no avail.

"Try me!"

Just then the barmaid rounded the corner from whence she had fled with two city guards in tow. "There he is!" she cried, pointing.

"The Night Flyer!" shouted one of the watchmen and raised his firearm.

"No, no," she insisted and pushed his barrel to the side. "The other one! The Night Flyer came to my rescue; 'twas the other one who assaulted me!"

Why now? Florentina moaned to herself as she twisted to put her foe between herself and them.

"But we have orders from the magistrate to arrest the Night Flyer," the second watchman replied.

That was it; she would not get what she came for. Florentina swiped her whip across his neck leaving an angry rope burn behind, shoved him toward the watchmen, and ran, scooping up her bola as she sped away.

"After him!" she heard the first man shout. The report of an arquebus rang out and she detected the ricochet off a nearby wall.

"No, no," the woman's voice entreated. "The other man!"

One peek over her shoulder confirmed, despite the barmaid's protests, the watchmen were chasing the Night Flyer while the true criminal lumbered into a dark alley in the opposite direction. Anger and frustration fueled her speed as she cut down a lane and rounded another corner, leaving them out of sight. Spotting a utility ladder set against the back of a tavern, she scampered up it and began forging a path along the gable.

"I think he went that way," one of the watchmen suggested as she spied them below.

"No, this way," countered the other. *At least I won't have to explain to Maddie how I got arrested,* she consoled herself.

The Night Flyer continued across rooftops until reaching one high enough for a safe launch. Then she pulled a cord to deploy her wings and gripping the steering handles, ran off the gable to soar in concert with the blackened sky. Here her perceived defeat waned, her spirits lifted by silk and wind which carried her home to the woman she adored. There would be another chance to find this secret society, this cadre of killers; there had to be.

CHAPTER 19

༶

Madelena, dressed in a white satin nightgown, paced the length of her bedchamber floor. Her lights were out save a single candle, and the rose velvet drapes matching the cushion of the settee were only halfway open. She did not want Alessandro to know she was awake and worried, but she couldn't sit still, much less lie in bed. *How long will it take?* she wondered as she made a pivot and padded barefoot back the other way. *Fiore said it could last far into the night, not to stay up, but... What a nervous wreck I would have been all those other times the Night Flyer was on a mission had I known! And yet...* Maddie paused for a moment, lost in thought. *She managed to return safe and sound without an ounce of worry on my part.*

Settling herself, Maddie glanced at the card which stood beside the candle on her small bedside table. It drew a smile from her lips, and she sauntered toward it. Feet aching from her hours' long march, she sat on the bed and picked it up. While nobody would mistake the artwork for Master Leonardo's, Madelena was touched Florentina remembered irises were her favorite flower, and these weren't half bad. "To my Valentine," she read aloud, a warm sensation growing around her heart.

She carefully opened the thick paper to read the verse again.

Moon who rules the sky by night
and stars with all their brilliance bright
pale before your beauteous light.

And looking up in wonder I
Dared to reach and touch the sky,
Into the unknown future fly.
And though I rise with wings as a dove,
My greatest heights are found in your love.

Fiore had not signed her name; any maid who may happen to peek inside might speculate the Night Flyer had left it for Madelena, and such maid would be correct. In an instant Maddie was struck again with awe, that the woman who taught her children to read and write, to speak French and Latin, geography, science, and mathematics; the woman who beguiled and bemused her; the same Florentina who lay in her bed and showered her with sweet kisses as often as they chanced arrange it, regularly performed death-defying feats, battled armed and dangerous men, and possessed the incredible daring to leap into the sky suspended above the unyielding stone and mortar of the city with little more than a few yards of silk to do what no one had ever done before—to fly. *And she loves me!*

Maddie brushed her lips to the paper, held it to her breast, and closed her eyes. "Come home to me, cara amore," she voiced in a hush as a prayer. After indulging in a deep breath, she returned the Valentine to its place and studied her room. Many a poor soul did not even own a bed, she understood, and in modest households the entire family may share one the size of hers. Its rigging was tight, the mattress soft over a firm foundation, the headboard and footboard crafted and carved by artisans who were only able to pursue their talents because the rich, such as her family, paid them to do so. Anyone could shove pegs into holes or strike nails with a hammer to make functional furniture, but because of merchants, bankers, nobles, and other wealthy citizens, those with gifts and abilities could take their time and create works of art rather than simply serviceable products.

She stroked her hand across the rich blue of her woolen blanket and the smooth silk of the pastel pillows scattered along the head of the bed. Her room was adorned with paintings and small sculptures, blown glass vases holding fresh flowers, fixtures of gold and silver, plastered walls with hardwood wainscoting and matching carved molding throughout. There was her dressing table bearing a box filled with costly jewelry, a meager collection of cosmetics and perfumes, an oval mirror, and round, padded stool. Against another wall stood a tall cherry armoire, a bookshelf with leather-bound volumes, for both enjoyment reading and reference books, and a woman's writing desk. A door led to a narrow closet for storing out of season clothing and wardrobe items she did not wear often. A modest hearth occupied one corner, emitting a humble glow as its fire dwindled.

Maddie considered she had lived a more than comfortable life, one of abundance, even extravagance, and yet some element had always been missing, something she couldn't quite put her finger on until Florentina. Genuine love was worth more than all the treasures in all the chests in all the world, and whether by fortune or design she had found it.

She paced more, sat on the settee and read a bit, then resumed pacing. After hours had gone by Maddie thought, *I'll just lie down for a minute to rest my feet.* She was beginning to doze off, caught in a half-awake, half-asleep twilight state, when she perceived a sound on her balcony. She opened her eyes to see a silhouette slip through the French-paned door. "Fiore?" She jolted up in bed and into wakefulness.

"Do not be alarmed," Florentina said as she pulled off her mask and cowl shaking lose her length of brunette hair. "I am home just as I promised."

Relief washed over Madelena like a rushing waterfall. Leaping from the bed, she ran to Florentina and wrapped her arms around her. "You were gone so long," Maddie breathed. She reveled in Florentina's tight embrace and felt safe. She tilted her head up while Florentina gazed down to her and their lips met to confirm all was well with the world.

* * *

FLORENTINA unbuckled her pack straps from her belt and lowered the flying contraption to the floor. Turning her attention back to Madelena, she cupped her smooth, ivory face in her hands and kissed her deep and long, wishing to dwell in impassioned unity forever. She cherished the sensation radiating from her heart, pulsing through her core, vibrating her fingertips and toes. Such unmistakable energy, the dynamic conscious awareness, a moment shared with her lover thrilled her beyond imagining. "You feel, taste divine," she uttered in a husky voice raw with desire.

Maddie raked fingers through Fiore's long, disheveled strands. "I had begun to wonder if you would ever return home. Did you kill him?"

Florentina studied the concern in Madelena's expression and shook her head, then placed a tender kiss between her brows.

"Did you find out anything, get information from him?" Maddie asked anxiously.

An audible sigh escaped Florentina's lips. "Only that if he told me, I wouldn't believe him."

Maddie brushed the scraped knuckles of Florentina's right hand and found the slit in her sleeve. "You have been injured," she declared, her brows drawing together in concern as she took Fiore's arm in her hands to examine it.

"You should have seen the other guy," she replied with humor. "'Tis a minor cut and can be tended in the morning. I have other plans for the few hours we have left before dawn."

"It is evident you fought him," Madelena stated and raised Florentina's bruised fingers to her lips.

"Yes, but we were interrupted."

Maddie led Fiore to her bed where they sat, and Florentina began to unlace her soft soled boots. "Tell me what happened," Maddie entreated.

Florentina relayed the story while she undressed. "A few more minutes and I could have gotten some information from him," she groaned. "But this much I did ascertain: the Spaniard is a hired professional, proficient in fighting skills with strong instincts, and he is more afraid of those who enlisted him than he was of the Night Flyer tightening a whip around his neck."

"At least you were able to save the girl from harm," Maddie consoled and kissed Fiore's cheek. Then those full, subtle, cherry lips wandered to her ear, her neck, her throat. Florentina felt the pulsing grow stronger and stronger, driving her to crave more.

Together they fell back onto the satin sheets, deft fingers exploring, thirsty mouths seeking. Florentina was aware of her own shortness of breath, increased heart rate, and inhibitions released. She was alive, and in Maddie's loving arms. As they came together, she let everything go save the intense pleasure of the moment and the overwhelming joy which filled her soul.

Florentina didn't remember falling asleep, but she was awakened by a light knock. "Mama," Betta's voice sounded. "Breakfast is ready. Why aren't you up yet? Open the door and let me in."

Maddie pushed up and rubbed a hand over eyes that barely had time to close. "I'll be right there, Sweetie. Mama overslept this morning."

"I'm going downstairs to make sure Matteo doesn't eat up all the best fruit," she replied and jogging footfalls trailed away.

Florentina and Madelena gazed at one another with bittersweet smiles. It had been glorious but ended too soon. "I'll get dressed and wait for everyone to arrive at breakfast," Fiore said, "then tiptoe down the servants' stairs, slip outside for a walk, and return before time for Mass."

A pained cloud of despair overtook Maddie's pink cheeks. "I wish it wasn't necessary; I wish—"

Florentina placed a finger to Maddie's lips. "I do it all the time, whether for you or for the Night Flyer. It is not a problem. I would do anything to be able to spend moments like this with you whenever it is possible."

Without warning, Madelena enveloped her in a tight embrace, pressing her cheek to hers. "It's not alright for me. Oh, Fiore, I love you so much; sometimes I feel I will burst! I want the whole world to know how happy I am, how lucky I am. Instead…" Maddie captured her lips and drank deep; only when her lungs demanded did she let go. "So many things are simply not fair," she concluded with a tear rolling down her face.

Florentina kissed it away. "All will be well, my love. Alessandro knows, and he has not forbidden us. It is all that matters."

Maddie nodded and tried to smile. "You are right; all will be well."

* * *

THE NEXT MORNING Madelena was excited to take Florentina and the children to see Margarita's Hope House where the renovations were almost completed. Francesco, the architect, was there to show them around. "Welcome good ladies," he greeted with a grin as broad as his wiry beard. "I think you will be pleased. I have incorporated everything you asked for, down to the fabric for the drapes and the colors painted on the walls. They have planted the garden in back, but not all is green yet. The kitchen is fully equipped," he explained as they walked. "I even included one of those new da Caprio pasta makers that is so popular."

"My goodness, Madelena!" Florentina exclaimed. "Now I understand how this consumed so much of your time." She glanced about at the shining floors, the spacious dining area with an abundance of tables draped with cream cloths and matching cushioned chairs, like a café. The walls were bright, the glass clean, and the hearths warm.

"Look outside, Betta," Matteo called as he skipped to the back door. "A covered walkway to an outdoor kitchen."

"Pansies!" Betta exclaimed as she followed him out and bent to smell the petite flowers.

Madelena took a deep breath. The building even exuded a pleasing aroma. "This is all acceptable," she stated in a businesslike tone to prevent the employee from too much self-congratulations. "I'd like to see the office, water closets, bathing rooms."

"Right this way." Francesco extended his arm in invitation, allowing Madelena and Florentina to walk ahead of him. They toured the upstairs and winded their way back to the office situated near the entrance. They were met by two children bounding with energy.

"You should see the kitchen," Matteo exclaimed as he skipped in front of his sister.

Betta swooshed in beside him. "It is bigger than ours!"

Florentina shot them a disapproving glare as they jostled for position. Her subtle correction was heeded, and they promptly stopped. "That is much better," their mother stated as they settled down. "It is to be expected for this kitchen be larger than ours," she explained. "It will need to feed more people."

Matteo tilted his head up at her with a considering expression. "It is not bigger than our house. How many people will live here?"

"Good observation, Cucciolo," Maddie said. "I am not sure how many yet. This residence will be open to women and children. I have been speaking with your Uncle Alessandro about a twin facility for men in the future if we have favorable results here."

"Mama, where's the water closet?" Betta asked with a look of consternation.

Maddie smiled and reached to take her daughter's hand. "There's one across from the office and another upstairs."

"I can go by myself," she declared with a lift of her chin. Betta then trotted off to the downstairs facility.

"I'll use the one upstairs," Matteo announced, started to run, then slowed to a pacer's rapid walk.

"Your children are lively," Francesco noted, then added, "and quite lovely as well."

"Grazie," Madelena responded. "Florentina, let's inspect the office." She opened the door and stepped into a functional space pleasing to the eye. It contained a desk and chair, several additional seats, some cabinets for files, and lacy curtains draped around a window facing the street.

"Have you started interviewing to hire staff?" Florentina asked.

"I need to soon," Maddie agreed. "Since Alessandro has acquired the *Gazette*, I can post the openings and date for candidates to come apply. Let's see," she mused as she studied the small office. "I'll require an administrator—a woman would be best—a cook, a custodian or two to keep the house safe—that position should go to a man. What do you think about a maid and gardener?"

"I think the residents would feel more like it was their home if they were assigned duties and chores; cleaning and caring for plants aren't difficult and do not require much special skill," Florentina suggested.

"Such an inspired recommendation," Maddie replied as she beamed fondly at Fiore who was testing out one of the chairs. Maddie took the seat beside her as flashes of Valentine's night enveloped her with heat.

Fiore asked, "How will you decide who gets a room and who doesn't, should more seek shelter than you have space for?"

The question jolted Maddie back to the present. She bit her bottom lip as her brows drew together. "It will require much thought and deliberation. Orphans who aren't already placed elsewhere should have first priority, followed by women with young children. I would certainly have a waiting list, but I suppose I would confer with the administrator and custodian, consider each applicant, and attempt to ascertain those in the greatest need—who would also be least likely to steal or destroy property. Working with the family business I have become quite adept at identifying a swindler."

Fiore's brown eyes sparkled at her with admiring light, causing her breath and heart rate to escalate. Unfortunately, the door was open with Francesco lurking about. "You are adept at a great many things, Donna Madelena," Florentina replied with obvious double meaning.

Betta sauntered in. "It will do nicely," she stated with authority, as if she were the one in charge. "The women and children should be happy here." The little girl aimed straight for her mother, who turned an amused smile to Betta.

"Indeed," she agreed and stroked Betta's smooth cheek. "Such is our intent."

CHAPTER 20

As February drew to a close, so did winter. The guild meeting day was cool and cloudy, indicative of the transition into spring. Giovanni Sacchi's suit was entirely black save for the silver stitching on his jacket. He wore a haggard, somber expression as he welcomed his fellow merchants at the entryway to the ornate hall, shaking hands and accepting tokens and condolences from his fellows. The few short weeks since his wife's death did not even mark the midpoint of his expected period of mourning; tradition dictated he wait a full year before embarking upon the search for another wife, should he choose to do so.

"Dear Master Sacchi," Strozza da Caprio acknowledged as he gripped the older gentleman's hand between both of his. "Such a tragedy, such a terrible loss," he lamented, his egg-shaped face drooping sorrowfully. "If there is anything I can do for you, anything my Veronica or I can do, the answer is yes."

"Grazie, Strozza," Giovanni replied regarding the shorter, heavier man's doleful countenance. "I will be sure to let you know."

The next to appear in front of him was Martino della Gazzada. *Ah yes, the husband of Isabella, one of Julia's friends,* Giovanni recalled as he regarded the average-looking man with straight brown hair which brushed his shoulders as was fashionable. He took the younger man's hand as it was offered to him.

"Isabella has not been the same since the funeral," he recounted. "I didn't have an opportunity to speak to you then as she was so distraught I dared not leave her side."

"The funeral was hard on all of us, Martino," Giovanni confessed. "I was not offended; in fact, so many citizens were lined up to offer condolences it became exhausting. This is a better time."

"I am glad I did not add to your burden, Master Giovanni," he replied, seaming relieved. "You are the best guild chairman I can remember."

Giovanni thought, *Because you have only been in the guild a few years and the leader before me was an incompetent twit!* Rather than reveal his private musings he simply said, "Grazie."

Blowing out a breath, Giovanni gave a nod toward Don Alessandro as he strode away from the door to prepare his notes for the meeting. The war was disrupting trade routes, and he had formulated a few proposals as to how they should deal with the matter; he had also written a list of other issues which demanded the guild's consideration. The new widower normally enjoyed being the center of attention, but all this grieving was becoming tedious.

In truth, he missed Julia more than he thought he would. The mansion was profoundly quiet. His eldest son Ambroso had traveled home for the funeral but returned to the university the next day. Pietro still lived with him, but engaged in an active social life as well as training for his sports and was seldom around. And while the head of House Sacchi was not as broken-hearted as he feigned, he was sorry he no longer had his energetic, attractive younger wife. He discerned she had been devious, manipulative, and never overlooked a detail nor a way to exploit it; those were actually traits he had admired in her. She had also been sweet, attentive, and had brought enjoyment and entertainment to his life.

However, the loss of a spouse was not about to get in the way of pursuing and promoting his business or stifling his personal plans. Giovanni may appear the part of a fop with silver hair, fine clothing, and eyeglasses, but deep inside he was a man of incredible action. With his fortune he would have no difficulty attracting an even more suitable consort should he decide to do so in the future. For now, he was focused on June and the vital deals and arrangements leading up to the pivotal day. He knew how to behave in public, but Giovannai's private bereavement had come to an end.

* * *

FLORENTINA SAT on a bench in the courtyard of Casa de Torelli under the evergreen boughs of one of the two ancient olive trees scouring Galeazzo Monetario's journal while the children filled glass jars with dirt for their seed sprouting lesson. A gentle breeze rustled the leaves, prompting her to glance up. A few advance buds tipped with the white of the flowers they would unfurl had already emerged on the olive tree's limbs. The gnarled trunk appeared much too broad for the delicate branches of the well pruned and tended family treasure. A black and white magpie took on a greenish sheen when it lit off into the sky. The occasional sparrow flitted around, landing to peck at the grass.

"Is this good?" Matteo asked as he thrust a clear glass jar of dirt into Florentina's line of sight.

"Did you remember to place a few pebbles at the bottom before filling it with soil?"

Matteo nodded while Florentina inspected his project. Then Betta placed her jar in her tutor's lap. "Is mine right?"

Florentina passed Matteo's back to him to study Betta's. "Good work, my little gardeners. Now for the next step." She removed two large dried beans from her pocket and handed one to each child. "Find a small thin stick to use as a tool. You need to plant your seed two finger widths—I think three of your finger widths—below the surface of the dirt, but you want it to be against the glass where you can see it sprout. Use your twigs to push the seed along the side of the jar until it is the proper depth. Any questions?"

"Why does it matter how deep it is?" Matteo asked.

"If it is too deep, the new stem will give up before it reaches the sunlight," Florentina explained. "If it is too shallow, the roots will not be able to hold the plant up properly as it grows and it may fall over or be washed away by the rain."

"It has to be just right," Betta declared. They both left her to her study while they completed their assignment.

"Did I do it right?" Betta asked a few minutes later as they both held their seed-bearing jars to their teacher. Betta placed three fingers to the side to demonstrate her planting depth.

"You both did well!" Florentina praised. "One more thing. Now you must pour in a little bit of water. The seed needs water to sprout, but not too much or it will drown."

Matteo giggled. "A seed can drown?" he asked in disbelief.

"Yes, it can," Florentina replied. "A quarter cup of water should be perfect. Each day we will examine our seeds for changes."

"What is it going to do?" Betta asked with excitement.

Florentina smiled and patted her shoulder. "You will see," she answered with a wink. "Now, carefully take your planting jars into the house, add the water, carry them up to your room, and place them on the windowsill with the seeds facing inside."

Once they were gone, she turned a page to again examine the drawing of a wheel with six spokes. She almost didn't notice Madelena slide in beside her. "Betta and Matteo are excited about some wonderful thing you taught them," she observed. Florentina's heart warmed at Maddie's melodious voice and the nearness of her presence.

"How a seed sprouts into a plant," Fiore replied raising her gaze from incomprehensible scribble into verdant eyes.

"Are you still contemplating the diary?" Madelena asked as she glanced over toward the little book.

Florentina sighed and held it out so they could both see it clearly. "It must contain more usable information somewhere. This seems to be one of the less nonsensical pages. This wheel appears on another page, but here it is larger and labeled with the city names. We presume these cities each have one or more members in the organization. They are the same ones listed on the ledger page." The wheel displayed six spokes passing through a center hub, creating twelve points along the circle's edge.

Maddie traced them with a finger, reading each name in turn. "Vienna, Venice, Florence, Paris, Milan, Rome, Grenada, Cologne, Lisbon, Prague, London, and Bern. Grenada is in Spain; the assassin perhaps?"

"Possibly," Florentina conceded. "But also notice which cities are across from each other. If we consider the lines drawn from one city to the other as significant, from the top, 'twelve o'clock' position down to the bottom 'six' place and so forth, they are: Vienna—Grenada, Venice—Cologne, Florence—Lisbon, Paris—Prague, Milan—London, Rome—Bern, Grenada—Vienna, Cologne—Venice, Lisbon—Florence, Prague—Paris, London—Milan, Bern—Rome, and back to Vienna—Cologne. Around, around, around they go."

"It is a wheel," Maddie stated the obvious. "A wheel continues to go around and really has no beginning or end."

"So, this could be a cycle of some kind, a repeating order," Florentina deduced. "The top of the page reads, 'when light equals dark they come together in secret, their plots and schemes to devise. Beware the horse that rears its head on a banner blue.'" Florentina paused to reread the line. "I hadn't noticed the word 'banner' before. This has nothing to do with Leonardo's horse or any actual horse—it is a symbol on a flag or crest, or a coat of arms."

"So it would appear," Maddie agreed. "This part about when light equals dark... do you think it means a time of day such as twilight or dawn, when the sky is equally dark and light?"

"That would be too frequent, I would imagine," Florentina replied deep in contemplation. "Another image of a wheel is on a different page," she recalled and flipped through to an earlier passage. "Here, it says, 'Beware the sign of the horse; they are as the months of the year or spokes on a wheel'. There are twelve months in a year, but even meeting every month, if these men had to journey from such far away cities as London and Prague to Venice or Rome, they would never have time to do anything but travel."

Maddie considered the page for a moment, then said, "Turn back to the big wheel drawing." Florentina obliged. "Twelve cities arranged in a particular order—a circle—but also with a mate across the wheel from it. It must be significant."

"The equinoxes!" Florentina's gaze shot to Maddie's as inspiration struck her. "When light equals dark, the two days of the year when daylight and darkness each comprise exactly twelve hours. Twelve cities, twelve points on the wheel, twelve hours of light and dark."

"You're brilliant!" Maddie's face lit with enthusiasm at the breakthrough. "Does that mean the society meets twice a year, on the spring and fall equinoxes?"

"It could be," Florentina replied, not daring to get her hopes up. "Let's see how that may work. We need to reflect on the order of the cities. You are likely correct about there being no beginning and ending; they just keep going around. They are not in order of size, wealth, or importance," she added as she studied the page.

"But look," Maddie noticed. "The right half, from Venice to Granada, are more in Southern Europe while on the left are more northern cities."

"Except Paris is farther north than Lisbon and about the same latitude as Bern," Florentina pointed out. "But you are correct in general." Then an idea sparked in her brain. "Maddie, when precisely, on what day did Vergilio die?"

"Let me see," she answered. "The sheep had just been sheered, and he was going to inspect the wool… March eleventh, a Friday. Why?"

Florentina's face radiated. "March eleventh was the spring equinox; it will fall on the same date again this year, less than three weeks away. Maddie, if we get this right, I can find them at their meeting!"

"Let us think clearly, then," Madelena replied. "If this horse society had anything to do with Vergilio's death, then it means they met in Milan last March."

"So where will they be this spring?" Florentina deliberated. "The cities could proceed around the wheel or they could move back and forth with the city each is paired with."

"If the order moves clockwise, as is logical since there are also twelve points on a clock face," Maddie reasoned, "then Rome comes after Milan."

"Yes, but if Rome is where they met on the fall equinox, then next would be Granada," Florentina considered. "However, if the line of the spoke connecting the cities indicates one as autumn and the other as spring…"

"Then Rome would be next," Maddie concluded, then second-guessed herself. "Unless it is Paris or London."

"But if these are like numbers on a clock," Florentina interjected, "the left half—the past six—should indicate the autumn meetings, the second half of the year, and then they start over after twelve o'clock, the top of the wheel, with Venice in the one o'clock spot."

"Such would indicate Milan last spring, followed by Bern this past fall and Rome this spring," Madelena calculated.

Florentina blew out a breath. "I must study this more tonight, but if what we suspect is true, I'll need to arrange travel to Rome very soon."

Madelena raised her chin and beamed at Fiore. "Correction. *We* will need to make travel arrangements very soon."

"Maddie, we could have interpreted this incorrectly; the man who wrote it was quite mad," Florentina warned. "And if a secret organization out to kill you is meeting in Rome, it is the last place I want you to be. It is too dangerous."

"That is where you are wrong," Maddie explained. "The assassin is here; they expect me to be in Milan. They would never search for me in Rome. The safest place I can be is within arm's reach of the Night Flyer." She flashed a dazzling smile at Florentina. "Besides, an educational pilgrimage to the Vatican, an expedition to introduce actual cultural sites to the children would be an excellent excuse for our trip. We'll bring Luca along to drive the carriage."

Florentina's expression was swimming in trepidation. "You want to bring the children? What if—"

"Safest place, arm's reach of the Night Flyer," Maddie repeated in earnest.

"Alessandro may not allow it, under the circumstances of these threats on your life. And he doesn't know I'm the Night Flyer," she added in a hush.

"You let me worry about my brother," Madelena said with a sly smile. "You use your powers of reason and deduction to determine the exact time and place of the conclave, and I will use my powers of persuasion on Alessandro."

Florentina frowned. "It's not that I don't wish to show you and the children the great attractions of Rome... I just prefer to keep you safe, is all." She spared a wary glance into Maddie's eyes which shone with excitement.

"Cease wasting energy on worry," she tenderly chided, adding in a whisper, "I want to kiss you now."

Anxiety flew away with the same swiftness the magpie had, while a cascade of amorous tingles raced across Florentina's skin even as Maddie's desire warmed her heart. She felt the color rise in her cheeks and glanced around to be sure they were alone. Light from the day was fading and the moon's reflection shone on the darkening blue sky above. "I must study every aspect, every possible meaning of this tonight," she uttered in necessity. "We can discuss it before breakfast if you like."

"Yes," Maddie agreed. "Then I can begin making our travel arrangements."

"I will miss you tonight," Fiore whispered.

"And I, you, vita mia," Maddie breathed in return.

CHAPTER 21

*D*on Benetto Viscardi tromped through the door into the pitiful great hall of his ancient manor house. He had started taking morning walks in an attempt to shake the mantle of melancholy which had thrust him into a loop of pointless emotions getting him nowhere. He wasn't confident it was working.

Benetto shrugged off his cloak and hung it on a hook beside the entrance. He spied his lovely daughter sitting on a faded couch by a small lamp table. A tiny spark struck somewhere deep inside him, struggling dauntlessly to blaze into life. Her uncertain gaze shifted from the writing paper, but Benetto perceived the love and joy beneath the hesitation.

He donned a smile and strolled in her direction. "Good morning, Tesoro mio," Benetto greeted with one of the pet names he had used for Agnese when she was little. "What are you doing?"

She glanced down at the paper then beamed back at him, light radiating in her pale blue eyes. "I am writing a letter to Antonio."

Benetto started to reply with a dismissive, callous quip reiterating his poor opinion of the boy and how she was wasting her time, but he stopped himself. Such a response would reflect the old Benetto, the tyrant who reacted without thought according to his ego and mood. *Isn't that what drove her away from me to begin with? I must relearn how to behave; I must consider Agnese's feelings if I hope to keep her in my life, else she will leave like Niccolo and Stefano did. This is my precious daughter; I remember the joy she brought to me when she was a child. I have lost everything—I cannot lose her too. No, I refuse to give in to old impulses. I must love her before I can expect her to love me.*

"I am certain it will bring joy and comfort to him on the battlefield," he pronounced inclining his head toward her with a smile. The words sounded foreign as they left his mouth, but at once he experienced the positive results of his decision.

"Papa!" Agnese dropped her quill into its ink well, leapt to her feet, and ran to embrace him. "It means so much to me you are supportive!" Benetto welcomed the kisses on his cheek and the enthusiasm emanating from his daughter. "I know you do not approve or even believe he will return, but Antonio will prove his character to you. You'll see. Oh Papa, I am so glad you are getting out of your room and returning to Mama and me. We can make a good life here, you'll see."

The tiny spark grew just a little, and he could sense the warmth chipping away at his icy heart. Benetto could not recall his timid, tacit daughter speak so many words at one time in years. Holding her in his embrace restored memories from long, long ago. As she slipped back to arm's length, he looked at her and responded with a genuine smile touching his eyes even as she had touched some long-forgotten place within his soul. He was baffled by the idea she could exhibit more happiness in this hovel than she had in their mansion... but perhaps the impetus lay beyond luxury and comfort. Could her newfound joy be fueled by something else, something his daughter generated from inside herself?

"I only want you to be happy," he said, and for the first time in ages truly meant it.

"Thank you, Papa!" She even sounded like the little girl from his memory. "Antonio has written to me as well," she said, then withdrew and bit her lip, her expression regaining its insecurity as she held her breath.

Wicked, bantam needles jabbed at his heart as if to prick it to life, and his countenance fell into dismay. "I do not wish you to ever be afraid of me, Agnese; not anymore. I am not the enemy. I only want... I only ever wanted..." *What can I say she will believe... or that I will believe?*

"I know, Papa," she breathed as she reverted to a relaxed state. "You only want what is best for me, for my financial security, arrange the most advantageous match; I understand." He, too, slid back into comfort, the tension he had not noticed creeping in subsiding. "But you must realize money is not the pinnacle; even if it was, Antonio's family is very wealthy.

I'm aware you do not get along with his father, but Antonio is not his father any more than I am you."

"I do want you to be happy and well taken care of," Benetto agreed as he walked toward the couch. A weariness assailed his body, and he decided to sit down. Agnese retook her seat beside him. "And I suppose my rivalry with Don Alessandro has tainted my view of his son. Let us not argue today. What news does the young soldier send from Napoli?" He wanted to ask how she received a letter without his knowledge, but supposed the response. Undoubtedly, she feared he would seize the letter and hide it from her or destroy it. Perhaps two months ago he would have.

"He says they have plenty to eat and are bored much of the time, and his commander prefers not to fight," Agnese volunteered. "They have not had a single real battle thus far, which is an answer to my prayers." Then she added shyly, "And he misses me, thinks of me every day, and those sorts of things."

Benetto nodded. "There is much boredom in the army," he confirmed. "Until the battle; then everything happens at once. But a siege can be a long, drawn out waiting game. I am glad for your sake he is safe and well."

"Thank you, Papa."

As he gazed on his daughter perceiving the love and joy on her dear face, it seemed to him another brick fell from the wall he had formed around his heart. For that one moment Benetto sensed an almost lost sentiment; he felt loved. In the instant, a part of himself from long ago, still as mist on the horizon, believed, just for a moment, that losing the business, the mansion, the fortune, the prestige, and the power was all worth it for her to look on him with such pure adoration. His mind instantly rebuked this notion, dredging up all the old arguments; but the new Benetto resisted, attempting to shut out the onslaught of negativity. He had not forgotten his daughter's words from Christmastime, on the day Niccolo had come to visit. *"But without love, what's the point? Without happiness, why bother to live at all?"* He had pondered those questions over the past weeks, seeking answers, searching for truth.

"Where is your mother?" he asked.

"I suppose she went to gather the eggs," Agnese replied. "In a bit I will help Marsilia with making breakfast and we'll call for you when it is ready."

Benetto's expression turned to confusion. Marsilia and her husband

Tomas had been the caretakers of the manor house when the vineyard was producing under the skilled oversight of the master vintner Amato Lorenzo, whom Benetto in his wrath had dismissed with the entire orchard workforce when he discovered the Night Flyer had salted the ground rendering the crops worthless for years to come. Now, unable to pay a full staff, the childless couple in their thirties were the only servants he could afford to keep.

"Why would you be doing work assigned to Marsilia?" he asked, quite baffled.

Agnese's laugh tinkled, erasing Benetto's concern. "Because, I want to learn to cook. I want to learn everything a proper wife should, even if we will have servants and staff; one never knows when we will not. Besides, sitting around being waited on is dull and vain. I could be a brilliant chef someday."

He knew all the great chefs were men and if his daughter did by some miraculous twist of fate ever end up as Antonio Torelli's wife, she would never need step foot in a kitchen. But if it made her happy... "Quite true," he replied, again straining against his old instincts to criticize. "I cannot wait to taste what the two of you prepare."

Benetto strolled out the door on the other side of the great hall onto a small covered portico furnished with a cedar plank bench with curved back support and a round café style table and two matching chairs. Glancing around at flowers blooming in their planters and hanging pots, he wondered if Tomas had put them there or if Daniella had. He recalled she enjoyed flowers.

Stepping out into the early sunshine, he cast his gaze upon the hills to his left. Nearby stood row upon row of grapevines clinging to their trellises, the first silvery leaves of spring beginning to peak their heads out into the world. Further away from the manor he spied fields widely adorned with daffodils, clover, and tiny wildflowers of lavender and white littering the green blades of grass that pushed through the withering yellow vegetation they replaced. Beyond the piedmont rose the distant snow-capped peaks of the magnificent Alps, as enduring as time. Spring was in the air, but again sorrow and anger threatened as he recalled he could not even claim the solace of a fine vintage to bottle with his name on the label. No edible grapes for Viscardi Vineyards thanks to the reprehensible Night Flyer.

Benetto sensed the heat begin to rise, but rather than give in to old emotions, he took a slow, deep breath, and focused his attention on a majestic eagle soaring effortlessly overhead. He had discovered getting angry did not solve anything. Neither had he the resources to hunt down this phantom of an enemy who appeared and disappeared like the wind in order to kill him as payment for his insults. Benetto had determined only two choices lay before him: wallow in his misery until his days on earth ended or try to make the best of things. "Good morning, Benetto," he heard Daniella's voice greet. "You are out early. Isn't it a lovely day?"

He turned his sights toward his wife, who seemed to trudge with noble effort up the path from the chicken house bearing a wicker basket. She wore one of her everyday wigs with a brimmed hat over it and a white apron tied around a modest blue and white dress.

"Good morning, Daniella," Benetto greeted. The smile came easier after his success with Agnese. "Come, sit with me for a moment," he invited, motioning toward the bench seat. "Why are you out collecting eggs?" he asked. "I was unaware you knew anything about chickens."

Daniella laughed, which put him further at ease. "I do this every morning; where have you been?" They sat together on the bench and Daniella lowered the egg basket to the paving stones and set her wide-brimmed hat on top of it. "It does not require a grand education to toss seeds to the hens nor to gather their eggs into a basket, but someone has to do it. Marsilia has sundry chores, and this gives me a reason to rise out of bed in the mornings." Then she turned her full attention to him. "I am glad to see you up and about early; it is good for you."

"I suspect you are correct," he replied as he studied her face. She wasn't wearing her cosmetics; then again why should she? Who would see her out here? He noticed the age lines, the double chin, the bags beneath her eyes. As Benetto considered she appeared older than she should, a pang of some long-lost emotion struck, and he tried to recall it to his awareness… concern; concern for someone other than himself. Since the reaction felt foreign his subconscious moved to dismiss it, but he held on. "I wanted to talk to you about a few things which have been on my mind of late," he stated.

"Very well," she responded with an expression of guarded curiosity.

Benetto had rehearsed what he wanted to say many times, but in the moment, he grew edgy, and rubbed his hands along the tops of his thighs as if he couldn't conceive of what to do with them. "Was it so long ago," he began wistfully, "when you and I were young, filled with hopes and dreams, and excited about life?"

"I was going to be the most beautiful woman in society, admired by all," Daniella recalled, "and you the most successful and prosperous merchant."

"And we were," Benetto confirmed. "No other could match your beauty when we wed."

She let out a dry, humorless laugh. "How times have changed!"

A veil of failure fell across Benetto's face. "I did reach the pinnacle," he replied, "before my great fall from grace."

"Oh, dear husband, it is not you I am laughing at, but myself," she explained. "My fall has far exceeded yours, and with no outlaw to blame."

Benetto tilted his head toward her, his gray eyes hazed like limpid pools rather than unyielding slate. "Why do you say such a thing?"

"Do you not recall? These past years you have stressed the fact with great regularity. I am well aware my days of attractiveness are long behind me."

"And that is what I wanted to speak with you about," he confessed. "How did we drift from a young couple who regarded each other with such hopeful expectations to this dreadful state?" He peered into her visage for a response, but his wife lowered her gaze in silence. He sighed and continued. "As I have contemplated all these things, seeking answers, to find the misstep here and the wrong move there, I have come across some regrets, primarily regarding my treatment of you. In the past, I uttered cruel words, dealt indifferently toward you, ignored your needs, and even acted impulsively to strike you in a way not proper. It was wrong of me and was in no way your fault. You know I possess a temper, and far too often I took out the anger or frustration caused by others on you because you were convenient. Daniella, I am truly sorry for my behavior; you deserved better."

He could sense potent emotion flowing from his wife and reached to take her hand. "You said you desired for us to be a family again," Benetto continued. "I would like to try. I don't know if a man my age can change his ways or not, but I have nothing more to lose, save you and Agnese. I should like to be a family again. I realize I have spoken harshly to you about your weight, how you have aged, the loss of your gorgeous hair, but these past months you have shown me there are other kinds of beauty. You didn't abandon me like everyone else. You stayed with me and never complained—not about my terrible moods or the losing of your luxurious lifestyle, which again was not your fault. You have repaid my ill-temper with patience; you have ever only tried to please me. That, Daniella, makes you the most beautiful woman in all the world."

Daniella gave his hand a squeeze while she lifted her other one to wipe away a stray tear. "I believe you can do anything you set your mind and will upon. You excel at being successful. Oh, Benetto, God has answered my prayers, you… you… thank you!" She leaned her head on his shoulder and he was comforted by her nearness. "I wonder if maybe the problem was, we each desired to reach our goal too much and took short cuts. Perhaps it is what has brought us to this."

Benetto reached an arm around her waist, drawing her tightly to his side. "I have considered that as well. There were times when I was blinded by ambition, laid ethics aside, and engaged in less than honest business practices. I was instructed in order to achieve my goals I must seize command, secure results, and rule with an iron fist, as it were; mayhap there were occasions when I pushed too far. The Night Flyer may be my mortal enemy, but what he said to me that night has lodged in my brain, needling my thoughts ever since. He said people didn't respect me; they were afraid of me, and it wasn't the same. He declared even my wife and daughter were terrified of me, and deep down I knew it was true. I could see it in your eyes, feel the dread in the air. Daniella, I don't want you or Agnese to fear me ever again. I should be your provider, your protector, not the one who causes you to flinch and draw away."

Daniella nestled her cheek into the side of his neck, rubbing her fingers over his in the hand she held. "If what you say is true, it is music to make my heart dance."

"With your help, I can be a better man, a better husband," he promised. "I know I cannot undo what I did in the past. I cannot take back bitter words nor restore time lost. I cannot bring the dead to life or recreate fair deals when I had deceived others. And you must understand I was taught to never let anyone make a fool of me, and ruthlessness was necessary to get ahead. I only ordered beaten or killed those scoundrels who stole from me, betrayed me, or cheated me in some way, only those who deserved it. But lately I have been having disturbing dreams. Niccolo said I created the Night Flyer, because I harmed or killed someone who was not deserving, and his relative took up the vendetta against me. He is doubtless correct, and somewhere along the line I got it wrong."

Benetto lifted his cheek from Daniella's head and looked down to catch her gaze in his. "I never committed murder," he said wishfully. "At least I didn't perceive it as such at the time. I believed I was dispensing justice, delivering what was deserved, but now... I fear I misjudged. Am I a murderer?" Doubt clouded his mind and his soul.

Sorrow filled her moist face, and she raised a hand to stroke his cheek. "Everyone makes mistakes, but as you say, you cannot restore a life that was taken. You can, however, become a better man if you truly desire it with all your heart."

"Do you believe in Heaven and hell?" he asked in candor. "When I was under the Night Flyer's blade, I assumed I was about to die, and I didn't know what would come next. I will never be a saint," he declared with a shake of his head, "but I do not want to spend eternity in hell. Just in case there is a God, you should know I have told Him I am sorry for thinking only of myself and for being too quick to take wrathful actions. We all sin, but I didn't have time to consider such things when I was busy conquering the merchant world. I ponder it often now."

"I believe God is just, but He is also merciful," she answered.

"A man does what he thinks is right in his own eyes," Benetto paraphrased the scripture verse. "It is time for me to begin doing what is right in the eyes of my Creator, but I will need you to do it. I am a bitter old failure of a man, and it is not who I want to be. I can't change without your help."

"For you to admit that," Daniella said with pride in her voice, "is such a monumental step in the right direction." Tears began to stream down her face, and she did not try to stop them.

Struck with sudden anxiety, Benetto moved to comfort her. "There, there, my sweet; what are these tears for? I didn't die; we have time to start anew, to be the family you wish for."

She looked at him with a bittersweet smile, then turned away, gathering herself. "Earlier I said the problem was *we* took shortcuts to achieving our goals, which includes me. I did everything society said I should to become the paramount of beauty—dyed my hair blonde, wore designer dresses and costly jewels, powdered my face white, and painted my lips, cheeks, and eyelids. I plucked the extra hairs from my brows and forehead so I would be stunning, so women would envy me, and men would envy you. I wanted to be beautiful for you, but also for myself. However, as they say, beauty is fleeting. The harsh dyes made my natural hair fall out. I gained weight in pregnancy and was never able to lose it. I admit, for years defined by melancholy, food was a solace to me in your emotional absence. Thus, I am fat. But those are not what is killing me."

"Killing you?" Benetto sat back, dazed in shock by her words. "What do you mean?"

"Oh, husband, I am ill," she answered with regret. "I have been for a few years. It is a slow progression, but my health continues to decline."

"Why did I not know this?" Panic raced into Benetto's chest. "Have you seen a physician?"

"Several, actually," she replied serenely, her tears having subsided as she relayed the story. "One gave me a tonic which I still take; it seems to help a bit. Another wanted to put leeches on me, and a third dismissed it as female hysteria. I have told Agnese and her reaction was similar to yours. I asked her to stop using the dyes and powders which are popular because I deduced they contain harmful properties. And I have spoken with numerous peers who suffer as I do, along with women who have not developed these ailments. And while my heart thrills over you wishing to rekindle what we had many years ago, it also strikes me as ironic since I am now dying."

"But, but," he frantically searched for words. "You can't die, not now." Benetto felt the sting of tears as a dagger pierced his heart. "I need you! You can't leave me. I… I… I…" Misery enveloped him stronger than even that of losing his fortune. He didn't know he could experience this level of pain.

As his distraught gaze sought hers, Daniella smiled sweetly at him, like a mother would to her child. She raised a hand to stroke his face and said with a touch of humor, "Don't worry, amore mio; I won't die today."

Maybe it was the duality of stoic optimism which resonated in her voice, or the expression of joy and love on her face, but the barricade Benetto had erected around his soul, the one Agnese had begun to chip away at, the impenetrable fortress of indifference to all but himself came crashing down in a single instant just as had the walls of Jericho so long ago, and he broke. Gathering her in his arms, Benetto leaned in and kissed his wife through his tears.

CHAPTER 22

"My feet hurt," Roberto grumbled as the troop marched along an uneven clay road, currently more mud than dirt. Conte glanced over at him with a scowl. "Stop complaining!" he dictated in a loud whisper. "Officers must set the example." The two junior officers trooped down the trail just ahead of Antonio and Papi with their enlisted charges in ranks to the side.

At least it isn't raining, Antonio thought as a blister wore on his heel from days of marching west from Barletta on their way to Cerignola, since hauling the cumbersome equipment slowed the convoy considerably. The commanders had decided to spread out the French forces and their army occupying Cerignola, a town best known for its olives, had need of artillery. Forty cannons and their accompanying crews had been sent to join the command of the esteemed Duke of Nemours, and those included the Milanese attachment. Captain Marseille rode astride a gray Andalusian, the young steed still dappled, with its thick, black mane and tail elegantly accenting the horse's strong, compact body. Spanish horses were ideal for light cavalry or officers' mounts. The French may have been praised for their fine wines, but even a proud Frenchman acknowledged Spain produced the most excellent steeds. Sergeant Beaufort marched alongside the men while forty teams of broad-hoofed heavy draft horses pulled the culverins and forty more towed supply and ammunition wagons bringing up the rear.

"It's not much farther, lads," Sergeant Beaufort stated in encouragement. Antonio suspected he had overheard Roberto's grievance as well as those expressed by the ranks in both verbal and nonverbal ways. "At least our camp will be beside a town, which means entertainment."

"You hear that, Torelli?" Papi grinned so wide all his teeth showed. "Women! Music, dancing," he speculated, wiggling his straw brows above lively eyes, "parties."

"I could use a diversion," Antonio mused aloud in response. "It would take my mind off my blisters."

Roberto said, "If the town has an inn, I want to purchase a hot bath in a real tub, and a pretty girl to scrub my back."

"I want my pretty girl to do more than give me a bath," Papi declared with a laugh. "Those camp women at Barletta were rather homely, and I didn't trust them to be without diseases. How about you, Antonio? No better diversion than a pretty, warm woman who is eager to please you."

Antonio shook his head. "I have a girl back home and I intend to be true to her."

"She isn't privy to what goes on here," Roberto mentioned over his shoulder. A breeze caught his red curls, and it seemed to Antonio the sun had multiplied his freckles. "You aren't even married."

"*I* would know," he answered, "and we are to be wed… one day. Besides, I suspect I will be too tired to do anything but soak my feet, have a few drinks, and pass out when we arrive," he added humorously sparking Papi to laugh.

Conte did not seem to approve. "How can you three consider drinking and whoring when there is a war on? What if we are attacked? We must stay vigilant at all times, isn't it so, Sergeant Beaufort?"

"Oui, Monsieur Foscari," Beaufort replied and spoke to them in French. "However, there should be time set aside for relaxation as well. I suspect Captain Marseille will assign us all to shifts so some may go into town one night and others the next. This is how it is generally done. The captain understands a soldier who is satisfied and content has more energy for fighting than a man who is tired and lonely."

As they walked along discussing their plans, a rider on a sorrel palfrey raced toward the columns and pulled his mount to an abrupt halt in front of Captain Marseille. "Shh," Antonio ordered, turning his full attention to the pair on horseback. He could not make out all the words because of the distance and the noise from the caravan, but he could see the alarm in the scout's expression and the frantic way he waved his arms.

"Halt!" shouted Marseille, holding up his right gloved hand. He barked quick orders in French, which the four Italian standard-bearers translated in hushed voices to their squads. "Load your weapons, draw your swords, form ranks here," he commanded as he pointed. "Sergeant Beaufort, Lieutenant Chevrolet, each of you take half of the company. The scout has spotted a Spanish patrol heading this way. We must defend our cannons!"

The shock thrust Antonio and his friends into a flurry of action as they tried to settle the squads under their command. "Men, do not panic!" Antonio commanded. He saw the sudden anxiety in their pallor of their faces, the round eyes and slack jaws of the ill-prepared, the shaking of their hands. "We are with the sergeant—to your right," he directed. "Line up on this side of the cannons."

Antonio sensed the adrenaline shoot through him like a drug and he felt just as shaky as his cannoneers appeared. They had drilled and practiced firing their big guns, not close combat. None of them carried an arquebus, and only the officers and Sergeant Beaufort possessed small firearms. Many did not even have a sword. At eighteen years old, Antonio's duty was to ensure they all did their jobs, which had not been difficult until that unforeseen moment.

Looking around, he tried to catch each man's gaze and infuse them with the confidence he did not retain. One gunman about his age shed tears and a wet stain appeared on his trousers. Another hadn't moved and seemed to be in shock. "Come on, men, this way," he motioned. He trotted a few steps to slap a hand on the stationary artilleryman's shoulder. "Come with me, Andrea; Sergeant Beaufort knows what he is doing. We are in excellent hands; there is no need to fear if you do what you are told." The man nodded and went where Antonio led him.

Sergeant Beaufort stood beside a wagon with its covering pulled back. "Any of you without a weapon, come quick and line up," he called. "I will supply you with a pike."

Antonio guided his squad into the line. One of the men said, "I have a sword; my father gave me a sword."

"Do you know how to use it?" Antonio asked as he scrutinized the man. With a nod, he moved his hand to its hilt. "Good. You stay beside me as I have a rapier as well." He saw a spark of assurance glint in the man's expression as he nodded and breathed a bit easier.

Beaufort spoke as he passed out the weapons. "Pikes are easy to use. They have long handles to keep your enemy far enough away he cannot wound you with his blade. We will form a wall with pikes and shields," he explained, handing a shield to every other soldier in the queue. "There are not enough shields for all of you, but no matter. Those without shields line up behind a man who holds one. It is essential no one breaks our defense. Stand at your post no matter what, unless the captain orders otherwise. We must protect our cannons."

Conte and his squad were next to Antonio and his with Papi and Roberto farther down the row. There were French squads as well, but most of them were with Lieutenant Chevrolet along the south side of the road. "Steady men," Conte instructed in a calming tone. "The patrol may see us and decide not to attack. We are a fearsome lot!"

"Did you hear Standard-Bearer da Parma?" Antonio called out. "Stand firm and show no fear; the Spanish will flee from you." Of course Antonio didn't believe that for a minute, but he had to tell them something; the big, burly fellow who lifted iron balls into the cannon barrels took one step out of position and vomited on the ground behind him while young Andrea appeared ready to bolt at any moment.

Beaufort had just finished directing everyone to their places when the loud report of gunfire began. "They have arquebuses!" a heavyset soldier cried, his eyes betraying his terror.

"Steady!" Antonio called out, but his palms were sweating. He gripped his loaded wheel-lock pistol in his right hand. Having practiced hitting targets, he felt comfortable using the newly invented weapon, and he was fast at under a minute reloading. But Antonio also realized in a battle, much could transpire in one minute. His mind ticked through the reloading steps while he scanned the forest and brush for the attackers. There was no point firing if he couldn't see a target.

A few more shots were fired, this time sounding like they came from his company. At once he spotted smoke from a gap in the trees and heard the loud report which followed, the projectile passing close enough for him to perceive its whiz. He fired at the smoky cloud and instantly began to reload his pistol.

Someone down the row cried out in pain and fell to the ground, but Antonio could not think about that now. A thousand thoughts crowded his mind, racing about in wild chaos, bumping into one another and shoving each other aside in a bid for supremacy. He ordered his hands not to shake as his gaze darted from the tree line to his task.

"I think you got him!" one of his squad members shouted.

SECRETS OF MILAN

"Stay focused," Antonio commanded somberly.

Just as he finished preparing his pistol, a cluster of pikemen burst through the underbrush, whooping and yelling to attack his section of the defense. "Hold tight!" he commanded with a deep voice of authority.

In the moment, with shouts and cries, arquebus reports booming, smoke and mud and a whirlwind of emotions swirling about him, Antonio drew forth his focus. He took a slow breath, careful aim, and from his position abaft the wall of shields and pikes squeezed the trigger of his wheel-lock and watched as a tiny lead ball struck a Spanish soldier in the chest. The impact caused the foe to fall backward, tripping the attacker behind him. "Hold your line!" he shouted again.

With no time to reload and no time for sentiment, Antonio thrust the pistol into his belt and drew his sword; he never had to use it. A signal sounded from somewhere in the forest, and the Spanish aggressors retreated. Some in the French coalition cheered, while others rushed to relieve themselves or simply dropped to the ground, grateful to be alive.

"I told you so!" Sergeant Beaufort roared, a broad smile peeking out from the brush of his hairy face. "Just a small skirmish. They wish to harass us, to rattle us, but our cannons are all intact."

"Good success!" Captain Marseille congratulated from atop his steed. "Now, let us be sure they have gone before we carry on. Medics, see to the wounded immediately! We shall be ready to move in an hour if they do not try again."

"Standard-bearers, post guards and report to me," Sergeant Beaufort called out. Antonio assigned Piero, an older Milanese enlisted man who didn't seem quite as shaky as the others, to stand as watchman while the rest regained their composure. The two medics, distinguished by their white tunics, worked their way through the ranks bandaging wounds and assessing injuries.

Antonio gathered with his fellow youthful officers around Beaufort. "Report," said the sergeant.

Roberto appeared even paler than usual beneath his sweaty red curls as he spoke first. "One of my men was struck by a Spanish arquebus ball." He paused, glancing back to a group of soldiers circled about one who lay on the ground. "I don't think he will live. I should go to him; I should be there." His distress pleaded with Beaufort as he rocked nervously from foot to foot. The sergeant nodded and Roberto trotted off.

Conte spoke next. "I have two injured, one may be serious." Conte's

French was impeccable and if not for his olive complexion and Italian colors, one might assume he was French with his groomed mustache and goatee. "My men stood their ground," he added with pride. *Perhaps he has the makings of a condottieri, but I have doubts about Roberto's chances.*

"Several of my soldiers have minor injuries," Antonio reported, "but one has a deep gash on his leg. I wish the medic to tend him sooner rather than later. We also need a count of enemy casualties. I know I shot one, and he went down."

"Yes, see to it," Beaufort charged.

Antonio nodded and patted Papi on the shoulder with another nod as he passed his friend. Papi looked different with his good humor stripped away. He heard Papi report as he walked past. "One of the auxiliary soldiers assigned to me is dead."

Poor Papi, Antonio lamented with a sigh as he returned to the skirmish field. On their side of the road three enemy combatants lay dead or dying; the lesser wounded were likely able to retreat with their fellows. He checked the other side commanded by Lieutenant Chevrolet and counted two dead. Returning to his side of the caravan, Antonio stepped deliberately over to the man he had shot and knelt beside his body. He lay in an unnatural pose, his eyes open, not closed as Antonio had expected. A large, crimson stain covered the chest of a youth younger than himself. A lump formed in Antonio's throat without him calling it forth. Upon closer inspection of the youth's face and uniform he recognized he was not even Spanish, but Nepalese—a fellow Italian fighting with the Spanish just as he fought with the French.

Lost in contemplation, Antonio did not catch the approach, but noticed the boots first, large feet posted at a forty-five-degree angle. "Sergeant," he uttered, recognizing the footwear. With his head still lowered over the body he asked, "What do we do with the enemy dead?"

"It is our practice to give them a proper burial just as we do with our own," he responded. "After all, we are all Christians." When Antonio continued to stare at the dead man, Beaufort inquired, "Is he the soldier you shot?" Antonio nodded. He wasn't certain he could speak without his voice cracking.

Sergeant Beaufort squatted beside him, most likely with notable effort considering his size and age. He placed a broad hand on Antonio's shoulder. "He is the first man you have ever killed, no?" Antonio nodded again, willing himself not to cry in front of his sergeant. "It is war. This is what it is. Either you killed him or he killed you, or one of those under your command. Your job, Torelli, is to protect your squad, keep them safe, whatever you must do. Understand that. We do what we must to win, but we also do what we must to protect and to survive. Any day which ends with you and me alive is a good day."

Antonio nodded, then swallowing replied, "Oui, Sergent. Je comprends." He reached out and brushed his hand across the dead man's eyes, tenderly closing his lids. "He was not even Spanish, but from Napoli, an Italian like me."

"Each man chooses his own side, his own path, his own destiny, does he not?"

"Perhaps," Antonio answered with reservation. "I did. But who knows about this boy? Was he conscripted by the Spanish? Did his father require him to join the Spanish army? Was he desperate for money? We don't know, and never will." *He will never marry nor have a child,* Antonio considered. *He will not return to his family or awaken in the morning. At least it was quick, and he suffered little pain. He is dead and me and mine are alive because I was a better shot. I killed a human being, a boy, an Italian boy.*

He felt the hand pat his shoulder again, then push on it as Sergeant Beaufort stretched up to stand. "You did well today, Torelli; you led your squad, none of them died on your watch. Such is the best you can do. Come," he invited, extending a hand in Antonio's direction. "The priests will take care of him now."

Antonio gripped his instructor's hand and rose to his feet, pricked to his core with an undefinable emotion. Beaufort was right, and yet... *Is this not what Papa always said? Did he not try to instill in me a disdain for war? I was afraid, but I did my duty; I kept my squad safe.* Antonio decided he had grown a few years' worth that day.

CHAPTER 23

⦿

March came in like a lion, giving Florentina the opportunity to teach the children basic properties of weather. "Aristotle wrote a book entitled *Meteorology* in which he explains how rain works. In a few years you will both be reading Aristotle for yourselves, but his books have too many big words for you right now."

"You tell us what he said then," Betta requested from her seat at the student desk in the children's chamber. Lightning flashed outside their window followed by a booming thunder clap. Betta sucked in a gasp and fear enveloped her visage. The child frantically leapt into Florentina's lap.

"It's only thunder," Matteo groaned and rolled his eyes.

But Betta's frightened little voice cried, "It sounds like the bombs going off in the church!" She buried her head into her tutor's shoulder.

Florentina instinctively wrapped Betta in her arms. "Thunder cannot hurt you," she pronounced in comfort.

"What causes thunder?" Matteo asked.

"There are many legends and sayings about what causes thunder," Florentina began, "such as the old Roman gods arguing and fighting to more modern tales of the angels paying bocce, or lawn bowling. They are fun stories, but far from scientific."

Betta clung to Florentina as the sky rumbled again. "What do the sci-ti, sci-en-tists say?"

Matteo scooted his chair a few inches closer while trying to maintain a sense of not being afraid as the window panes rattled. Rain struck the house as violently as if it stood beneath a waterfall, and the wind howled through any crack it could find. "Aristotle teaches us the heat and brilliance of the sun causes water vapor to rise up from the earth into the sky where it gathers to form clouds. When the vapor is condensed very tightly inside the cloud, it reforms into a liquid and falls back to the earth again. The greater the pressure exerted on the cloud, the heavier and stronger the rain will be."

"There must be tons of pressure in that cloud!" Matteo exclaimed. Then his expression drew into concentration. "If water goes up into the clouds and then falls back down, that explains why green places have more rain than deserts. Deserts don't have rivers and lakes like we do, so there's not much water for the sun to turn to vapor. But..." He wiggled and scratched his head, all the while maintaining a pensive countenance. "Are deserts dry because they don't get much rain, or do they not get much rain because they are dry?"

Florentina radiated approval. "Matteo, you are such a smart boy! Do you know what you did?" she probed, and he shrugged. "You took information I just shared with you and added it to something you had already learned to draw a conclusion. Then you asked more questions!"

"Weather is interesting," he replied.

"Yes, it is," she agreed, and reached a hand to muss his acorn hair. "But you have all the makings of a brilliant scientist. If you keep your sharp mind thinking along these lines, there is no limit to what you can discover or achieve."

Betta, who was being left out of all the praise, tugged on Florentina's sleeve to catch her attention. "But what makes the thunder?"

Returning her bright gaze to the girl in her lap, Florentina explained. "Aristotle scientifically deduced thunder is caused by wind striking the cloud. Notice how there is always a great deal of wind in storms which produce thunder?"

Matteo peered out the window at the two olive trees' limbs being violently whipped about and he nodded. "I'm glad I'm not out there," he noted. "We are safe in our sturdy house."

"You hear your brother, Betta?" Florentina asked as she stroked the girl's silky blond hair. "This is a strong, safe house. The storm cannot hurt us."

"I know," Betta replied. "But your lap is comfortable, and I just like to sit here."

"Very well," her tutor allowed as she tried to hide her pleasure. Florentina adored the children, and it made her feel loved, needed, and part of the family whenever they all laughed and played together, or when tender, affectionate moments presented themselves. She recognized she should require Betta to sit in her own chair as was proper for conducting lessons, but she also understood the child was prone to nightmares about the crashing church building and the noise of the bombs. *It is more important for her to feel safe,* she concluded. *Besides, she is only five years old.*

Florentina continued with the lesson while the early March storm raged. "The most famous myth about lighting involves Zeus, the king of the Greek gods. The story says Zeus had the power to command lightning and whenever he was angry, he would throw lightning bolts at the earth. We know lightning can cause fires and that it is very hot, but no one knows for certain what it is made of. Aristotle explained the phenomena in a much more intellectual way. He said lightning goes together with thunder inside the cloud during a storm. It always looks like the lighting happens first, then the thunder, but actually they happen at the same time. You see, Aristotle discovered light moves faster than sound, which is why when something is far away, we can see it before we hear it. We can tell how far away the lightning is by counting after the lighting strikes. If the lighting is very far away, we may not hear the roar, but if it is close, the thunder will clap right after the lighting flashes, or even at the same time."

"What difference does it make?" Matteo asked in curiosity. "Why would we need to count?"

"Because," Florentina replied as she shifted Betta in her lap lest her leg go numb. "Like I said, lightning can catch trees and wooden buildings on fire; it can also hit people and kill them, so lighting is dangerous. But if it is far away, no one has to worry."

"Is this lightning far away?" Betta raised big blue eyes to Florentina and seemed to be holding her breath as she waited for the answer.

Florentina eyed the little girl with a serious expression. "I want to tell you two true things; will you trust me?" Betta nodded. "Good. One: this is a powerful storm, as often occurs when spring arrives. Some scientists believe it has to do with the position of the stars in the sky, why spring often has such violent storms when other times of the year do not. The lightning is not far away, which is why the thunder is so loud. Two: you are perfectly safe inside this house. No rain, thunder, or lightning can hurt you. It is made of strong bricks and mortar, smoothed with stucco, and has a lightning-proof clay tile roof. There is nothing to catch fire." Florentina's mind moved forward into thinking, *however, if an earthquake were to hit... but I'll not mention that possibility.*

Betta hugged Florentina and declared, "I'm going back to my chair now."

Florentina beamed at her and then turned her gaze to Matteo, who bounced in his seat, his focus on the storm. "Matteo?" Florentina called to regain his attention. "Could you repeat to us Aristotle's explanation of the elements of a storm—the rain, lightning, and thunder?"

Matteo jumped to his feet and stood up tall and straight. He then proceeded to reiterate the lesson, only requiring a few prompts from his teacher.

* * *

It was easier than Maddie thought it would be to convince Alessandro to allow them to take the journey to Rome. He seemed satisfied with her plan to have Luca drive their carriage and watch over them, and even she imagined the skinny lad would provide none but token protection. Florentina had discussed her findings and conclusions with Madelena as well as several related passages from the jumbled diary, and they came to a decision to follow through and see what would happen. Besides, Maddie had only been to Rome on one other occasion long ago and she looked forward to seeing the sights with her children and the singular woman who had captured her heart.

Maddie hadn't left the estate with the storm raging outside; even Alessandro decided to catch up on his letters and excuse any workers who could not make it to the production house. But the idea of being forced to stay inside made Madelena antsy. She sorted through her clothes deciding what to pack, checked if anything needed to be washed or mended, peeked in on the children's lessons, and roamed the house like a cat in a cage. Presently, she ventured into the ladies' parlor where Portia sat playing with the puzzle box Florentina had made special for Maddie. Madelena had brought it out after Epiphany so everyone could enjoy it.

Glancing up, Portia commented, "This is more difficult than it appears."

"Keep testing possibilities and you'll get it," Maddie replied. "Where is Pollonia?"

EDALE LANE

"She managed to leave for her school before the storm hit," Portia said.

"Lucky for her!" Maddie exclaimed with a laugh.

"Are you sure you would not like me to watch Betta and Matteo for you while you and Florentina visit Rome?" The question seemed to come out of the blue for Madelena and she scanned the hallway for any roaming staff members.

"No," she answered as an uneasy sensation worked its way into her chest. Madelena closed the parlor door and took a few tentative steps toward Portia. "Why would I?"

Portia shrugged and set the puzzle box on a lamp table beside her settee. "It would be nice for the two of you to be able to get away and have some alone time."

Maddie felt lightheaded and placed herself into a seat before her knees buckled. She sensed all the blood drain from her face and licked dry lips before she spoke. "Has Ally been talking to you?"

"He didn't have to." Portia faced Maddie with a genuine smile. "You both do an admirable job of displaying appropriate deportment and speech, especially when servants are about. But dear, there is no way you can hide the glow on your face when she is near, nor she stifle the essence of love and joy that radiate from her to fill a room when you are in it."

"Does everyone know?" Maddie waited breathlessly, frightened but struggling to keep her dignity.

"I do not believe so," Portia answered in a comforting tone. "I don't think they pay such close attention, but even if they suspected, no one would say anything; they enjoy working for us too much to risk losing so prime an employment."

Madelena swallowed and attempted to steady her breathing. She nodded, and lowered her head, not knowing what her sister-in-law's opinion of her might be.

"Maddie, do not feel awkward or ashamed, not with me," Portia implored. "You may forget you were still a girl when Ally and I married, and I moved into your family's home. I watched you grow up. I knew about the tryst between you and that maid. Your brother and I thought it was a phase you would grow out of, and soon afterward Vergilio began courting you. We were happy for you because you would have a family of your own. But deep down, I think we both discerned you were playing a role, the one everyone expected you to."

Portia rose, stepped across to the twin settee, and slid in beside Madelena, who sat silently with her chin still lowered, one hand brushing aside a tear. "Maddie, do not fear, please," she soothed. "Alessandro completely adores you, and I completely adore him. We have never seen you happier. I may not understand the attraction, but I am convinced your feelings are real and valid; I would never be so insensitive or thoughtless as to dismiss them as otherwise. I am your family and your friend, and we all love Florentina. She is so good with the children—all the children, mine included. Trust me."

"Oh, Portia!" Maddie turned to her brother's wife and hugged her, tears of relief now flowing unbridled down her cheeks. "Thank you for being so understanding, so accepting. I didn't want to be different; I just am."

"There's nothing wrong with different," Portia said as she returned the hug.

Madelena sat back and mopped at her cheeks. "I have wished so much I had someone to talk to, someone to share my happiness with. I told Ally, who already knew—the man doesn't miss a thing! But it's not the same. You are like my big sister, and I so much wanted to tell you, but I was afraid. I didn't want you to think less of me. I didn't want you to avoid me or hate me or look at me in some judgmental way like most people would. I didn't believe you would, but I just couldn't risk it."

"Sweet Maddie," Portia breathed as she helped wipe away a stray tear from Madelena's cheek. "I could never think less of the truly remarkable woman you are simply because your love is unconventional. You are still the same person you have always been. I loved the little girl you were, the young wife and mother you became, and now, seeing the grace with which you have handled tragedy and the courage you employ facing these attempts on your life, I have nothing but admiration for you, and I am so glad you have found The One."

Portia's affirmation called forth a fresh spring of tears of joy and Maddie beamed through them with glistening green eyes and a jubilant smile. "Thank you so, so much! I cannot even express what this means to me. I have always admired you, and tried to follow your example, to emulate you. But deep down inside, I was ever aware I desired something... different. Oh, Portia, you are so wonderful!"

She embraced the petite blonde once more and sniffed, then sat back beaming. "And thank you for offering to keep the children, but we want to show them the grand sights of Rome. Perhaps I'll take you up on your offer another time, just for a short weekend getaway."

Portia smiled at Maddie and took her hands. "I would love to do that for you. Another time, then."

Madelena was relieved and overjoyed both of her closest family members not only knew her secret but understood and were not bothered by her relationship with Florentina. They must still keep their love hidden from everyone else, but at least now she did have someone she could confide in and share her joy. With the tempest roaring outside, inside her heart Maddie experienced a calm peace; she felt safe.

* * *

THE NEXT DAY the storm had passed and Florentina and Maddie both packed for their trip. While Madelena helped her children with their bags, Florentina shuffled items in the top portion of the ornately carved chest her father had crafted for her, the one with the secret compartment. Angela was in their shared room gushing on about how exciting this was, and had Florentina ever been to Rome, and how she wished she could go. Florentina politely responded but in truth hoped the girl would find somewhere else to be so she could check her Night Flyer gear. *I'll have to do that after she is asleep.*

"You should pack this dress," Angela suggested lifting one from a hook on the wall. "I think it is the best one you have, and you'll need something nice when you go to St. Peter's Basilica."

Florentina took the dress Angela handed her. "Thank you," she said and stuffed it into the trunk. *I'll also need bandages and ointment in case of injuries,* she thought as she ticked off her mental checklist. Once she had included everything she could while her roommate bubbled about, Florentina proceeded downstairs for dinner.

The family she loved being a part of sat around the big table. When Alessandro had concluded blessing the food, he looked out at them all with pride and excitement beaming from his handsome face. "I have an announcement to make," he declared, drawing everyone's attention. "Today I received a correspondence from Rome. House Torelli has been selected as the new source of silk for the Vatican."

Mouths dropped, eyes popped, and Portia proclaimed, "That is spectacular!"

"It appears the Pope became dissatisfied with their previous merchant from Venice who ran into some supply problems they blamed on the Spanish-French War in Napoli or some such excuse. The cardinal who wrote the letter wished me to bring samples of our finest crimson and we will settle on all the particulars for the order in person. We are going to outfit bishops, cardinals, and the Pope himself!"

"Ally, the Vatican is the most prestigious contract in Europe!" Madelena exclaimed. Betta and Matteo grinned from ear to ear, most likely because everyone else was happy and excited. Florentina suspected they had no idea what supplying silk to the Vatican meant. "When do they want you to go?"

"Immediately," he said. "It seems I'll be joining you all on your journey tomorrow. I know you have already arranged your accommodations, but it doesn't matter as I've been invited to stay in guest quarters at the Vatican. You all stay as long as you want in Rome, and I can hire a ride back home when my business is concluded."

He took his wife's hand in his and gave it a squeeze while his children heaped praise on him and cheered about the honor bestowed on the family. "Portia, would you like to accompany me?"

"I would love to see Rome in the springtime, especially for such an occasion as this," she gushed. "But it is Pollonia's coming out this spring and I can't miss her first ball. You understand, don't you, my dear?"

Alessandro smiled and nodded. "She will be the most beautiful young lady of the season and I shall need scare all her suitors away when I return."

"Papa!" Pollonia giggled. "I won't accumulate suitors in one week. Don't worry about me; but if you see the Pope tell him I said hello." They all laughed and continued to discuss the wonderful fortune while enjoying delicious rigatoni, salad, fresh bread, and fine wine.

While Florentina was likewise thrilled about Alessandro's good fortune, she wondered how this would affect her mission and hoped her lover's brother did not get in the way. He certainly looked as if he could handle himself with his impressive physique, but this underworld society employed professional assassins and she did not wish him to be harmed, especially on account of her activities. She was also doing her best to keep the Night Flyer's identity a secret. Florentina smiled and offered her congratulations while a sea of anxiety whirled within.

CHAPTER 24

Upon their arrival in Rome on March ninth, Alessandro and Luca helped Madelena, Florentina, and the children get settled into their room at the inn. Luca's room was across the hall, and Ally ordered him never to let the women out of his sight whenever leaving the inn. Then Alessandro took his bags through the north gate of St. Peter's Square to the visitors' quarters assigned to him. The building was strategically arranged between the barracks for the Pope's guard and the clergymen's dormitories. The Pope's residence was nearby, connected by corridors to the Sistine Chapel and the neighboring St. Peter's Basilica. Since everyone was tired from the long journey, they decided to settle in and meet the next morning in St. Peter's Square after having their breakfast.

Betta and Matteo were all energy and so glad to be out of the carriage that Maddie and Florentina—with Luca along as bodyguard—were obliged to take them to the nearby Piazza Navona to play. Their inn, the Albergo del Sole al Pantheon, boasted an ideal central location to all the attractions they wished to visit. A few blocks stroll to the west was the bridge over the River Tiber to the Vatican. Even closer to the southeast was old Rome with the ruins of the Colosseum, the Forum, and other ancient sites. And less than five minutes' walk away stood the unparalleled Pantheon, an architectural marvel, and the best-preserved structure from antiquity.

Maddie sat on a marble bench beside Florentina in the partly paved, partly green area of Piazza Navona, which had not long ago been the site of a market place. But the market moved, and the city appointed the rectangular expanse between the rise of tall edifices on either side as public space. Several carriages pulled by hackneys or cobs rolled along the edge designated for vehicles while dozens of people enjoyed the fine weather, taking a stroll or bringing their children out to play. The afternoon sun meandered across a blue sky spotted by the occasional fluffy white cloud. Maddie wanted to kiss Florentina right there in the magical City of Love; she settled for enjoying her nearness.

"Did you know this piazza is built on the site of the ancient Circus Agonalis?" Florentina commented, rousing Madelena from her amorous musings. "They played sporting events here."

"I wonder if they had a game like calcio." She wondered aloud.

"I'm certain they had many games," Florentina deduced.

Maddie watched the wiry, youthful, fair-haired Luca play with Matteo and Betta with contented satisfaction, and the expression on Florentina's face revealed she felt the same. "Where will you search on Saturday? How will you find their secret meeting place?"

Florentina turned a thoughtful look to Maddie, her intelligent eyes now indicating uncertainty. "I will work on it," she said. "I brought the diary for more study and I shall watch for clues as we tour the city. Perhaps I will spot something which corresponds to a random passage that will give it meaning. Otherwise..." Florentina glanced back to see Luca toss a squealing Betta into the air and catch her. "I pray for good fortune."

After dinner in a quaint café, they returned to their rooms to retire for the evening. The rented chamber was small, but well furnished with two windows to provide cool air. In its center was one large bed, not as comfortable as Maddie's at home, but suitable. All four of them piled in.

"Tell us a story, Florentina," Betta requested before opening her mouth in a wide yawn. She hugged her Lena doll as she curled into her sleeping position.

"Tells us the story of Rome, about Romulus and Remus," Matteo specified.

Dressed in a delicate white gown and a long, gray tunic, Betta and Matteo snuggled into positions between Florentina and their mother. Maddie met Fiore's gaze with a mix of delight and unfulfilled longing. Three nights of unbridled desire in the Eternal City would be sublime, but this was satisfying in a different way. They were establishing bonds as a family unit, and that is what Maddie saw them as becoming. Deep abiding love was more than passion—although passion certainly deserved a place. Love was being content with having one's heart touched when her body could not enjoy her sweet caress. She was certain her face glowed with adoration as she felt a tingling sensation wash over her skin.

Florentina responded with a wink and a smile. "Once there were two twin brothers, Romulus and Remus, who were abandoned at birth beside the River Tiber. They would have died except a she-wolf found them there. Being a mother herself, she had compassion on the infants and nursed them with her own pups." Maddie settled down into her pillows, enfolded her small daughter in one arm, and listened to the story with rapt attention. Long before the fratricide, they had all fallen asleep.

* * *

ON THE MORNING prior to the equinox, the family met in St. Peter's Square and Luca was released to have the day to himself and go see whatever he liked. Alessandro led the way toward the impressive basilica followed by Madelena holding Betta's hand, Matteo, and Florentina, wearing the dress Angela had chosen for her. Maddie had worked hard to rid it of wrinkles.

They were approached by a diminutive young man with a studious face and an eager expression donning the black robes of a priest. "Are you Don Alessandro Torelli?" he asked.

"Sì," Alessandro replied as he stopped in front of the priest, practically resting his chin on his chest to make eye contact with him. "I am here to see Cardinal Francesco Barberini. I have the letter he sent me and I am expected."

"Sì, sì," he responded with an air of genuine hospitality. "I am Father Angelo di Pietro, administrative assistant to Cardinal Barberini. Please call me Angelo; everybody does. The cardinal asked me to greet you. He said, 'look for a very tall, distinguished looking man; you cannot miss him,' and he was quite right. Welcome to the Church of St. Peter and the birthplace of our Church."

"Grazie, Angelo," Alessandro replied.

"Cardinal Barberini is in a meeting this morning," Angelo explained, "but he is happy to meet with you this afternoon. Is this your family?"

"Yes," Alessandro answered with a charming smile. "Let me introduce you. This is Madelena Carcano, my sister and a partner in Torelli Silk; her two children, Matteo and Betta, and their tutor, Florentina de Bossi. They were planning an educational pilgrimage to your fine city anyway; I was merely fortunate to be able to accompany them."

"Ladies, children, so glad to meet you," Angelo said and bowed to them with his hands clasped behind his back. Maddie wasn't sure she had ever met a grown man his height before as he was shorter than she and much shorter than Florentina, about Bernardo's size except with a slighter build. *Do they not feed the low-ranking priests here?* She wondered.

Then his face lit with inspiration. "Since you are here early and wish to see the sights, would you do me the honor of allowing me to show you around? One morning is not enough to view every holy site in the Vatican, but we can visit the most essential ones, no? Please, it would be my pleasure."

Betta and Matteo's enthusiasm could not be concealed as their wide grins and round eyes displayed unequivocal delight. Alessandro replied, "We would very much enjoy your tour, Angelo. But I'll inform you Florentina is quite an expert on art, so be sure to include any works of the masters as you lead us around."

Angelo raised a sparkling visage to Florentina. "I will show you all the masterpieces; you will never forget what you see here today," he proclaimed. "This way, please. May I present St. Peter's Basilica," he said, stretching forth his arm.

Residents of Milan were accustomed to walking past, strolling in, and gazing skyward at the second largest cathedral in all of Europe, the Duomo; St. Peter's was the singular one to surpass it. However, it was not the cathedral alone which presented itself, but a huge semicircle of high Roman style columns supporting roofs over porticos and the facing structures forming a bowl around St. Peter's Square. In the middle rose a mighty monolith, aiming toward the heavens.

"What is that?" Matteo asked as he pointed to it.

"It is an Egyptian obelisk," Angelo explained. "Emperor Caligula brought it from Heliopolis in Egypt to decorate the spina of his circus; today this obelisk is all that remains of the Roman circus which once stood on this spot. We keep it here at the Vatican to remind us this became the site of martyrdom of many Christians when they were persecuted after the Great Fire of Rome in AD 64. Nero blamed the fire on

Christians and many were put to death on this site. According to tradition, it was in this circus where Saint Peter, the founder of our Church, was crucified upside-down."

Betta scrunched up her nose and gave her mother a questioning look. "Upside-down?"

Maddie gave her hand a squeeze. "When the Romans condemned the Apostle Peter to death," she expounded, "they decreed he should be crucified like his master, Jesus, had been. But Peter protested, insisting he was not worthy to die in the same manner as his Lord. Therefore, the Romans crucified him upside-down so it would not be exactly the same as Jesus' death."

Matteo gazed up and up at the towering monolith until he had to hold up a hand to shade his eyes from the brightness of the sun overhead.

"But," Betta questioned with grave concern etched across her face. "Why did the Romans want to per, persa…"

"Persecute," Florentina supplied.

"Yeah, why persecute Christians?" she concluded sorrowfully, empathizing as young children do.

Madelena lifted the troubled child into her arms as she viewed the question through a new lens. "Because they were different," she said. "People are afraid of what they don't understand, they hate what they fear, and they attack what they hate. Christians brought new ideas and beliefs which were not at all what the people were accustomed to. Leaders feared the new ideas would diminish their power over the masses, maybe render them obsolete." Maddie had never talked down to her children, and though she understood Betta may not comprehend every word, she would catch the general drift. "So, they decided the best way to deal with these strange people was to eliminate them. They lost all their rights, some were arrested, others beaten, and many were killed." Madelena was mindful of the multiple layers beneath her explanation. She, too, was one of those "different" people that some in society would persecute if they were aware.

"All because they believed in a different God?" Matteo asked, turning his attention to his mother.

However, Florentina answered him first. "Ideas and beliefs are very powerful, Matteo. Some people kill others over ideas."

Matteo tilted his head as he peered up at the priest, his brow furrowed with concentration. "But we persecute people who are different," he

SECRETS OF MILAN

voiced with unease. "Jews don't have equal rights, and Florentina teaches us history. Back during the plague, some Christians falsely accused Jews of causing the plague and killed a lot of them. And, and the crusades," he added with emphasis. "We killed Muslims. Do we persecute Jews and Muslims because they believe differently than us? And doesn't that make us just as bad as the Romans who killed St. Peter? And shouldn't we be better than that? I think we should be better than that."

Out of the mouths of babes. Maddie's heart swelled with pride. *Florentina is not merely encouraging Matteo when she praises his intelligence. He can truly make connections and draw conclusions beyond what is expected for his age.* She brushed a hand over his head affectionately.

"Well," Angelo uttered and looked very uncomfortable beneath the child's scrutiny. "The Church has an official response to your questions; however, in light of the points you make, I am not certain it is a sufficient defense." He sighed and shuffled his feet. "Men are not perfect, only God is. Therefore, we are subject to err as we have in the past and will no doubt do again in the future. Thankfully, God's grace is bountiful; he forgives when we truly repent." Raising his head and brightening his tone, Angelo directed, "Come. There is more to see inside."

"I notice the scaffolding and stacks of building materials," Alessandro stated as they crossed the square toward the majestic columns to the entrance of St. Peter's. He glanced over his shoulder to wink at Maddie and grin at Matteo. She knew the glow of pride he sent and returned a bashful smile.

"Sì," Angelo said brightly. "Pope Alexander VI has commissioned renovations and additions to be constructed and they are just getting ready to begin the project. There is always some grand construction plan underway in Rome. The Eternal City—the city eternally being built!" he said with a laugh.

The interior was immense, the dome high, the art exquisite, but nothing was overdone. "First and foremost," Angelo explained, "this is a house of worship. We wish the embellishments to enhance, not overwhelm."

It was awe-inspiring, Maddie thought, just to walk through the sanctuary where the Pope would speak, hold Mass, and bless the Eucharist. They could stay until Sunday; it would be worth it for the experience.

"This way." Angelo led them through a corridor off to the north side of the nave. "You must see the Sistine Chapel."

*   *   *

FLORENTINA HAD VISITED ROME BEFORE, but when she was much younger. Now she truly appreciated every detail. She was struck again with wonderment and reverence as she lingered along the murals, soaking in the images, marveling at the artistry, and recalling the Biblical stories depicted in the scenes. She did not possess that kind of talent, but she had true appreciation for it.

"Pope Sixtus IV commissioned the best artists to paint the frescos: Domenico Ghirlandaio, Sandro Botticelli, Pietro Perugino, and Cosimo Roselli. See, here is *The Life of Moses,*" Angelo motioned to his left toward the southern wall, "and over there *The Life of Christ,*" he lifted his right hand to indicate the northern wall. "You should take your time to absorb the spirit of the chapel."

The murals were high on the walls, above a tier of draperies, so nothing or no one would impede a view of them. A third tier was marked by arched windows, between which were paintings of various popes. Spreading over the long dome above was a blue canopy gilded with stars. Florentina marveled at the vibrant colors, the attention to detail, the everyday activities of the characters, and the emotions expressed on their faces. She had studied the greats enough to recognize each artists' work as she scrutinized his panel. Here was *The Trials of Moses* by Botticelli. Angelo was right; beyond the art, the chamber had a decidedly "holy" feel to it.

As they strolled along, Betta slipped her hand into Florentina's. She gave it an approving squeeze and smiled down at the little girl. She paused at *The Delivery of the Keys* by Perugino, which depicted Jesus handing Peter the Keys to the Kingdom just outside of Heaven's gates.

"Is that what Heaven looks like?" Betta asked as she strained to stare up at the painting.

Florentina lifted her for a better view. "No one knows what Heaven looks like. This is what Perugino imagined when he painted it. What do you think Heaven is like?" she challenged.

Betta thought for a moment. "I think it has green grass, flowers and fruit trees, and a really big sweets shop, only you don't have to pay for the treats because everything in Heaven is free."

Florentina smiled and hugged Betta close. "Your vision is as valid as anyone else's."

"An interesting fact about this chapel," Angelo said as they completed the walk around. "It was constructed to the dimensions of the Temple of Solomon, as given in the Old Testament. We will be exiting through the same way we entered because it has no exterior egress, but is only accessible from the Papal Palace. We will not enter the Papal Palace, but the corridor returns us to St. Peter's Basilica."

Florentina could have stayed in the hallowed sanctuary for hours more and still not have had her fill. But they had many sites to see, and Alessandro's meeting would be soon. She set Betta back on her feet, took her hand and followed the men, Maddie, and Matteo into the corridor, appreciation vibrating through her being. But as she watched Madelena's smooth gait, the subtle way her hips swayed, how she held her head high with dignity fitting her station, she appreciated the woman she treasured even more than fine art. The chapel may be a sacred place, but didn't the divine dwell in every human soul? She loved Maddie's soul.

"You will not want to miss this," Angelo chimed in excitement as he led them back across St. Peter's toward the south transept. "This way is the Chapel of Santa Petronilla, an old circular building which was the mausoleum of Emperor Honorius near the end of the 4th Century. Only a few years ago the French Cardinal Jean de Bilhères de Lagraulas, a representative in Rome, commissioned a sculpture to serve as the Cardinal's funeral monument. It is...," Angelo paused before opening the door to the ancient sanctuary. "Breathtaking."

CHAPTER 25

Madelena, Florentina, Alessandro, and the children followed the diminutive Father Angelo di Pietro through an arch into a side chapel. The atmosphere shifted to one less grand and more intimate. The air was closer, the scent of wax more pronounced in the small chantry. Positioned in a place of prominence, well-lit by natural light from the windows along with spirals of white candles on black iron stands sat a life-size representation of Mary holding in her lap the body of Jesus after being taken down from the cross. "It is the *Pieta*," Angelo said with a touch of reverence in his voice. "The young artist, Michelangelo, is, shall we say, not a holy man. He is gruff, difficult, and forgets to bathe. But God in his infinite wisdom has deemed to gift him lavishly. Never has any sculptor been blessed with the ability to draw such life from stone."

"It is," Alessandro began to speak as they all gathered around to marvel at the exquisite representation of the Holy Mother and her Son. As he neared, he shook his head. "I have no words."

"The *Pieta* has such an effect on many people," Angelo said. "Michelangelo—remember his name, for you will be hearing much about him in years to come—claimed the block of Carrara marble he used for this was the most perfect block he had ever encountered. When the cardinal asked how he could chisel out of rock something like this, he replied, 'I do not carve the piece out of the rock; I release it. I see what is inside and then chip away what does not belong.'"

SECRETS OF MILAN

"I've heard of Michelangelo," Florentina said in a distracted voice as her attention was fully on the sculpture. "Cesare mentioned him to me, but I have not met him. Isn't he in Florence now?"

"I believe so," Angelo replied.

The children had completed a full circle around the piece and were examining details. Betta reached a little hand and stroked the marble. "It is so smooth, Mama," she said in wonder.

Madelena stroked the leg and foot of Jesus, awestruck by the realism; the marble had so high a polish as to feel like brushing the frozen surface of water. "Yes, baby, it is very smooth to touch."

Matteo had to stroke it too. "I can see the nail marks in His hands and feet," the boy commented. "But I don't see any blood."

"I would think carving blood would not come across looking right," Florentina said.

Then Angelo spoke. "The young master artist said it was his intent to create 'the heart's image.'"

Alessandro stood thoughtfully eying the *Pieta* while Florentina discussed its artistic qualities with Angelo. "See the overall shape of the work," she motioned, "like a pyramid with Mary's head, most likely her face, as the focal point."

Madelena shifted her attention to the focal point, and the others' voices faded from her ears. A beautiful, youthful face, far younger than one would expect for the mother of a grown man, but an image very frequently selected to depict Mary. Idealized as she was in a Catholic's heart, Mary was forever young. The sorrow was apparent, but her features were not twisted in anguish, rather the grief of having realized the inevitable. *Had she always known?* Maddie wondered. *And if she had comprehended from the beginning she would live to witness her son's death, would she have still said, 'be it unto me as you have spoken?'* She exhaled a slow steady breath, her thoughts turning inward as being a mother herself she empathized with Mary, this marble Mary who seemed so real and yet so perfect. *What agony I would undergo if I was to see my son die, to suffer pain and humiliation and be executed for a fictitious crime. And Portia—dear sweet, understanding Portia! Her son's life is in actual danger on the battlefield. Whatever will we do if he does not come home safely?*

Peering into Mary's face, Maddie asked in silent prayer, *Could you comfort her? Did you suffer such loss as this so you would be able to console other mothers in their time of sorrow?* She heard Matteo and Betta's voices as well as Florentina and Angelo, but she was not listening to any of them. As she stepped around to the left side of the figure, she stood on tiptoe to peer into the face of Jesus. They were always being reminded of Christ's agony on the cross, but this face was not tortured or desolate; it was peaceful. As Maddie considered those aspects, she sensed Alessandro's hand press the small of her back in a comforting gesture. Until that moment, she had not realized a tear had streaked her cheek. She wiped it away with a casual sweep of her fingers.

"He looks peaceful, content even," she observed in wonder. "Do you think Jesus' expression is correct?"

Ally considered and then gave a nod of approval. "If I had just saved the world, I would feel absolutely wonderful about it, even if I had suffered great pain to do so."

"Yes," Maddie agreed, a smile trying to form on her bereft countenance. "He died knowing He had won, so He wore a pleasant visage. She is the one with the broken heart, but… it's like she knows, too."

Ally leaned into her, his potent presence reassuring. "It is no small thing to save the world."

In the midst of the Torelli family's appreciation of the young Michelangelo's masterpiece, a man poked his head into the chapel. "Cardinal Barberini is ready to meet with Don Alessandro now," and scurried away before Maddie had turned her face from the *Pieta*.

"Ah, very good," Angelo stated with a broad smile. "I will show you to the cardinal's office." Reluctantly, Madelena followed, casting one more glance over her shoulder before exiting the chamber.

They made a quick detour by Alessandro's room so he could pick up his case of samples since Cardinal Barberini's office was near the guest housing. The grand edifice was a classical styled building to the north of the St. Peter's complex. A substantial man with salt and pepper hair draped in red silk robes and a golden cross pendant waved and smiled in greeting. "Don Alessandro," he acknowledged, extending a hand.

Ally shook it and returned cordially, "Cardinal Barberini, so nice to meet you."

Standing in the shade of the massive portico, Roman columns rising to support the roof, it seemed to Maddie as if she had been transported back in time. Vatican architecture was so different from the familiar brick, stucco, and terracotta roofs of Milan.

"My sister and her family," Ally motioned with a sweep of his arm.

"Welcome to the Vatican," he greeted with a warm smile. "I hope you are enjoying our fine city. Father Angelo, perhaps there are other points of interest here in the Vatican you can show to our guests while Don Alessandro and I discuss the business at hand."

"Indeed!" Angelo sang. "There are many; which would you like to see first?"

"Isn't there a famous library here?" Florentina asked with anticipation gleaming on her countenance. Maddie felt the love swell in her heart to gaze at the youthful excitement she sensed exuding from her partner.

"Sì!" Angelo replied with a nod. "The Vatican Apostolic Library is one of the oldest and most renowned in the world. In contains historical texts, codices, books, and incunabula in Greek, Latin, Hebrew, Italian, and many Byzantine manuscripts as well."

Maddie was pleased by Florentina's delight but was still too emotionally overwhelmed to march straight into another treasure-trove. "If no one minds, I will sit here on the portico and wait for Alessandro. You go on and enjoy the library."

Florentina gave her a questioning look as if to ask if Maddie was feeling well. Maddie smiled and nodded, then sat to rest on a granite bench beside a potted plant while her brother and the cardinal stepped into the administrative building.

It was a pleasant day. Madelena watched people go by, noting how the populous was overwhelmingly male; only a few nuns and laywomen strolled about. She supposed one may get used to all the majesty of the locale if he lived here every day, but she doubted she could. *Florentina will never fall asleep tonight after this little venture to Heaven,* she thought. Then leaning against the stone wall, Maddie closed her eyes and let the sights, sounds, and feelings of the morning coalesce within her.

After a time, she heard Ally and the cardinal exit a door near her seat. "It has been a pleasure, Cardinal Barberini," her brother's voice boomed. "I can have your first order shipped as soon as I return to Milan."

"The pleasure is mine, Don Alessandro," the hefty middle-aged clergyman assured him with a smile. "Go with God and come back soon!"

With a hearty laugh, Barberini re-entered the building and Maddie joined her brother. "I take it all went well," she presumed.

Ally nodded and turned an oddly spiritual aspect toward her and extended a hand. "Walk with me." She took the hand he offered, and he led her on a rambling promenade around the grounds. Discerning his introspective mood, she remained quiet, waiting for him to speak.

Presently, he stopped in the orchard situated at the north end of the gardens, fresh leaves and blossoms on every tree, and collected both of her hands, turning her to face him. "I want to thank you," he said in a candid tone. "You are the reason we got this account."

Madelena started at his words and shook her head with a confused chuckle. "Why do you say such a thing? I never even spoke with anyone from the Vatican."

"Neither did I," he answered in wonderment. "You know I am not a religious man," he began, and she nodded. "But I am aware there are many truths to be found in the scriptures, wisdom to be gleaned from their words. There is a principal of sowing and reaping that goes something like, whatever a man sows, that he shall also reap."

"Yes, I recall the passage," she said, still unaware of how it related.

"You convinced me to invest a sum of money into purchasing and refitting a building for your charity house, an economic venture with no prospect of financial gain. In fact, it promised to cost us money every year in the future," he reflected. "I didn't particularly share your vision, but you were so enthused about the project, I simply could not say no. So, I financed Margarita's Hope House, not because I am an altruistic or virtuous man, but because I wanted to please you and make you happy. Then I just left it all to you and haven't given it a great deal of thought until now. Do you know how much we are making off the Vatican contract?"

His dark eyes glistened as they bore into hers. Maddie shrugged. "Exactly ten times what I spent to buy and renovate Margarita's Hope House. Tenfold!" He took a breath to let his words sink in for a moment. "You wanted to do something to help poor people in need, those who fell on hard times, who fell through the cracks of the safety net spread by the Church, and because you asked it of me, I sowed the seed. I put up money which I presumed I would never see again because of your kind heart. A few months later, with no courtship on my part, not so much as a letter of inquiry, I received notice the Vatican has decided upon Torelli Silk out of all the merchants on the peninsula. I was taken completely by surprise," he admitted with a look of wonder. "Do you know how much our wealth will grow because of this one client?" But he answered before she could. "Of course you do, because you are the one who keeps the records." He

SECRETS OF MILAN

shook his head, lowered his chin, and rocked their clasped hands to and fro.

"But I didn't do anything," Maddie replied. "I had no conception that—"

"Precisely," Ally interrupted and leaned in to kiss her forehead. "And I suppose that is how it works. If the purpose of donating the money was to receive a financial reward, then we would never have received one. But your motive was pure and as a result we have reaped a tenfold harvest—an unbelievable amount, and for just one year."

Alessandro released her hands, rubbed the back of his neck, and swallowed. "I have been giving this thought on the whole trip down here," he mused, gazing out into the orchard. Returning his focus to her, he said, "For years now you have been helping out, an unofficial partner in our family business. I have noticed in smaller businesses from time to time a widow takes over ownership when her husband dies. Vergilio was not a full partner yet, but one day I expect he would have been. To be honest, you contribute more expertise than he did. What I am coming around to propose is this: I want to make you a full partner, legally. I want to put your name on the legal documents where it belongs."

Madelena was flabbergasted. She knew he enjoyed having her work with customers and keep the books, and she did benefit financially, but she never expected actual recognition. "Ally," she uttered, almost too stunned to speak. "But the other master merchants—"

"I am beyond needing to care what other people think," he proclaimed. "We are at the pinnacle, Maddie. We are richer than all of them, so who cares? If a woman is smart, talented, and skillful, why shouldn't she be recognized for it? Maybe we could open a new door in our society and lead the way for others. Why, one day women may even be admitted into the guilds! Honestly, there is no reason save insecurity and pride that women have not already been allowed to assume such positions. And when I am hemmed in by women such as you and Florentina, how can I deny you? Portia does not aspire to such goals, but she is a wonder in her own right. It is time, Maddie. You deserve this."

Overjoyed, astounded, and still a bit stunned, Maddie threw her arms around Alessandro and hugged him. "I don't know what to say, except... thank you!"

She sensed the strength and goodness in this honorable man, this confident, successful, wise man who was her big brother and hero. He loved her; he always had, which she considered odd with their difference in age. Joy and victory permeated her being as she reveled in the moment. This had certainly been a day to remember—and it wasn't over yet.

The two caught up with Father Angelo, Florentina, and the children in the nearby garden where Matteo climbed a tree and Betta flitted from one flower to the next like a butterfly. "Look at me, Mama!" Matteo called as he hung upside down, his knees clinging tightly to a sturdy limb.

"Come down from that tree!" she commanded. "It is time to go."

"Good!" he replied as he maneuvered his way to the ground. "I'm hungry!"

Maddie's eyes found Florentina's with a mutual exchange of affection promising much conversation, and hopefully more, to come.

"I will take us all to eat a late lunch," Alessandro announced. "And isn't the Pantheon near your inn? I think I should like to see it."

"In fact, it is only a block or two away," Florentina confirmed. "You missed the fabulous library," she gushed. "Don't you want to tour it first?"

"No!" two children's voices chimed in unison, followed by Matteo's mournful cry of, "Food!"

CHAPTER 26

After a long and exciting day, Florentina held Maddie's hand across two sleeping children in the bed they all occupied. She felt like she could swim in those verdant pools of eternal light forever and never tire. It had been a wonderful day, but she was no closer to discovering the location of the secret society's meeting. *Tomorrow,* she thought. *Some clue will present itself; it must.*

Maddie whispered joyously through a glowing countenance. "And Ally said he is making me a full legal partner in Torelli Silk, which may pave the way for other women in the business world."

"That is marvelous," Florentina cooed in a hushed tone. "And well deserved." She gave Maddie's hand a squeeze and threw a silent kiss her way.

Madelena winked and blew a kiss in return. "So, what is your plan for tomorrow? You must think the meeting will be held at night."

"Surely it will be after dark, although not necessarily late at night," Florentina supposed. "We shall search for clues while we tour Old Town. After dinner I will need to sneak out somehow."

"I know!" Maddie winced as her exclamation came out louder than she intended. Determining both children still slept, she continued. "After supper you could say there is this bookstore you must explore, and since we would likely be bored Luca and I can take Betta and Matteo for sweets for dessert."

Florentina's expression sparkled. "Brilliant," she whispered. "That will also explain why I have not yet returned by their bedtime." A warm sensation began to sweep over Florentina from her head to her toes. "I love you Maddie," she breathed. "We will solve this and keep you safe."

Maddie laced her fingers around Fiore's as her eyes darkened with pleasure. "I love you, too, and I have all confidence in you." Florentina reached deep to find the same assurance for herself and to thrust it forth with boldness; all she found were the jumbled words in a diary, the supposition they were in the right city on the correct day, and an extensive list of questions. The equinox was tomorrow. This would be it… or it wouldn't. "Go to sleep, my love," Madelena's melodious voice coaxed. "You need rest to be ready for tomorrow."

"Will you sing to me?" Florentina asked. "It may help."

Maddie raised up on her elbow and began to stretch across her sleeping youngsters; Florentina met her halfway for a tender goodnight kiss. With a light caress of Fiore's cheek, Maddie nodded, then settled back into her spot on the bed. The wispy lullaby sent Florentina into dreams.

* * *

FLORENTINA, in her regular day dress and straw brimmed hat, stood in the hallway with Betta to one side and Matteo to the other while Madelena knocked on the door across the hall. "Luca, are you ready for breakfast?" she called. "Alessandro wants you to accompany us around the city as he is returning home today."

A sleepy looking, lanky young fellow with sandy hair standing in tufts opened the door. "Can I meet you downstairs in five minutes?"

"That is acceptable."

The women and children proceeded to the dining hall and ordered their food. "How will we know where to go, what to see?" Maddie asked. "There is so much and I do not know my way around Rome."

"I can help you out!" declared a sprig of a lad about Bernardo's age with black hair and an olive complexion.

Florentina offered him a considering appraisal. "And who might you be?" she inquired.

He jerked a thumb at his chest. "I am Paulo. My uncle runs the Albergo del Sole al Pantheon." His grin was charming, his dress casual, and his enthusiasm clearly practiced. "I know all the places visitors want to see, the best routes to find them, and my fee is the most reasonable. You have to watch out," Paulo warned, changing his expression like a mask. "There are guide boys in Rome who will take advantage of ladies such as yourselves, charge way too much and leave you lost far from your inn." Then he pulled back his shoulders and the grin returned. "Not Paulo! I am the best tour guide in the city—just ask my uncle."

Florentina and Maddie exchanged glances as they both worked to swallow laughter. They were then met by Luca, dressed and hair properly combed. "Is this boy bothering you," he huffed out in his most intimidating manner. Maddie could hold her laugh back no longer, and it spilled out. Paulo shrunk, and Florentina reassured him with a smile.

"No, Luca," Madelena said. "He is offering to show us around. Do you think you could handle him should protection from a youth become necessary?"

Luca eyed the boy, younger and smaller than himself and gave a curt nod. "Come, sit, Luca," Florentina suggested motioning to the empty chair, "and eat. Paulo is going to start our tour soon."

Maddie reached into her handbag and removed a few coins. "Half now, half when we are done." He gave her a courteous bow and took what she offered.

After making introductions and completing their breakfast, the small group stepped outside to a damp, overcast morning. The paving stones and ground were wet and some moisture still clung to the air. Matteo looked up to Florentina. "Is it going to rain?"

She inhaled deeply, sampling the air, then peered up to study the clouds. "It rained last night, which may or may not have drained those clouds," she stated. "But it is likely if it does rain, it will be light and not last long."

Betta turned fretful eyes up to her tutor. "But no storms?"

Florentina whisked the little girl up, tossed her into the air with a twist that whirled her around, and catching her, drew Betta into a tight embrace. "No, Piccolo, no storms today." She kissed a giggling Betta and upon setting her feet to the cobblestones, tickled her, producing more giggles and a squeal.

The laughing child backed away saying, "You are silly, Florentina!"

"I'm silly?" Florentina replied with feigned offence, pretending as though she may cry.

Betta nodded her head, then added, "But I love you anyway."

The child's words warmed Florentina's heart, and the sentiment inspired her to reach across for Madelena's hand. But remembering Luca and their young guide were standing there, she let it drop to her side. The two exchanged a knowing glance and proceeded to stroll down the street.

"What would you like to see first?" Paulo asked as he skipped ahead.

"Old Town Rome," Florentina said, "and the Colosseum."

Maddie nodded her approval, and the lad waved his arm. "This way!" As they sauntered along Paulo pointed out shops and eateries. "This is one of the best rated cafés in Rome," he said pointing to what Florentina deemed to be a newer building. "You may want to eat there tonight," he suggested.

Florentina walked beside Madelena, the children ahead of them trying to keep pace with the energetic Paulo and Luca playing the protector marched a step behind. She may not be able to hold Maddie's hand, but she felt the connection so strongly it didn't matter. She was walking through the City of Love with the woman she loved and intended to memorize every moment.

"We get to the Forum first," Paulo announced just as the ancient columns came into view.

"It is larger than I expected!" Madelena exclaimed upon viewing a vast expanse of ruins which filled a low area and continued up the side of a hill.

"That's because there were many magnificent temples and other buildings here back in old Rome," Paulo explained.

"What's a forum?" Matteo asked.

Florentina replied, "The Roman Forum was a meeting place where people would gather to discuss important topics such as politics, religion, and philosophy. Other times they would talk about less serious things such as sports or the weather. Many prominent men taught their ideas here, especially during the days of the Republic. They would hold elections and trials here, have grand processions for special occasions. It was the heart of the city."

Paulo glanced over his shoulder with surprise. "You know about the Forum?"

Maddie smiled. "Florentina possesses considerable knowledge about many subjects."

Soon they stood in the midst of the ruins, gazing out at an unreal architectural graveyard. Great columns reached skyward, supporting no roofs and surrounding no walls. There were massive arches unconnected to anything, partially destroyed temples, and heaps of stones. Wild blackberries sprung up in out-of-the-way places, weeds pushed between cracked granite squares, and vines scaled the ancient facades. Matteo scrambled up onto a stack of mortared stone which obviously had once been part of a wall. Betta struggled to imitate him, but wasn't tall enough to reach. Florentina gave her a boost.

"You two be careful," Maddie cautioned.

"Yes, Mama," they chimed together.

"That looks like part of an old aqueduct." Florentina pointed to a crumbling erection of archways supporting a long stretch of stonework.

"Why is everything in such a state?" Luca asked. "It appears as though bombs destroyed the town."

Betta trembled at the word "bombs", but Maddie stepped closer to her with a reassuring smile.

Paulo laughed. "They didn't have bombs a thousand years ago!" He stopped laughing when he caught Luca's sullen mask of embarrassment at his question. "But the city was attacked by barbarians on several occasions." Florentina lifted Betta from the stone wall as it came to an abrupt end, but Matteo insisted on jumping down. "Then no one repaired them; they just constructed new buildings. There was once more to see here and the damage not so bad, but then..." Paulo stretched out his explanation for emphasis. "The occasional vandal had always snuck in here to collect building materials, but about a hundred years ago the government decided they could make a little extra money to charge people for licenses to quarry stone. It wasn't long until the Pope wanted to be part of the scheme, so they passed a new law. Then the church started hauling out huge quantities of stone to repurpose for their new construction. Then whole ancient temples were torn down, like the Temple of Venus, the House of the Vestals and others I can't remember."

"And now this is all that remains of what was the greatest city on earth," Florentina lamented as she peered down at a mighty fallen column broken in three places.

"At least most of the Colosseum is still there," Paulo said brightly. "Or half of it," he amended. "This way," he motioned. "You'll be able to see it just... over... there!" he pointed in triumph.

As they approached the massive stadium, Betta and Matteo uttered sounds of disbelief. Then Luca asked, "Isn't that where they fed Christians to the lions?"

"Shh!" Madelena scolded him, pressing a finger to her lips. He shrunk under her stern gaze.

"More persecution stories?" Matteo asked as he took Betta's hand in an effort to stay her distress.

"It only served such a gruesome purpose for a brief time during Roman history," Florentina interjected. "Before, it was a grand arena for sports, theater, and gladiator fights."

Nearby another family strolled along, gawking up at the mammoth erection with a young local boy pointing and expounding about the stadium's history.

"It is SO BIG!" Matteo emphasized as they drew nearer. The lesser damaged side stood three, possibly four levels high in a ring of colossal archways with a solid rim at the top. Its other side raised two levels high, marked by a circle of arches. The travertine limestone and brick-faced concrete construction bore a light earthy coloring similar to many of the Forum ruins.

"It was the largest amphitheater ever built," Paulo replied. "They say it could hold 80,000 spectators, more than twice the number of people who live in Rome now."

"Whoa," Luca exhaled in slow astonishment.

Paulo continued his tour speech. "The interior is a mess, but in its day the Colosseum boasted a great floor covering the arena, with trapdoors that tigers could pop out of. In the basement were rooms for the gladiators and cages of wild animals."

Gazing up at the massive edifice, Florentina wondered at how an architectural marvel of this magnitude could have been engineered almost a millennium and a half ago. *Were they more advanced than we are today? And why is it only recently the knowledge of their era has been rediscovered? If mankind had not fallen into a dark age for a thousand years, what would we have accomplished by now?*

As they circled the enormous stadium which comprised the southern terminus of the Forum complex, Florentina's eye happened to catch a street sign. She froze, her brain speeding through reams of information until she pulled out the piece she needed. "The Appian Way," she said out loud.

"Sì," Paulo confirmed as he bounded over to the sign. "It was the most famous road in the old Roman Empire."

"Indeed," Florentina agreed. Maddie strode up to stand close beside her, studying Fiore's face while waiting breathlessly for her to think. Then Florentina recited, "On the Appian Way, Quo Vadis—where are you going? Look to the left; the dead cannot answer." She couldn't help the fact Luca would think her words odd gibberish; she sensed Maddie was focused with her.

"You must mean the church," chimed Paulo. In an instant something clicked in Florentina's mind, and her intuition was blaring.

"There is a church called Quo Vadis?" she asked in disbelief. Her heartbeat sped as excitement coursed through her veins.

"Yes, yes," Paulo replied. "It is not the most popular on our tours, but some visitors ask to see it. Let me tell you the story behind the church. It was built on the spot on the Appian Way where the risen Jesus appeared to St. Peter when he was fleeing persecution in Rome. Supposedly St. Peter asked Jesus, 'where are you going'—quo vadis in Latin—and Jesus said, 'I am going to Rome to be crucified again.' And that made Peter realize he had to go back to Rome and be crucified himself so Jesus wouldn't have to endure his suffering all over again."

"The story doesn't make sense theologically," Florentina mused, "But people love their stories. Tell me, Paulo, does this church have a cemetery?"

He shrugged. "I don't know about now, but the histories of the area say back in the old days, when Christians were being persecuted by the emperors, they dug catacombs into the sides of the hills to bury their dead. Some of them even used the caverns as places to hide."

Florentina, whose mind raced through wild possibilities and vivid scenarios, heard Maddie ask, "Could you please take us to the Church of Quo Vadis? We would like to see this landmark."

"Certainly," he chirped with a broad grin. "It isn't far."

CHAPTER 27

⁂

They followed young, wiry Paulo past the city walls along a rough paved highway, lined with trees, wildflowers, and spring green to the sound of songbirds whistling out their tunes. The first rays of sunshine peeked through the clouds, signaling the threat of rain had subsided. They passed two tall, abandoned cylindrical stone structures with crumbling bases, which Florentina supposed to be ancient shrines of some kind.

"It is small," Paulo said, "Just a sanctuary, really, but the footprints of Jesus are there."

"Footprints of Jesus?" Madelena asked incredulously.

Paulo shrugged. "As long as I can remember there has been this marble slab with two foot impressions in it. The priests say they are the footprints of Jesus from when he appeared to St. Peter. I guess they figure a risen Christ's feet would do something to the stone that bore their prints into it, otherwise, how did they get there?" He laughed at his own story then as they came to a fork in the path Paulo announced, "Here it is—the Church of Quo Vadis."

Off to the left stood a small Romanesque chapel with a sign bearing its designation. "It was built centuries ago," Paulo stated, "but obviously after Rome became Christian. Would you like to come inside and see the footprints?"

Betta and Matteo nodded eagerly, but Florentina continued studying the sanctuary. *Look to the left; the dead cannot answer. It didn't mention footprints. The dead—it must refer to a burial site.*

"Are you coming, Florentina?" She only vaguely registered Maddie's voice, so deep was her concentration.

Florentina shifted her focus from the church building to her lover. "I need to search around out here," she answered in a hush. "Take your time inside." Madelena nodded and followed the others in.

Florentina struck out across a field behind the chapel which was both to the left side of the Appian Way and to the left of Quo Vadis. She wasn't certain what she was looking for, but hoped to recognize it when she found it. She rounded clumps of trees and unkempt shrubs, stopped to examine a decaying, dried-up well, and then raised her focus to the landscape. About a hundred yards further from the road she noted a small rise, possibly a steep hill or shallow cliff; it was hard to discern with the vegetation in the way. She hadn't found any gravesites or holes in the ground, but maybe dug into the hillside. Florentina quickened her pace and lengthened her stride toward the embankment.

The farther from the Appian Way she ventured, the thicker the foliage. It was not dense forest by any means, but like an overgrown meadow that had not been grazed in a few years. As she high-step marched through thick weeds and briars, Florentina came across a narrow dirt path appearing to be an animal trail. Pausing, she followed it with her gaze. *It seems to lead toward the ridge; may as well follow it than have to explain why the hem of my dress is in tatters.*

Florentina scanned her surroundings, seeking a headstone or forgotten monument or anything unusual. Nearing the sharp incline, she spotted a vast growth of untended wisteria, the vines sprawling everywhere as they branched out from twisted, crooked trunks. Though untamed and unruly, the purple blooms, which rather resembled bunches of grapes, hung all along the short cliff side. The glycine, as it was known in Italian, was a favorite in gardens running the length of the peninsula, but the lovely, early blooming vine had been imported from the Orient, therefore it seldom grew wild. *Someone must have planted this here long ago as it has clearly been neglected. But why plant it this far from the church building or the road? Who would come back here to appreciate its beauty?*

The minor earthen trail ended at a very large, very old climbing wisteria shrub with a thick trunk that appeared to spiral wrapping around itself many times. The branches and vines spread out to both sides and up to the crest of the embankment about twelve feet above. It was encumbered with purple blooms, and Florentina considered collecting a few, not only to refresh their room with a pleasing aroma, but because she knew they were poisonous and toyed with the idea of extracting the toxin to repurpose in her fight with the assassins.

She reached to touch the velvety racemes and brushed back a branch laden with them, only to her surprise there was a dark void rather than a wall of dirt. A spark shot through her, and she tugged at the vine to peer behind it. *YES!* She silently cheered in triumph. The ingress stretched at least five feet from the ground to her chin, perhaps higher except the branches were too thick to shove aside. She peered inside to total darkness, stale air, and wait… She thrust a hand in along the side and felt rock, possibly pumice, but definitely not dirt.

Her heart and brain were racing so, she did not hear the footsteps approach and jumped when Matteo called out, "A cave!"

Sucking in a breath, Florentina whirled around, dropping the vines and branches to form a curtain over the opening. Before her stood the whole entourage. She straightened her hat and brushed her hair back. "Let's explore it!" Matteo suggested with great gusto. "It will be an adventure!"

"Oh, you don't want to go into that dirty, dark hole," Florentina cautioned. "It is black as pitch and we have no candles. Besides," she added for good measure. "It is filled with spiders, bats, and rats. You won't be able to see your hand in front of your face, much less identify what bit you."

Betta frowned. "I don't like spiders or bats and rats."

"Why'd you walk all the way over here?" Luca asked as he huffed out a breath. "I'm getting hungry. Doesn't anyone want to eat?" He glanced up at the sky and evidently noticed the angle of the waning sun. "We must have missed lunch altogether."

Florentina shot him an exasperated expression and placed fists to her hips. "I came over to inspect this beautiful growth of wisteria, and no one said you had to march over too."

"More flowers!" Matteo groaned and rolled his eyes. "Luca is right; let's eat!"

Glad Matteo had abandoned the spelunking idea, she nodded. Betta reached her arms to Florentina saying, "That was a long walk." Florentina lifted her up and situated her on her hip.

"Why not ask Luca to carry you?" Maddie suggested.

But Betta shook her head. "Florentina carries me when my feet are tired."

Maddie raised a questioning brow at Florentina, who replied with a subtle nod.

"I will show you the very best place to eat," Paulo beamed. "Just follow me. Back to the road, everyone."

* * *

FLORENTINA HAD MANAGED to relay what she found to Maddie when they excused themselves to the water closet at the café. "The cave I found has to be the place," Fiore had told her, and they finalized their plan. Now, with Paulo having been paid and sent on his way, they stood outside the fine eatery pleased with his suggestion.

"Where to next?" Betta asked.

"I was thinking," Maddie said with a twinkle in her eye, "of taking you all to the sweets shop for dessert."

"Yeah!" the children cheered; Luca appeared happy as well.

But Florentina said, "I really wanted to go to the bookstore we passed this morning, and it closes soon. Luca, why don't you stay with Madelena and the children since no one is trying to harm me, and I'll meet everyone back at our room tonight?"

Matteo shook his head in disbelief. "More books? I thought we'd never get you out of the library yesterday!"

Betta stepped up to Florentina with a sad guise on her face. "But then you will miss out on the treats."

Florentina knelt down to look Betta in the eye. "Maybe you could save a few of those almond stuffed dates rolled in sugar for me," she proposed with a hopeful expression.

A big grin brushed away the concern on Betta's face. "I sure can."

Florentina stroked her cheek. "You be a good girl now, and I will see you later."

"I am always good!" Betta beamed, drawing a laugh from her tutor.

Florentina stood and caught the little boy's attention. "Matteo, you help Luca watch over your mother and sister."

"I will!" he declared as he tried to stand taller, chin raised and puffing out his chest.

With a nod to Luca, she shifted her focus to Madelena, conveying all the emotion she could not voice in one singular gaze. Then Maddie said, "Don't buy too many books."

Florentina relaxed. "I won't," she promised. "See you tonight." Then by strength of will, she turned and started down the street in the direction of the Albergo del Sole al Pantheon.

* * *

With an hour of light remaining, Florentina was in no hurry as she knelt beside her trunk, pressed the hidden buttons, and reached into its secret compartment. She lifted out her black wardrobe, belt still holding her dagger in its sheath, and her repeat firing crossbow. She checked the cylinders and reloaded bolts to the two empty ones. Setting the weapon aside, she considered the other items she had brought. *I will have no need of these wings inside a grotto, and will probably have no room for throwing a bola, but the whip...* She retrieved the bullwhip and set it with her other supplies. She selected two vials of noxious gas potion in case she was overwhelmed and needed a quick getaway. Florentina sighed when viewing the empty syringe. She had only a trivial amount of opium to begin with, but had taken what remained as a pain killer after being injured in the church blast. *I will need to acquire more of that drug.* Neither would bombs be useful underground as a cave-in would trap or kill her as well as any enemies. She wasn't even completely certain she would find anyone down there, but it was worth a try.

Florentina withdrew two more pieces of equipment: a roll of kite twine and a small brass lantern; a tin of matches was already secured in one of her belt pouches. Those would prove invaluable for exploring catacombs. She changed clothes, equipped her gear, and took a peek in the mirror. In five minutes, she had transformed from intellectual tutor to dangerous vigilante. It was time.

The last rays of the sun passed below the horizon just as she reached the hole in the hill behind the wisteria. The Night Flyer paused to light the lantern's wick and close the little door made of a thin, transparent sheet of horn the same as the side panels. Holding it by its top ring in her left hand, she ducked beneath the heavy boughs of purple blooms into the unknown.

Florentina raised the light high and studied the sides of the corridor, running her fingers along the walls. *Tufo,* she thought. *A soft, volcanic rock, easily excavated.* The passage led down into a black abyss in which her small lantern appeared like a firefly. After about fifteen steps descent the grade leveled out, and she came upon a niche cut away into the wall, a *loculi* upon which a body would have once laid. Now the six foot by two foot indentation, which was about two feet from the floor, held only dust. A few more steps and there was another, this one with a second hollow above it. *It would make sense the older graves, the ones placed here first, would be nearest the entrance. They likely continued to dig farther in and branched out as more space was needed. That is why there are no bones. These loculi are empty.* The dank air felt as primordial as the bodies which had long ago returned to dust and the close walls of the corridor pressed in on her, but she persisted until arriving at an intersection. A portion of the passage continued straight, but added splits to the left and right.

The Night Flyer retrieved the roll of twine from a pouch on her belt and fastened it securely to a jagged edge of rock sticking out from the surrounding wall. She had no idea how many tunnels there would be and needed to leave a trail to follow or she would never find her way back out again. Florentina paused, closed her eyes and listened, trying to decide which direction to go. She was met with silence. Then she turned down the wick of her lantern until it snuffed out and waited for her vision to adjust to the total darkness which enveloped her. When she opened them, Florentina smiled. She registered a faint hint of light emanating from the passage to her right. Leaving her lamp off so as not to be noticed herself, the Night Flyer felt her way along the *ambulacra* toward the dim illumination, her heart pounding faster with every step.

At the fork, she followed the light to the left this time, trailing the string behind her. Now, as she stealthily placed each foot with slow deliberation, Florentina could detect the low sound of voices up ahead. *How many will there be? Will there be guards posted? Stay focused! Watch, listen, stay alert,* she reminded herself. The illumination grew nearer, brighter with every step, and she began to make out a few words, then some feet shuffling, and the voices ceased. She stopped dead in her tracks, flattened herself against the wall and waited in breathless anticipation of being discovered. As the minutes passed and no one came, she breathed easier and resumed her surreptitious advance. Soon she spied light spilling from an arched opening into what must be a sizable cavern or *cryptae* ahead.

The Night Flyer set down the darkened lantern and tied the end of her twine to its ring, then slipped across the corridor to flatten up to the far wall. Ever so silently she slinked along, edging closer and closer to the hollowed-out chamber deep in the bowels of the earth. The international cadre who hired assassins to do their bidding would be within, plotting some evil no doubt. The first thing she needed to do was take a peek inside, ascertain how many there were, how well they were armed, get the lay of the land. Then she could plan her next move. A few muffled voices once again echoed down the tunnel whose walls were lined with shelves for the dead. She was not concerned about ghosts at the moment, only the living.

The Night Flyer had almost reached the opening when a tall figure draped in a charcoal woolen cloak and hood rounded the corner from the lit room. He stopped right in front of her and crossed his arms over his broad chest.

The blood drained from her cheeks, her heart pounding like a thunderstorm, and she felt as though she may faint. "Alessandro!" she gasped in a voice choked with shock.

He inclined his head toward her. "Florentina," he greeted.

CHAPTER 28

Florentina's pulse raced, she couldn't breathe, and stars flashed before her eyes, just as if someone had struck a blow to her head. *This isn't right. Something went wrong,* she reasoned as her whole world crashed in on her. Disbelief, panic, and a sickness that threatened to render her completely helpless whirled inside her, until from the tumult she seized upon rage. She could not stop shaking, but she could focus all the myriad of emotions into fury.

The Night Flyer took a step back, whipped her knife from its sheath, and held it up in front of her, steeling her jaw and stared energetic daggers into Alessandro's eyes. "You..." Her lip quivered and the sick sensation pushed against her throat. "You tried to have your own sister killed!"

"No!" thundered the emphatic reply. Alessandro sliced the air with a decisive hand. "Absolutely not! I am devoted to Maddie, as are you."

Still shaking from ultimate shock, she asked, "The other women and Vergilio?" *How can this be? How can he be part of an underground criminal enterprise? I thought I knew him!*

"I know nothing about Julia and the Countess; Vergilio's death was an unfortunate necessity," he stated more calmly and lowered open palms in a nonthreatening gesture. "Listen, we are not what you think. You may as well put the weapon away as you know I could render you unconscious before you could tickle me with it." Alessandro paused, taking a slow breath as he waited for her, but Florentina could not move. "We both have questions," he admitted. "There is an alcove just around the corner where we can sit and resolve everything. Just a moment." He held up his index finger, fixed her with a sincere gaze, and disappeared through the archway into the lit room.

Florentina's knees threatened to buckle beneath her. She knew he was right, especially in her current condition. Without much debate, she slid the blade back into its case on her belt. Alessandro emerged from the large chamber holding a candelabra in his right hand. He caught her upper arm, which she was glad for as it steadied her, and led her a few yards away into a *cubicula* to one side of the corridor. There he guided her to a stone shelf carved out of the tufo where she sat before falling. Immediately, Florentina lowered her head between her knees in an effort to forgo the blackout she felt coming. She sensed Alessandro's large frame settle on the bench across from her. "What, why, how…" The questions attacked her brain like a hurricane while her heart mourned as though a dear loved one had just died.

"I am a member of a secret society called the Cavalieri Dell'unità," he began in a calm, soothing tone. "We are not your enemies and we are certainly not trying to kill prominent women of Milan, although I suspect I know who is."

"But." Florentina tried to speak through a mass of confused thoughts. "Your trip to Bern wasn't at the equinox. It was weeks later."

"No," he replied in a surprised intonation. "Several of our members could not attend on that date so we postponed the meeting so all could be present."

"How did you know?" Florentina asked as her head began to feel steadier. "How did you know I was the Night Flyer?" She drug off her mask and hood, releasing her long, brunette braid to tumble past her shoulder. Might as well do this face to face.

"I have suspected it for some time," Alessandro said with a pleasant expression. "I knew for certain the night you threw the assassin off Maddie's balcony—an action for which I am ever in your debt."

"Maddie was right; you know everything." Florentina was finally able to look up without dizziness.

"Not everything," he replied with an easy smile. "But with the exception of Iseppo's betrayal, I do know what goes on in my own house.

Really? Why would the Night Flyer keep showing up there?" He laughed, clearly trying to put her at ease. "But how did you find us?"

Florentina took a deep breath and licked her lips. "When the Night Flyer burned down Don Benetto's house, he feared I had been sent by a secret society, a group of powerful men who were out to get him. He had a diary which I confiscated, written by a lunatic named Galeazzo Monetario. It is filled with riddles and scribbles about this group with the sign of the horse—ah, Cavalieri! That part was correct. He seemed to think you want to take over the world. Anyway, I did what I could to decipher the madness and here we are."

"Galeazzo Monetario," Alessandro repeated in recognition. "We wondered if he had written anything down."

"Who was he?" she asked. "Viscardi said his body was fished out of a canal, and it was supposed he fell in drunk, but he didn't believe that report."

"He was a relation of one of our membership, and both drunk and lunatic describe him well," Alessandro concurred. "His mind was... well, he talked to people who were not there, was paranoid to an extreme, and had a phobia of horses. Naturally he was an embarrassment to his noble family. He had a habit of stalking those he perceived as enemies. A year ago last fall, we caught him spying on our meeting. He was babbling wildly, accusing us of everything from incest to Satanism. His relative among our number promised he would take care of him and swore no one would believe anything he said anyway. I couldn't tell you if he fell into the canal or if he had help; it was never discussed."

"But I thought I was tracking down a murderous criminal enterprise," Florentina said with dismay. "Just who is the Cavalieri Dell'unità?"

"I told you we are not who you thought we were." Alessandro leaned his elbows on his knees to shift closer to her and his face took on a purposeful expression. "The Knights of Unity is an international organization with a mission of saving the European people from the savagery and waste of war. We work behind the scenes, influencing political and church leaders, structuring alliances within the worlds of banking and trade, using information when possible and bribery when necessary to achieve our goal—a unified Europe."

"A new Roman Empire?" Florentina's eyes widened.

"No, no," he dismissed. "Not an empire; more like a confederation of independent states. The Swiss are leading the way and have already begun to unify in a confederation. We were making great strides toward the same on the Italian peninsula. The Medicis and the Sforzas had established a surreptitious alliance and Venice was on the verge of joining. There was even talk of proclaiming a Tuscan coalition and then…" he lowered his head and shook it. When he spoke, there was heat in his tone. "Then the French and the Spanish brought their futile competition over whose nation is the greatest to our lands, spending young men's blood like game pieces so one could claim Milan and another claim Napoli. They don't care how many must die or how financial and scientific progress is disrupted, as long as their kings can boast and indulge their egos and stuff their coffers with gold. This constant infighting will be our downfall in the long run."

"It would seem an impossible task to convince the kings and dukes of Europe to just all get along," Florentina voiced earnestly.

"It will not happen in my lifetime," Alessandro admitted, "but the Cavalieri was founded before my generation and will outlast me. I had hopes Antonio would inherit my seat at the table, but," he sighed. "We shall see. It may take hundreds of years to accomplish, but accomplish it we must; it is our only hope. Can you imagine the progress we could make and the speed with which we could achieve it if nations spent their resources on advancement rather than destruction? We could end poverty," he speculated, "and transform transportation with innovations such as your flying device. Your Master Leonardo has envisioned such wonders, and if governments invested in those rather than more and deadlier weapons, the sky, even the stars would no longer be limits to mankind." Florentina soaked in his words, feeling herself pulled like the tide in a direction she had already favored.

"But with every generation," he expounded, "weapons grow more lethal and wars more devastating, leaving death and misery in their wake. Economies crushed are forced to begin again, and the toll in lives is unconscionable. Not only France and Spain, but Prussia, Russia, the Holy Roman Empire, England, and the rest. Now they have a New World to fight over! We do not propose a single government to oversee such a diverse population, rather each country should retain their sovereignty in domestic matters while forging military and economic alliances which guarantee no European nation will attack another, that all will come to the aid of one who is attacked from the outside, and there should be free trade between all member states. One of the Cavalieri proposes a uniform currency, which would be convenient indeed. Men and women with vision comprehend what the future holds: if we do not come together to form a military and economic alliance, within a few centuries or less, we will destroy each other. Then powers from the East will sweep in to take our soil and enslave the survivors. It is inevitable. We join as European nations in unity, or we perish from the face of the earth."

"You make a compelling case," Florentina said. Being draw in by the passion of his speech, her body and emotions had become steady. The color had returned to her face, and she was more intrigued than afraid. "By all indications, this is the most noble of causes, so why the secrecy? Why not shout it from the rooftops? Surely most people would agree with you."

Alessandro sighed, offered her a sage smile, and sat back against the wall. "Do you recall the Knights Templar?"

"Certainly," she replied. "Everyone has heard of them. They were heroes of the First Crusade."

"But do you recall what became of them?" he asked, raising a brow. "On Friday, October 13, 1307, King Philip IV of France ordered the arrest of all the French Templars on false charges of everything imaginable. They were tortured until they confessed to crimes including idolatry which they did not commit. This allowed the king to confiscate all of their lands, property, and treasury, which were substantial. Next Pope Clement issued a papal bull instructing European rulers to arrest all the Knights Templar and confiscate their properties. These men were then tortured, those who were not killed in the raids. Within a few years the pope disbanded the order altogether and any remaining Templars were forced into hiding."

Florentina eyed him in consideration. "You believe the French king and then the Pope merely wished an excuse to seize their wealth?"

"Most assuredly they did," he stated. "But beyond that there were rumors. Some claimed they were guarding the Holy Grail. Others attributed to them massive treasures which have never been found. The Templars were not hoarding treasure for the sake of their own wealth; they had grander, nobler goals. Those in positions of power were aware of their stake in banking and of economic innovations they proposed; also, the fact they were spread across several countries could be conceived as members of the order having dual citizenship. The biggest secret, which was no longer a secret, was the holy warrior society had adopted a disdain for war and violence. So they were a triple threat—they processed land, wealth, and a new idea. Because they did not keep their secrets well enough, they were destroyed."

"So," she mused in response, "you think these greedy kings and a worldly pope would violently oppose your ideas of unity and prosperity?"

"Without a shadow of a doubt," Alessandro confirmed.

Then Florentina cocked her head and narrowed her brows at him. "Your Cavalieri wouldn't happen to have been started by those Templars who survived the purge by going underground, would it?"

"I can neither confirm nor deny that supposition," he answered. "However, it is imperative no one outside our circle find out about our existence or our mission. It is too vital for us to succeed."

Florentina swallowed and sobered. "And Vergilio?"

Alessandro sighed and rubbed the back of his neck. "Vergilio was a competent merchant and treated Maddie with respect, but he had two notable flaws: he was far too concerned with the affairs of others, and he talked too much. We have one undisputable rule—no one can know about our organization outside of our membership. I told Vergilio I had a meeting to attend, and he said he wanted to come. No, I insisted; it was personal and did not concern the business. Then I sent him off to the countryside to inspect the wool. I thought he did as he was told, but no. He must have followed me, which I was not expecting. He walked in on our meeting, engaged in casual conversation, and then started asking a lot of questions. He made himself a liability, one the seriousness and necessity of our mission could not afford. If the French magistrate were to find out about us, or the pope, we would all be dead and with us our great-grandchildren's future."

"You killed him," she said.

"Not personally," he confirmed, "but I had to agree to the decision reached by the majority."

Florentina nodded with her chin pointing toward the floor. Then she raised her head, put back her shoulders and met his eyes in resignation. "I know about your secret society," she professed. "So now you will have to kill me."

Alessandro's lips curved into a smile. "Florentina, when have you ever known me to waste an asset?"

"But—" she began with surprise.

"You may know my secret, but I also know yours, which makes us even. Who is the number one most wanted criminal on the magistrate's list? Who is every constable and watchman in Milan eager to arrest? All I need do is turn you in should you breathe a word of this to anyone; but unlike mad old Galeazzo and chatterbox Vergilio, I don't believe you would, especially since we find ourselves with the same short-term goal—discovering who is trying to kill Madelena."

At that, Florentina popped to attention and sat forward with intense interest. "Do you have a suspicion?"

Alessandro nodded. "We think it is the Shadow Guild, at least we call them by that name. We have no idea what they call themselves."

"Who or what is a Shadow Guild?" she asked with furrowed brow. "Another secret society?"

Light twinkled in Alessandro's telling expression. "What? You thought there was only one?" Then he wiped the laugh from his face. "They are our archenemies, though we have not yet been able to find one another. We did uncover a copy of their manifesto; Florentina, they worship chaos," he said in disgusted disbelief. "This manuscript outlines what they stand for and we can link some acts of violence over the years to them, but most of it is cryptic, laced with riddles, and frankly makes no sense. We have actually talked about you, the Night Flyer," he said, then looked her straight in the eye with an intensity he had never shown her before. "The Night Flyer found us; we are hoping she can find the Shadow Guild, too; end this threat to Maddie's life and allow us to concentrate on our primary mission of establishing a European Union."

With no hesitation, Florentina declared, "I will do anything and everything humanly possible to keep Maddie safe and to bring down those cowardly chaos worshipers who would send assassins to kill her. I would do so with or without the request or blessing of the Cavalieri," she confirmed. "But having a copy of the manifesto and anything else you can tell me about this Shadow Guild will be of great assistance."

Alessandro nodded. "I'll get it for you. I see you didn't wear your wings," he commented. "I would love to try them some time, but I am not certain I would have the courage."

A brief smile crossed her face. "I didn't think I would be doing much flying in the catacombs, and my wings are designed for someone of my size and weight; I doubt they would hold you aloft at all." Then her face turned pensive as she absorbed what he had told her. Everything Florentina knew about Alessandro, every word and action she had witnessed, how he dealt with his family and his business, reinforced her deep belief he was a good man. How was she to reconcile that with the fact he had been a party to murder, the murder of his sister's husband?

"Alessandro," she began with hesitation. "I am having difficulty reconciling who I know you to be with what I have just learned about…" Florentina sighed and wiped her brow. "In my role as the Night Flyer I killed two men, but both were in self-defense. Therefore, I bear no guilt over their deaths. But—"

"I admire you for choosing mercy with Benetto," he interrupted. "He was your prime target, the object of your vendetta. He was the one who killed your father, or ordered it done."

"He didn't even remember," she uttered in despair. "I had to remind him when I forced his confession."

"And yet you allowed him to live."

Florentina nodded. "He was just an old man, stripped of his wealth and power. I accomplished what I set out to do, and I am no murderer. So I chose to give him to God, walked away, and have given little thought to him since that night."

Alessandro inclined his head toward her. "Noble indeed. I wish all our choices were between actions which are clearly bad or good. How easy it would be to walk a noble path. But sometimes our choices are hard. Sometimes they aren't between right and wrong, but between two deplorable options. At times there is no righteous alternative. Suppose on that night Don Benetto had reached up and pulled off your mask. What if he then recognized who you were—a woman who works for the Torelli household? Even if he were to promise not to tell anyone, could you for one minute trust his word? Could you have afforded to choose mercy then?"

Florentina threw her head back and closed her eyes, emitting a mournful sigh. She didn't want to think about the scenario, and yet it struck her with the same agonizing decision which must have faced Alessandro and his companions. "Please don't ask me that," she uttered in a tone of desolation. After taking a deep breath, she returned her gaze to his, swallowed, and nodded once. "Point made." Then she leaned forward with the most serious visage. "Maddie must never know. It would destroy her."

"I am glad you agree with me," he said.

More secrets to keep from Maddie. Another sick feeling welled in her heart, but Florentina comprehended the vital necessity of this one. "The manifesto?" she asked.

"Come." Alessandro rose, took up the candelabra, and offered her his other hand. "I have some friends who are eager to meet you. They have become quite the admirers of the Night Flyer."

Florentina replaced her mask and coif, then took his hand to pull herself up. She felt much stronger than when the sight of his face nearly caused her to faint dead away; but she also seemed to have aged a few years in the span of half an hour. "It is no small thing to save the world. You said that to Maddie when we viewed the *Pieta*. I see it's what you are trying to do here."

"Not in the eternal spiritual sense," he confessed. "But maybe in a more physical realm sort of way, or at least to save our part of it."

Not such a bad aspiration, she thought, and walked with him into the lighted chamber to face the Cavalieri.

CHAPTER 29

⌘

The Night Flyer had no need of the lantern as she walked back to the inn under the luminescence of a full moon. At first she had been surprised to discover three women among the twelve members of the Knights of Unity; perhaps their participation had influenced Alessandro's view on the expansion of women's roles. Then again, he had never been intimidated by a strong woman—nor a strong man either. No one exchanged names, rather referred to each other by their city designations, a wise routine. While Florence had been lovely and Paris charming, it was bristly old Prague she felt an immediate connection with. She imagined an endearing grandfather beneath the rough exterior.

She carried the manifesto in a large pouch tied to her belt where she had once or twice transported hand bombs. *What will I tell Maddie?* She pondered as she steadily placed one foot in front of the other. Once inside the city gates she passed a few people still lingering in the streets. To avoid being conspicuous, she had removed her mask and held it folded up in her fist. Passers-by may have thought it odd to wear black and a hood on so warm a night, but truly the scattering of tavern hoppers paid little attention. *I can't tell her I discovered the secret society only they were altruistic futurists, and she must never know of her brother's complicity in Vergilio's death —that is certain.* She held no doubt about the matter. Perhaps one day she would discover Alessandro's association with the Cavalieri, but she must never learn the whole story. The idea of keeping more secrets from Madelena tore at her heart like the talons of a raptor, but she deemed the alternative to be worse. *I can say I found the manifesto in the catacombs*, she reasoned, and pleased with the narrative her mood lightened.

The desk attendant had left for the evening when the Night Flyer entered the front hall where a dim oil lamp burned. She ascended the stairs with her thoughts on the kisses and caresses awaiting her when she presented herself to Maddie safe and unharmed. While she longed to create a way, some pretense or explanation, or even devise a secret passageway to find herself present in Maddie's bed every night, there was a more pressing matter at hand. *I will have to give this manuscript an initial read tonight so I can mull over its contents. Once we return home, I shall begin dissecting it in earnest.*

Topping the stairs, Florentina noted the hallway was dark save light spilling from the bottom of the staircase and a small lamp near the back stairs at the other end of the hall. All at once she perceived the figure standing outside the door to their room fiddling with the lock. She froze, her penetrating glare blazing heat as it bore into him. He must have sensed her presence because before she could rush him, he glanced up, detecting her. In an instant, she swung her crossbow into position and fired off two rapid shots. One bolt lodged in the door frame but the other swiped him as she heard a muffled yelp and the steel bolt skip across the floor. Then he was off, like a destrier racing across a battlefield, toward the back stairs, and she lit out in pursuit. She slid her mask back over her eyes as she hurtled after him.

Oh no, you don't! she swore to herself as she kept pace with him, unable to gain strides and catch him. Now she could have used her bola! If she fired her weapon while running full out, she would surely miss, especially at night; if she stopped to aim her shot, he could get away, so she ran.

The Spaniard dashed out the back door of the inn and down a deserted street with the Night Flyer fast on his heels. Tonight he wore an umber doublet over a forest green tunic and black leggings. He had let his beard grow again, Florentina noted, not that shaving it had disguised him much. She knew he would have his sword. As before, she would prefer to capture him and force him to give her information, but one way or the other, this ended tonight. She would not allow him another opportunity to try to kill Madelena.

The assassin glanced over his shoulder to spy the Night Flyer in full pursuit. He started to dart across the avenue, then swerved back to his original path. *He may be attempting to evade crossbow bolts, not aware I quit firing them,* she thought as her feet pounded the paving stones. One block, then a second he ran, and she gave chase. Then he spun on a dime and zipped off the street between the mighty granite columns of the Pantheon.

The Night Flyer chased the Spaniard through the massive pillars which stood over thirty feet high supporting the roof of the relic's portico. Here intelligence dictated she stop and take her time, lest she meet with a fatal sword thrust from behind one of the stone posts. Taking silent steps, crossbow in her hands, she stalked across the floor laid out in large light and dark marble squares. Above her a dim glow was reflected in the brass ceiling. Her strides continued toward the open gold-plated bronze door. When nerves sought to spider their way through to her brain, they were squashed by Florentina's iron determination.

She paused at the entryway to listen, then with her back against the doorpost, peeked around into the rotunda. Eerie bluish moonlight streamed in through the hole at the top of the dome for which the building was famous. There was no time to marvel at the world's largest unsupported dome, nor to question what mysterious materials had been used in its construction. In the pale light she could see the geometric patterns of circles and squares arranged throughout the swirling marble floor. Around the interior sphere stood columns, barrel vaults, and covered platforms displaying sculptures of long forgotten gods and emperors.

A brush of movement dashed from behind one of the statues, and the Night Flyer fired her weapon. She rushed into the huge chamber, the sound of her steps echoing as did those of her foe. He had evaded her shot and now stood across from her with his sword drawn. She squeezed the trigger, releasing another bolt, but he dropped to the floor and rolled away from it, springing back to his feet like a large cat. This time she moved as if to fire, but he did not dodge. Instead he began to twirl his blade in front of him like a windmill. The Night Flyer fired, but the shot was deflected by his sword and bounced across the marble floor with the clatter of defeat. *One bolt left; this is not working.* Florentina looked at her weapon and cursed audibly, then let it fall to her side by its strap.

"So sorry, Night Flyer," he taunted as he began to slowly circle, spinning his rapier in his right hand. "All out of arrows. Now perhaps you will fight me like a man."

Not exactly like a man, Florentina thought as she snapped out her whip.

"Following Madelena, I presume? Waited for her brother to leave town before striking? I'll bet you didn't count on me showing up." She cracked the plaited leather, and the sound was deafening with the chain of echoes from the oculus.

"It seems we are both in the habit of following Madelena," he replied. "Ready to dance?" The Spaniard swept out with his rapier, making a polite bow without ever taking his attention off her.

The Night Flyer was light on her feet as their battle began. Her initial goal was to keep him out of striking distance with her whip which landed a few stinging pops on his arm or shoulder, but he kept moving in such a way she was unable to wrap her lash around his sword as she had done before. As they circled each other trying to get a bite in, she observed the assassin switch his blade to his left hand and reach into his belt. She suspected he was drawing his dagger to have two weapons with which to attack. As he stepped out of the direct beam of moonlight into a shadowy spot, she noticed his hand move in a blur and then felt a razor-like slice across her side and the impact of metal ricochet off a rib bone followed by a clink on the floor.

Florentina's eyes popped wide as she realized she had been struck by a throwing knife. She scurried into shadow, clamping her left hand over the wound. *Bleeding, but not too deep. Lucky he missed center mass; just swiped me, that's all.* To let him know his aim had been off, she scored his cheek with the tip of her whip, pleased by his audible hiss. She would have to move in closer. Doing so, she cracked her lash toward his sword held ineptly in his off hand. This time it connected and coiled around his hand and weapon like a serpent. She gleamed with delight until she saw the glint of steel in his right hand.

The Night Flyer made a quick jerk to pull her opponent's weapon free, only to discover it did not budge. In a decisive fluid motion, the Spaniard sliced through the braided leather of her bullwhip, allowing a short lead to fall at her feet. She was stunned for only an instant while he scraped the body and tail of her lash from his blade. She tossed the crop into her left hand and drew out her knife with her right. *I'm not quitting until I have you!* she swore to herself. Florentina hastily wrapped the four feet of whip she still had around her left forearm as a bracer and charged him, dagger in hand. *Get close enough he can't use the sword.*

As they grappled, she felt the blood soaking her tunic from where his thrown blade struck, and pain with every twist and turn shot through her.

But up close under the luminescence of the moon she could make out wounds she had inflicted on him as well, and the knowledge stoked her confidence. When he raised his blade to strike, she sidestepped and cut his arm with her knife, then danced just out of reach. He swore and spit, swapping hands between his sword and dagger. She spun at his next chop and kicked out one foot to sweep him, but the Spaniard hopped over it nimbly.

"I am on to your tactics, Night Flyer," he boasted. "You caught me off guard at our first meeting; it will not happen this time. Why not fly away home while you still can?"

"Why are you trying to kill a good woman who has done you no wrong?" she called in return. "Do your bosses pay you so well?"

"The pay is excellent," he shrugged. "But maybe I enjoy the work." He flashed her a toothy grin that infuriated her, but understanding it was probably what he intended, she tamped down the rage.

He won't tell me anything, she thought, *and he thinks he's won. Besides, if he enjoys his work, he would find someone else to kill. I have to take him down.*

She danced a few more circles with him, trading strikes, one of his digging into the leather coiled around her left forearm. Then she stumbled—on purpose—inviting him to move in for the killing blow. When he was right on top of her, sword raised to strike, she jerked up her crossbow, aimed at his core, and pulled the trigger. The last remaining bolt sped into his chest, piercing flesh and bone.

With shocked, round eyes he stared at her in disbelief before staggering, dropping both of his blades, and falling backwards. The crimson blood appeared black as it pooled on the marble in the moonlight. In the temple to all the gods, now the Basilica of St. Mary and the Martyrs, the Spanish assassin died without Florentina discovering his name or who had hired him. *At least Maddie will be safe until this Shadow Guild can hire another killer.*

* * *

MADELENA LAY awake on the side of the bed nearest the door, the children having fallen asleep hours ago. She thought she had heard Florentina return earlier, gotten up, walked to the door and waited. The sound of rushing feet alarmed her. After some debate, she had opened the door to find the hallway empty. She re-locked the latch, paced a while, and then laid back down. Her mind raced with wild possibilities, conjuring up the best and worst scenarios. It seemed as if every cell in her body stood on edge in anxious anticipation when she heard the sound of a key rattling tumblers in the lock.

As she skittered to the door her thoughts and emotions were reeling with excitement. "It's me." Hearing the familiar voice from the other side swept all fears away and as soon as Florentina was inside Maddie wrapped her arms around her tall, lean frame with a heart beating wildly.

Florentina refastened the latch and responded in kind. This felt so right to Maddie, being held close in her lover's arms. Her lips eagerly peppered Fiore's cheeks as they found their way to her lips. Even as she reveled in the satisfying heat of the life-affirming kiss, Madelena determined something was wrong. A warm, wet sensation had pressed through her nightgown to her own skin. She pulled back and eyed Florentina warily. "You are bleeding!"

"Shh," Fiore reminded her of sleeping children. "I ran across our Spanish assassin; seems he followed you here. He got a piece of me, but we need not worry about him anymore."

Maddie touched Florentina's side and raised her hand to see blood in the light of one candle. "Let's get you out of those clothes and see how bad it is," she whispered and began tugging at Fiore's tunic.

"I'll have to mend the tear," Florentina breathed with regret.

"Never mind the cloth," Maddie chided. "It is the tear in your side I am concerned about. So he's dead?"

Florentina nodded and allowed Maddie to pull the silk blouse over her head. "I brought some medicines and bandages in case of something like this," Fiore said. "It isn't bad, really. His blade deflected off my rib and didn't strike anything vital."

Maddie's eyes flashed. "It struck you, and that is vital to me." She returned her focus to studying the cut. "It needs suturing. I should call a physician."

"In the middle of the night?" Florentina shook her head. "I'll visit the apothecary when they open in the morning for some catgut and do it myself."

"If you are sure," Maddie offered reluctantly. Then she raised her clean hand to stroke Fiore's face. "Did you find them, the secret society?"

Florentina shook her head in regret. "I did not find what I was looking for," she replied. "But I did discover this in the catacombs." She reached into a pouch at her belt and took out the paper manuscript. "It is their manifesto. It will tell us much more than we knew before. I must have missed them, or the meeting was so deep in the tunnels as to not be found. But someone left this text. Maddie, they worship chaos," she said with concerned sorrow. "The church bombing was likely only the beginning of what they have planned."

"Chaos?" Maddie's heart sank. She had speculated a group of men who opposed women gaining rights and influence had targeted herself and the others, probably Vergilio having discovered their plot. But this… this was so much broader and with deeper, deadlier implications.

"Do not fear, my Love," Fiore said with ardent confidence. "We will sort it out, find them, and put an end to this threat. At least there is no assassin hunting for you tonight." Florentina brushed her lips. "Let me put a bandage on this cut and then properly show you how very delighted I am to have you in my life."

On a fervent impulse, Madelena once again enveloped Florentina in a tender embrace. "I know, vita mia," she breathed against her throat. "We will figure it out together. I love you so very much!" When their lips met, it was with all the promise and vitality of a lifetime.

SNEAK PEEK - BOOK THREE

I hope you have enjoyed reading *Secrets of Milan, Book Two of the Night Flyer Trilogy*. Here's a taste of Book Three, *Chaos in Milan:*

When chaos strikes at the heart of Milan, it is up to Florentina's alter-ego the Night Flyer to stop it. As Florentina and Madelena's love deepens, so does the well of danger surrounding them. The race is on to discover the mysterious Shadow Guild and uncover who is behind the deadly rampage, but Florentina's mission is hindered by the authorities who blame the Night Flyer. Can the Night Flyer prevail, or will Maddie's love be ripped from her arms?

Chaos in Milan is the third book in Edale Lane's *Night Flyer Trilogy*, a tale of power, passion, and payback in Renaissance Italy. If you like action and suspense, rich historical background, three-dimensional characters, and a sweet romance, then you'll want to continue the Night Flyer saga. Order your copy of *Chaos in Milan* today!

ABOUT THE AUTHOR

Edale Lane is the author of an award winning 2019 debut novel, *Heart of Sherwood*. She is the alter-ego of author Melodie Romeo, (*Vlad a Novel, Terror in Time*, and others) who founded Past and Prologue Press. Both identities are qualified to write historical fiction by virtue of an MA in History and 24 years spent as a teacher, along with skill and dedication in regard to research. She is a successful author who also currently drives a tractor-trailer across the United States. A native of Vicksburg, MS, Edale (or Melodie as the case may be) is also a musician who loves animals, gardening, and nature. Please visit her website at: https://pastandprologuepress.lpages.co/

OTHER BOOKS BY EDALE LANE

Merchants of Milan, book one of the Night Flyer Trilogy Get It On Amazon
Secrets of Milan, book two of the Night Flyer Trilogy Get It On Amazon
Chaos in Milan, book three of the Night Flyer Trilogy Get It On Amazon
Missing in Milan, book four of the Night Flyer Series Get It On Amazon
Shadows over Milan, book five of the Night Flyer Series Get It On Amazon
Heart of Sherwood Get It On Amazon
Viking Quest Get It On Amazon
Daring Duplicity: The Wellington Mysteries, Vol.1 Get It On Amazon
Perilous Passages: The Wellington Mysteries, Vol. 2 Get It On Amazon
Walks with Spirits Get It On Amazon
Sigrid and Elyn: A Tale from Norvegr Get It On Amazon
Meeting over Murder Get It On Amazon
Skimming around Murder Get It On Amazon

Visit the Past and Prologue Website:
https://pastandprologuepress.lpages.co/

Follow me on Goodreads (Don't forget to leave a quick review!)
https://www.goodreads.com/author/show/15264354.Edale_Lane

Follow me on BookBub:
https://www.bookbub.com/profile/edale-lane

Newsletter sign up link:
https://bit.ly/3qkGn95

Manufactured by Amazon.ca
Bolton, ON

38354802R10125